The Journal of Henrietta Grasso

The Journal of Henrietta Grasso

A Novel

To Annie,
Greetings from the Parkland
Library —

Carolyn D'Alfonso

Carolyn D'Alfonso

June 6, 2015

Author's photo and book jacket design by Sean Simpson www.simpsonsphoto.com
Cover image by Florenita di Rotellini Massimo & C. s.b.c., Campi Bisenzio, Florence, Italy c/o Fiorentina LLC www.fiorentinaltd.com
Calligraphy by John C. Seedorff

ISBN – 10: 150591275X
ISBN – 13: 9781505912753
Library of Congress Control Number: 2015900197
CreateSpace Independent Publishing Platform
North Charleston, South Carolina

D'Alfonso, Carolyn, 1951-
The journal of henrietta grasso/Carolyn D'Alfonso
1. Philadelphia – Fiction. 2. Antiques – Fiction. 3. Art – Fiction. 4. John Singleton Copley – Fiction. 5. Love stories – Fiction. 6. Historic houses – Fiction. 7. Past life regression - Fiction. 8. Ghosts - Fiction. 9. Time travel – Fiction.

PRINTED IN THE UNITED STATES OF AMERICA
10 9 8 7 6 5 4 3 2 1

To
JCS
With Love
For incomparable days past
and
Laughter on late Sunday evenings

Table of Contents

This journal belongs to <u>Henrietta Green</u>

The Story

There are defining moments that change the course of one's life forever.

With these words begins the magical journey of a young woman whose distant past meets the present day and who travels back in time and across the ocean to fulfill her destiny.

Henrietta Grasso has inherited her family's antiques shop, a three story townhouse on Pine Street in Philadelphia known as Antique Row. It begins with the discovery of a ruby ring hidden in an antique Chippendale secretary, a never before seen portrait by the most famous artist in 18th century America and a love story on the eve of the American Revolution.

"Perhaps when the gods smile upon us,
we can have more than one great love in our lives
and that the second great love is really the wiser,
truer version of the first."

Antique Row

December 1981

Philadelphia

There are defining moments that change the course of one's life forever.

My father's death was such a moment. A year after he passed away, a series of remarkable events started to unfold and I, not wanting to forget, recorded them in my journal.

And so, as with all stories, I shall begin at the beginning...

I am the proprietor of H.R. Grasso & Daughter, a dealer in fine antiques in Philadelphia. You could say I'm a little obsessed with beautiful things. I have an intuitive sense, an emotional connection to finely rendered objects. It has served me well in the business started by my parents in 1955, the year before I was born. After graduating from the University of Pennsylvania with a degree in art history and a graduate program at the Winterthur Museum in Delaware, I was ready to take my place in the three story townhouse at 814 Pine Street on Philadelphia's Antique Row. My name is Henrietta Grasso named after my father and maternal grandmother. My lean, lanky frame comes from my father while my dark hair, green eyes and fair skin are courtesy of my mother. My parents specialized in 18th and 19th century American and English furniture and upon my entry into the business, broadened their scope to include sterling and porcelain.

My father, Henry Richard Grasso, was tall with light brown hair, a classic Roman nose and twinkling blue eyes. He wore Brooks Brothers and penny loafers, had a rich baritone voice which he used to sing at Handel's Messiah sing-a-longs. Gregarious with a curious mind, he was always up for an adventure. He loved architecture and history and enjoyed taking me on long meandering walks around the city looking for hidden streets and forgotten byways. When I complained that I was tired and hungry and couldn't go another step, we would happen upon some hole-in-the-wall place for a delicious meal. One of his favorite walks was on Spruce Street; you could literally walk from east to west, from the Delaware River to the Schuylkill River and travel back in time through three centuries of architectural styles from Colonial to Colonial Revival.

My mother, Charlotte Harrington Grasso Tuttenham, is petite, well-mannered and quite beautiful. Her personality is the complete opposite of my father's. She was a war bride, an English beauty from the Cotswolds who never *quite* shared my father's enthusiasm for his home town. So, upon my graduation from college, feigning home-sickness *and* showing shrewd business acumen, she returned home to open a branch of the business in Bath, promptly divorced my father and married a wealthy businessman from London named Arthur Tuttenham. Fortunately for me, my parents remained on friendly terms and continued to do business together. Mother still comes to visit when she has an occasion to be in the states and there is always an open invitation to visit her in Bath. She and Arthur live in the Old Rectory, a 17th century house made from the local Bath stone, a rich honey colored limestone, surrounded by antiques, heirloom roses and a pair of English Springer Spaniels, Naomi and Isabella.

I live in a cozy apartment looking out on the treetops on the third floor of the shop furnished with antiques from my parents' former home at 922 Clinton Street. On a snowy winter morning in Philadelphia it's lovely to have my morning coffee in the George III tester bed in the blue bedroom, the gas fire lit, knowing I just have to walk down the stairs to go to work. At the end of the day the red sitting room with its jewel toned Heriz carpet provides warmth for dining by the fire in the evenings; the French doors looking out to the pocket garden below. Cloaked all in white in winter and forsythia and daffodils in the spring, it is the perfect place to spend a quiet afternoon or evening dining *al fresco* with friends, weather permitting.

The Star Ruby

December 1982
Philadelphia

It was on such a snowy morning, I was listening to *Winter* from Vivaldi's Four Seasons playing on WFLN Radio, as I drank my morning coffee. I had an appointment at the Society Hill home of Pamela Stuart on South 3rd Street to discuss her furniture collection. Mrs. Stuart lived next door to the Powel House, considered to be the finest Georgian townhouse in Philadelphia. Now a museum, it has always been one of my favorite places. I think I fell in love with antique porcelain when I first saw the Old Paris dessert service at the museum. I said goodbye to my staff, James and Melinda and said I hoped to be back in a few hours unless I found a "hidden treasure." These words, so prophetic, haunt me still. Mrs. Stuart said she was selling her home and moving to an apartment on Washington Square nearby. "Sadly, I won't be able to fit all of my furniture into the new apartment and am interested in selling select pieces," she said over the phone.

Standing on the marble steps at 242 South 3rd Street, I tapped lightly with the brass s-shaped Nantucket style door knocker. An elegant silver-haired woman dressed in a dove gray cashmere sweater with matching slacks and a necklace of gray south sea pearls answered. Pamela Stuart was the widow of Girard Bank President, Peter Stuart and a former debutante from Bryn Mawr. She greeted me warmly saying, "You must be Ms. Grasso. Thank you for coming on such a cold morning, we can start in the library and afterwards have a hot cup of tea." We walked into the room and I immediately recognized an 18th century Philadelphia Chippendale secretary. It was mahogany with a graceful swan's neck pediment and a magnificent hand carved phoenix bird rising above multi-paned glass and fretwork doors. Below the

3

doors was a fitted interior with pigeon holes over four graduated drawers with bracketed feet. The brasses looked original and the glass panes on each door numbered 13, reflecting the number of the first American Colonies. The phoenix is a mythical bird that lives 500 years and then upon death rises from its ashes. I have always believed in signs and synchronicities. Perhaps this was a sign from my father to begin this new phase of my life.

A few hours later after tea and having selected a collection of Chinese export blue & white porcelain, miscellaneous furniture pieces and the secretary, I exited Mrs. Stuart's home feeling like a child for whom Christmas has come early. I knew I would have no problem reselling the pieces but the Chippendale secretary was mine! It would fit perfectly in the red sitting room filled with my reference books and writing implements.

James scheduled the pickup at Mrs. Stuart's with our furniture handlers for the following day and Melinda and I spent the afternoon decorating the shop for Christmas. The smell of fresh balsam filled the air as we set up the tree and hung wreaths and garland. We filled the sterling George II punch bowl with fresh lemons and pine branches and placed the green and white Copeland Spode Fitzhugh china on the pie crust table. The showrooms would look so festive with the new purchases just in time for gift giving. The rooms on the first and second floors were set up as though in a home with a front parlor, dining room and library on the first floor and bedrooms and sitting rooms on the second. On display in one of the bedrooms was a Georgian doll house from my mother's shop in Bath, a perfect Christmas present for a lucky little girl.

The next day the furniture delivery arrived and the handlers carried the secretary to the third floor. I could hardly wait until the evening to clean and polish it with my custom blend of lemon and olive oils. Finally after a quick supper, I started to remove the drawers from the pigeon holes. I first opened the center door which revealed three drawers which I removed. I then pulled out the drawers to the left and my fingers found a wooden peg. As I pulled on the peg, the back of the center section fell away and revealed yet another drawer — a secret compartment! Curious, I opened the drawer and found a small heart shaped maroon leather case.

There nestled in ivory satin was the most beautiful ring. It was a gold ring with a round pinkish-red stone cut in a smooth cabochon encircled with pearls. It seemed to glow from within. I took out my jeweler's loupe that I used for identifying silver and porcelain hallmarks to get a better look. As I turned the ring over I saw an inscription on the inside which read:

"Far Above Rubies" JSC to CB 1768.

I felt a sudden energy go through my body and a sensation of deep sadness. This ring was not part of my purchase and must be returned. I promptly called Mrs. Stuart and informed her of my discovery and arranged for a time to meet the following morning at her home.

Mrs. Stuart welcomed me at the door and we walked into the front parlor where a fire was burning brightly in the grate. We sat together on the yellow damask camelback sofa and when I handed her the ring a strange expression crossed her face. She rose slowly and asked me to follow her into the sitting room at the rear of the house. There over the mantel was an 18th century portrait of a beautiful young woman with dark auburn hair in a French lace trimmed claret red satin gown and on her hand was *the ring*. "This is a portrait of my ancestor, Caroline Blackburn Stuart." She had the look of a true English rose with a pale pink complexion and clear blue eyes staring knowingly at me. "She was born in 1750 and died in 1827. It was painted in 1768, family legend has it, by John Singleton Copley when she was 18 years old but it was never finished and is unsigned. She had just arrived from Boston and was engaged to marry Charles Stuart. It must have been commissioned as a wedding portrait." I wanted to return the ring but Mrs. Stuart insisted that it was rightfully mine since I purchased the secretary. I suggested the fair thing to do was to have the ring appraised and then she could decide. She agreed.

Back at the shop I called a dear friend, Samuel Jacobson and made an emergency appointment to meet him at his place of business on Jewelers' Row. As I walked down Sansom Street near 7th Sam saw me through the plate glass window painted with the name *Samuel M. Jacobson, Estate Jeweler* in gold lettering and waved. He was wearing his standard uniform; Harris Tweed jacket, matching tie and John Lennon style gold wire rimmed eyeglasses. The shop gave off a familiar aroma of Middleton's Cherry Blend, his favorite pipe tobacco. Sam gave me a warm hug. "How are you, my sweet Henrietta? I've missed you." My father used to bring me to Sam's shop to help him pick out estate pieces of jewelry for my mother. Sam said I had a good eye, even at a young age. He laid a black velvet pad on the glass counter and I removed the ring from its case and handed it to him.

He looked at the ring through his jeweler's loupe for a long moment and said, "This is a star ruby, notice the six points of light radiating from the center of the stone, these are natural seed pearls surrounding the ruby and the setting is 18 karat gold, Georgian, mid 18th century, probably pre-Revolutionary War, but the stone could be much older." I brought his attention to the inscription inside. "Oh yes, this is a quote from the Bible, the Old Testament, Proverbs 31:10: *Who can find a virtuous woman? For her price is far above rubies.* The star ruby is rarer than traditional rubies and in ancient times was thought to have mystical properties." Sam measured the ruby at 10 millimeters, took a few Polaroid photographs, said he would check the most recent auction records and if I could find evidence of a provenance, it would increase the value.

We made plans to have lunch together at our favorite restaurant in South Philly, The Saloon and I walked out the door wondering if the initials JSC stood for John Singleton Copley, one of the most famous artists in the 18th century. Why did he give this ring to Caroline Blackburn Stuart and what was the significance of the inscription inside the ring?

I decided to take a trip to the main library at Logan Square to see if I could find some answers. Designed in the elaborate Beaux Arts style and opened in 1927, the library was modeled after one of a pair of buildings on the Champs-Elysees in

Paris and a centerpiece on Philadelphia's Benjamin Franklin Parkway. Among the library's seven million items was an extensive art reference department.

Reading Copley's biography (1738-1815), I came upon the name of Joseph Blackburn. Blackburn, an English portrait painter, established a painting studio in Boston in 1750 and was an instructor to Copley. What was his relationship to Caroline? I continued with the works of John Singleton Copley but could not find the portrait of Caroline Blackburn Stuart.

I found a portrait of the artist painted in 1784 at age 46 by Gilbert Charles Stuart. Copley was a breathtakingly handsome man, fair haired and blue eyed with patrician features. He would have been 30 years old when he met Caroline, aged 18, in 1768 in Boston. His biography stated he married Susanna Farnham Clarke in 1769, the daughter of a wealthy tea merchant in Boston. But what happened during that year of 1768?

Christmas Eve arrived with a light dusting of snow as if on cue. James, Melinda and I, after a holiday toast of sherry and an exchange of gifts, called it an early day so they could leave to be with their families. I planned to meet my closest friend, Phoebe Ingersoll, at my apartment for a simple meal of wine, crusty bread and homemade French onion soup from the Head House Tavern recipe before going to hear the choir during midnight services at Christ Church. My favorite church to attend was St. Peter's on Pine Street but Christ Church was where George Washington and Benjamin Franklin worshipped and where my parents always took me on Christmas Eve. Phoebe, looking like a Christmas angel, petite, blue eyes and curly pale blonde hair, arrived in good cheer. She never failed to brighten my day when we were at Penn together and was a great comfort after my father died. A brilliant student, she was now an assistant professor of art history at the university.

Over supper, I was excited to show her the ring and tell the intriguing story of finding it hidden in the secretary and then seeing the painting. Phoebe's eyes sparkled as she said, "Can you get a photograph of the painting? I can easily do the research to see if it exists among Copley's known works. If not, this could be very exciting. Just think what a stir an undiscovered painting by John Singleton Copley would cause in the art world! I have some time now that the students are away for Christmas break. How would you feel about discussing this with Dr. Spiller?" Robert Spiller was an American art scholar specializing in 18th century painting and our former professor at Penn. Now retired, he and his wife, Dorothy lived in their country house in Chestnut Hill. "I think we should invite ourselves to tea and bring Pamela Stuart," I said. We decided to contact the appropriate parties after Christmas and so, dressed in our holiday best, headed off to the concert.

Christmas morning was overcast, cold and damp with more snow predicted. I was invited to Phoebe's family home in Haverford for Christmas luncheon but begged off; not feeling in the mood for celebration. I turned on WFLN just as Handel's *Messiah* was playing and I thought of Dad. Fortifying myself with two cups of coffee and a few cranberry and almond biscotti, I sat by the fire, telephone in hand. Dreading the obligatory Christmas call to my mother and step-father, I slowly dialed the number. "Darling, Happy Christmas, it's so good to hear from you," my mother said. I could hear the dogs barking in the background and people talking and laughing. "We have a few friends over for drinks; everyone, it's Henrietta calling from America." I talked with my mother and then she put Arthur on the phone. "Henrietta, how's our favorite girl?" Unfortunately I had never had much to say to my step-father, even on a good day. We spoke briefly and then with relief I ended the call. He was a very kind, decent man, just not my father.

Every year my father and I would brave the elements to visit Independence Park on Christmas morning and there, sitting on a park bench, he would re-tell the story of George Washington crossing the Delaware on Christmas Day. He would recite Thomas Paine's words as Washington had delivered them to the Continental Army:

> "...*These are the times that try men's souls: The summer soldier and the sunshine patriot will, in this crisis, shrink from the service of their country; but he that stands it now, deserves the love and thanks of man and woman. Tyranny, like Hell, is not easily conquered; yet we have this consolation with us, that the harder the conflict, the more glorious the triumph. What we obtain too cheap, we esteem too lightly: it*

is dearness only that gives every thing its value. Heaven knows how to put a proper price upon its goods; and it would be strange indeed if so celestial an article as freedom should not be highly rated..."

Afterwards, I could feel the past all around us as we quietly walked back home through the streets that once belonged to Colonial Philadelphia. Mother would have a pot of hot chocolate heating on the stove and freshly whipped cream waiting for our return. Dad would then take two small beautifully wrapped packages in gold and silver from his pockets, one for Mother and one for me, something he bought from Samuel Jacobson, and say, "Look what I've found, Santa must have forgotten to put them under the tree." How I missed him, especially at Christmas.

A few days later Pamela Stuart, Phoebe and I arrived at Dr. Spiller's door. His wife Dorothy set a beautiful tea table in the solarium amid blooming amaryllis and fragrant paper whites. The table was set with Mrs. Spiller's Minton Green Cockatrice china, a, lively pattern of birds, flowers and scrolls in rose, green and gold on a white ground with dramatic wide green borders. In the center of the design was a phoenix-like bird which reminded me of the Chippendale secretary.

"So, what is all this mystery? You have had me in suspense since your phone call," teased Dr. Spiller. Pamela removed the photograph from her purse and handed it to him. He gazed at the photograph, took a breath and slowly exhaled. "I have never seen this painting before but it does look to be in the style of Copley before he left America for England in 1774. In England, he painted scenes from historical events, military battles, but there is the opinion that his best portrait work was behind him. He liked to paint in his portraits personal objects that were of significance or sentiment to the sitter, a rococo device called *portrait d'apparat*. Notice the book she is holding in her hand, Edmond Spenser's poem *The Fairie Queene*. It's quite a remarkable portrait." I then showed him the ring and the inscription. "So...the plot thickens. Were they in love? I know that Copley was married for many years until his death and never returned to America. Let me research this further and then plan a visit to your home, Mrs. Stuart. I must meet this mysterious Caroline

Blackburn Stuart in person." We said our goodbyes and walked out into the late winter afternoon.

The next morning, too restless to stay in bed, I rose early and put French Roast beans in the grinder for my morning coffee. Eager to get back to the library as soon as the doors opened, I hoped to find a copy of Spenser's poem and learn more about the star ruby. As I hurried out into the cold morning, I bid a brief hello and goodbye to a bemused James and Melinda.

At the library, I found a modern edition of Spenser's book and read from the introduction:

"...*The Faerie Queene written during the years 1590-1596 was one of the most influential poems in the English language. Spenser brilliantly united Arthurian romance with Italian Renaissance epic. Each book of the poem recounts the quest of a knight to achieve a virtue... In Book I The Knight of the Red Crosse is called upon to slay a dragon to achieve the virtue of Holiness. Accompanying him is Una a beautiful maiden who represents the symbol of Truth. They fall in love but the knight and his lady are torn apart and suffer trials and tribulations until he finally confronts and slays the dragon. The betrothal of the Knight of the Red Crosse and Una at long last takes place but they cannot marry because he must fulfill his pledge of six years of service to the Faerie Queen...*"

I suddenly understood why Copley had added the book to Caroline's portrait. A deep sadness filled me again as I mourned for this man and woman who lived over 200 years ago. Lost in my own world, I looked up from the book and realized I was still at the library. Wiping my eyes, I left my chair and walked back to the stacks. I found what I was looking for, *The Mythology of Gems* and read the following description:

"*The star ruby is a rare variety of ruby. This magnificent gem displays a sharp six-rayed star which seems to glide magically across the surface of the gem, a phenomenon known as "Asterism". The ancients regarded the star ruby as a very powerful talisman, a guiding star for travelers and seekers. Traditionally, star rubies were worn by knights in battle to protect them from the enemy. The stone was so powerful, it was said to continue to protect the wearer even after being passed on to someone else. It also gave the wearer the ability to develop psychic gifts..."*

This was becoming very personal for me. The ring was the connection, the link between these two people. I recently became interested in the study of psychometry. It is a psychic ability in which a person can sense or read the history of an object by touching it. Such impressions can be perceived as images, sounds, smells, tastes, even emotions. I knew I had to dig deeper to find the answer...

New Year's Eve arrived and I had almost forgotten that the Powel House was having a Candlelight Ghost Tour and a "Toast with a Ghost" champagne reception. Pamela invited me to accompany her; it sounded like fun and I looked forward to the evening, I didn't want to be alone on this night. Every New Year's Eve my parents used to host a midnight champagne supper at our Clinton Street home for family and friends. Earlier this year I had the extremely emotional task of dismantling my parents' home to prepare it for sale, so I understood what Pamela was going through. I decided to wear a vintage Balmain dark teal velvet lace mini dress and the Tiffany green tourmaline and diamond earrings my parents had given me. When I arrived at her home, Pamela looked striking in midnight blue velvet with a sapphire and diamond necklace and matching earrings.

We were welcomed at the entrance to the Powel House by costumed guides dressed as Samuel and Elizabeth Powel. Samuel Powel, the last mayor of Philadelphia under the Crown and the first mayor of the city after the American Revolution purchased the home in 1769 at the time of his marriage to Elizabeth Willing. They must have known the Stuarts and Caroline Blackburn. We walked up the stairs to the ball room on the second floor. Iced champagne was being served in crystal flutes. We each took a glass, Pamela greeted another museum member and I excused myself to go on the ghost tour.

Being in this historic house in candlelight, harpsichord music playing, the guides looking like 18th century portraits, the aroma of cloves and bergamot in the air, I felt as though I had gone back in time. I lost track of what our guide was saying, something about the spirit of the Marquis de Lafayette when I noticed a man and women in the shadows.

They were dressed in period clothing, probably members of the museum. They looked familiar so I approached them to say hello. The woman started to cry and the man handed her a lace handkerchief. Embarrassed, I turned away to give them privacy. When I turned back they began to fade and just melted away. I thought this was part of the ghost tour, some staged special effect. I went back downstairs to look for Pamela and she was talking with Tom O'Neil, the tour coordinator. "Great special effect with the fading man and woman upstairs in the back parlor," I said. Tom and Pamela gave me puzzled looks. "No special effects, Henrietta, perhaps it was the champagne," smiled Tom. "Speaking of champagne let me refresh your glasses for the toast at midnight." Pamela started to speak but I interrupted her and said, "I must just be imagining things…" Tom returned with three glasses as the tall case clock in the entry started to chime the midnight hour. "Happy New Year!" everyone shouted and applauded but I, unsettled, continued to sip from my glass.

January 1983
Philadelphia

The new year began on a happier note. We experienced record sales leading up to Christmas and it was time to replenish our inventory. James and Melinda were both attending estate sales on the Main Line so I was holding down the fort. Sipping a cup of Darjeeling tea in one of my favorite china patterns, Coalport Indian Tree Coral, the phone rang. It was Samuel Jacobson. "Happy New Year! Did I catch you at a good time?" asked Sam. "Happy New Year Sam, perfect timing. I was hoping to hear from you today, what did you determine about the ring?" He took a deep breath and said, "Well, I think you're going to like hearing this. The most recent auction record of a natural untreated star ruby of similar size sold at Sotheby's for $49,999.00. Yours could be worth far more, as I told you, if you can prove provenance. For example, an original bill of sale, if a person of significance made or owned the ring or a letter referencing the ring." I was at a loss for words, a rare occurrence for me. "Sam, I must contact the owner and discuss this with her to see if she can shed more light on the ring. I will let you know what I find out. Thank you and it is indeed a *very* happy new year."

In the afternoon I was scheduled to meet Dr. Spiller and Phoebe at Pamela Stuart's home to view Caroline Blackburn Stuart's portrait. Phoebe, true to her word, had researched the complete works of John Singleton Copley and over the phone said she had a big surprise for all of us. Pamela warmly welcomed us to her home; we already seemed like old friends. We walked back to the sitting room and I once again looked upon the arresting face of Caroline Blackburn Stuart. Pamela turned on all the lamps; the afternoons were dark this time of year, so Dr. Spiller could get a good look at the portrait.

After what seemed like a long time, Dr. Spiller spoke. "I believe this is the work of John Singleton Copley even though it is unfinished and not signed but we will have to do further testing to authenticate it." Pamela was so thrilled that she opened a bottle of her private reserve, Pedro Domecq Sibarita sherry and we raised our glasses in a toast. Phoebe, who could barely contain her excitement, then said, "Remember how Dr. Spiller noticed Caroline was holding the book of Spenser's The Faerie Queene in her hands? In the process of reviewing Copley's body of work, I found a picture of a painting at the National Gallery in Washington, DC entitled *The Red Cross Knight* painted in 1793. It is a self-portrait of Copley as the knight and the woman in white holding Spenser's book is definitely Caroline Blackburn Stuart." Phoebe took a color copy from her brief case and there was the painting of the Knight of the Red Crosse and his Lady Una. We were definitely getting warmer and it wasn't just from the sherry.

Everyone was leaving when I asked if I could speak to Pamela privately. She went to see her other guests to the door and I was briefly alone in the sitting room with Caroline's portrait. Even though the ring was still in its case, I started to feel that energy again and the sadness was more intense this time. As I heard Pamela coming back to the room, I quickly composed myself.

"I have more wonderful news to share with you today," I said as I gently withdrew the ring from its ivory satin nest. "According to Samuel Jacobson, my estate jewelry appraiser, the ring is worth approximately $50,000.00 and could be even more valuable with the connection to John Singleton Copley." To say Pamela was speechless was an understatement. I continued, "Therefore I think we should keep the painting and the ring together as they were during Caroline's lifetime. I am returning the ring to you but before I do, there is one more thing I want to try." I hoped she wouldn't consider me to be slightly unbalanced when I told her I wanted to try psychometry using the ring as a conduit to the past. "My dear, you have done so much for me already, you have brought back excitement and romance into my life. I thought those days were behind me but life has a way of surprising us when we least expect it." She also promised to search for further information on the ring as she continued to pack in preparation for her move.

The next day I called Phoebe at her office at school. Luckily I caught her between classes. She and I attended a weekend seminar in October given by Dr. Frederick Wendt on reincarnation, past life regression and survival of the human soul after death. He was also an expert in psychometry. Dr. Wendt was an adjunct professor in the psychiatry department at the university's medical school. Phoebe thought it was an excellent idea to talk to Dr. Wendt about using psychometry with the ring. She called his office and invited him to meet us at his favorite restaurant on the Penn campus, La Terrasse, for drinks after work. "How can I resist being asked out by two of the prettiest – and smartest young women in Philadelphia? Just don't tell my wife, she's the jealous type." We knew Martha his wife from the seminar; she was beautiful and accomplished - a former student of his and co-author of his acclaimed books on the topic. It was going to be an interesting evening...

"So, let's review the basics of psychometry," Dr. Wendt said as we settled in with our drinks around the table at La Terrasse. "It is a psychic ability in which a person can sense or "read" the history of an object by touching it. Impressions can be perceived as images, sounds, smells, tastes, even emotions. For example, he continued, "A person who has psychometric abilities – a psychometrist - can hold an antique glove and be able to tell something about the history of that glove, about the person who owned it, about the experiences a person had while in possession of that glove. The psychic may be able to sense what the person was like, what they did and even how they died. Perhaps most important, the psychic can sense how the person felt — the emotions of the person at a particular time. Emotions especially, it seems, are most strongly "recorded" in the object." *This explained the deep sadness I experienced when I held Caroline's ring*, I thought.

We talked a little more about his successful experiments with psychometry and as I listened, a sense of relief washed over me that I wasn't just imagining things. Finally, as Dr. Wendt was getting ready to leave, he said, "Here are two signed copies of my book on the topic with instructions on how to begin the process. Take your time reading them and call me if you have further questions or concerns." Then he smiled and said, "Now I must get home to Martha, she will have supper waiting." We thanked Dr. Wendt and sat down to finish our drinks. "Will you do this with me Phoebe?" I asked. "I'm a little afraid to be alone and I need someone to record my impressions." Phoebe quickly responded, "You know I would *never* let you do this alone, of course I will be with you."

We decided to meet at my apartment the following Friday night. "First, let's review the procedure," Phoebe said after she arrived, notebook in hand, as we sat in the red sitting room. I nestled into the high back dark blue velvet wing chair by the fire and she made herself comfortable on the matching camelback sofa, put on her tortoise shell framed eyeglasses and started to read from Dr. Wendt's book:

"1. Hold an item in your hands. A personal item works well since it is in constant contact with the wearer and the energy imprinted on it should be strong.

2. Focus on the object you are holding. Close your eyes if it helps you to concentrate. Direct your energy to the object in your hand. Let your thoughts rest only on the object.

3. Visualize a link forming between the energy of the object you are holding and your own energy. See the energy merging into one energy field.

4. Relax, and see what images come to mind. Pay close attention to what you are feeling and sensing, as well. Impressions may come to you in the form of images,

thoughts, sensations or even a certain smell. Take note of any impression you may receive.

5. Notice whether the object feels differently in any way. Notice whether it feels hot or cold.

6. Accept any feeling, thoughts or impressions that you receive. If you are using psychometry to read for another person tell them everything that you have experienced. They will tell you if anything you describe to them is familiar and how accurate your impressions have been. If you are practicing psychometry in order to develop the skill, write down all of the impressions that you have received, and keep a journal to track the strength and accuracy of your skill as you continue to practice and develop.

"Sounds simple enough," I said. "Now, let me get the ring." I rose slowly, walked over to the secretary and withdrew the ring case from one of the pigeon hole drawers. "Just relax, Henrietta, take a deep breath and remove any expectations," said Phoebe. "If nothing happens, it's OK and we can then have a glass of wine and enjoy the start of the weekend."

But something did happen - and almost immediately when I removed the star ruby from its case. As I held the ring in my hand and closed my eyes, the first sensation was that of smell; the strong, heavy combined odors of turpentine and linseed oil, and leather. This time the ring felt warm to the touch accompanied by a sense of happiness instead of sadness. I could taste oranges and sherry on my tongue – all my senses were engaged now. Images started to emerge, vaguely at first, a room with light coming in through multi-paned windows. I could hear horses' hooves coming from outside in the street, church bells ringing, the ticking of a clock. And I heard the words, softly spoken -

> "…Her angels face
> As the great eye of heauen shyned bright,
> And made a sunshine in the shadie place;
> Did neuer mortall eye behold such heauenly grace."

The Star Ruby

They were there. Caroline Blackburn was seated in her claret red gown holding the book of Edmund Spenser's *the Faerie Queene* and John Singleton Copley was sitting at his easel watching her and working on her portrait. *And on her hand was the star ruby.* A blue & white bowl of oranges rested on a table with a glass decanter filled with sherry and two glasses. Then, slowly, the scene began to fade and I was once more back in my red sitting room.

Emotionally spent, I sank back into the wing chair and related everything to Phoebe. "I saw them, Phoebe! They were the couple I saw at the Powel House on New Year's Eve." "This is fantastic," said Phoebe. "It really worked! Dr. Wendt will be so pleased you were successful. And think how useful a tool this will be for your research. You can publish your findings." "Spoken like a true professor, Phoebe, publish or perish," I said and smiled with relief. "Now I think I really need that glass of wine."

Saturday morning, Pamela called me on the phone and said, "Please come as soon as you can." Her voice sounded urgent. "Is everything alright, are you ill?" I asked. "No, no I'm fine. I have something to show you, something we have been looking for." I flew out the door, saw a yellow cab, hailed it and was on her doorstep within ten minutes. She opened the door even before I had a chance to knock. "Come into the library, I have something very special to show you." The library was filled with packing crates scattered around the room, she had been in the middle of removing her books from the shelves. "I was looking at my books, trying to decide which ones to take with me and which ones to sell or donate when a book on the top shelf fell to the floor in front of me." It was the 1590 edition of Book I of Edmund Spenser's *The Faerie Queene.* "It was here all along. When the book fell it must have dislodged this." In her hand was a letter, yellowed with age. Pamela handed it to me. There on the front was the name *Miss Caroline Blackburn in care of The Stuart Family* hand-written in script. The letter had once been sealed but the hardened red sealing wax was cracked. I could still make out the markings. Pressed into the wax were three elaborate initials *JSC.* "I wanted to wait to open it with you," Pamela said softly. My hands trembling, I gently pried the seal open trying not to further destroy it or the paper and carefully opened the letter. I slowly read it aloud:

Boston, September 28th 1768

My Beloved Caroline,

I write this with great trepidation. On the King's orders, General Gage has recommended deployment of two regiments to occupy Boston due to the unrest. I fear greatly for my family here and think of you so far away in Philadelphia. I have been commissioned to paint the General's portrait and that of his wife which means I shall not be able to come to you as I had planned. I have completed Mr. Revere's portrait in exchange for his creation of your ring. How I long to be with you in these dark hours so we can offer comfort to each other. Remember when you were just a young girl and I would come to your uncle's studio for my lessons? I shall always think of your sweet disposition which has grown ever dearer to me over the years. You have become a beautiful woman. I know I must not say these words to you now that you are betrothed to Charles but I cannot help but think what might have been, what still could be. Spending these hours with you, painting your portrait have been the happiest I have ever known. Remember the poem we read of the Knight of the Red Crosse and Una. Someday I shall paint our portrait as the Knight and his Lady. I know you cannot wear my ring but know that when you hold it in your hand, I shall be thinking of you and loving you always, my Rarest Love, far above Rubies.

I Remain Forever Yours,

JSC

After a long silence filled with much emotion, I said, "They were *there* at the Powel House. That's why they looked so familiar. They were the couple I saw on New Year's Eve, I'm sure of it. I was supposed to see them; it was the last time they were to be together." I removed the ring case from my pocket, placed it in her hands and then related my wondrous experience of the night before.

I looked at Pamela and we both smiled through our tears. Pamela finally said, "It's as if they wanted us to find the ring and the letter, to tell their story. And you, my lovely Henrietta, have a special connection to them and helped them come through, I'm sure of it." We hugged each other knowing we also had formed a special connection and in that moment I felt a long forgotten sense of joy.

February 1983
Philadelphia

The Historical Society of Pennsylvania, founded in 1824 was known for its extensive collection on regional history covering the 17th, 18th and 19th centuries. The Society was extremely pleased to announce the opening of a new exhibition at their headquarters at 13th and Locust Streets on February 14th, 1983 to celebrate a very special acquisition to the collection. The exhibition was titled:

A Price Far Above Rubies – Love in the Time of Revolution

The exhibit designers under the direction of donor Pamela Stuart and guest curator Henrietta Grasso had created a remarkable installation. The walls were painted a deep red, the signage a warm gray with white text and the display cases were each lit with tiny pin lights creating an intimate atmosphere. On the center red wall was the portrait of Caroline Blackburn Stuart dressed in her claret red gown in the original hand-carved gilded frame. To the right was the 1784 portrait of John Singleton Copley by Gilbert Stuart on loan from the National Portrait Gallery in London. On either side of the portraits was a pair of antique bronze mirrored Adams style wall sconces from E.F. Caldwell courtesy of H.R. Grasso & Daughter. On the opposite wall, Copley's 1793 painting of the Red Cross Knight was on loan from the National Gallery in Washington, DC. In one display, the letter from John

Singleton Copley to Caroline Blackburn was placed on a claret red moiré fabric with Copley's 1770 pastel self-portrait on loan from the Winterthur Museum. In another, Edmund Spenser's 1590 edition of Book I of *The Faerie Queene* was opened to the title page. The 1768 Day Book of Paul Revere listing the commission for a ruby and pearl ladies ring for J.S. Copley and Revere's original drawing of the design was on loan from the Massachusetts Historical Society. And in the center display in its original maroon leather heart shaped case nestled on ivory satin was the star ruby surrounded by seed pearls, the six points of the star shining brightly for all to see.

Late in the afternoon, the day after the celebration at the Historical Society of Pennsylvania, I took a walk to St. Peter's Church at 3rd and Pine Streets. Built in the Georgian style, most of the church remains as it was in the 18th century. This was the church where Caroline Blackburn was married to Charles Stuart and where she was buried. This was also the site of my father's grave. As I walked through the tranquil churchyard I passed the graves of notable 18th century Philadelphians: Colonel John Nixon, who gave the first public reading of the Declaration of Independence on the steps of the State House on July 8, 1776, Commodore Stephen Decatur, naval hero and Charles Willson Peale, a contemporary of John Singleton Copley who painted the first portrait of George Washington. I came to my father's grave first —

Henry Richard Grasso 1918-1981
Dearly Beloved Father Who So Loved This City

"Dad, it's been an amazing last few months, you would have enjoyed helping to solve the mystery. I miss you so much." The Stuart family grave further down the path was planted firmly in the earth and the words carved into the stone simply stated *Charles Peter Stuart 1740-1793, Caroline Blackburn Stuart 1750-1727* and the names of their children, John and Caroline. And lying there, as the last rays of winter sunlight filtered palely through the trees on the aged stone, was a single ruby red rose.

The Solitude

March 1983
Philadelphia

Spring came early to Antique Row in Philadelphia. As I looked out the French doors of the red sitting room, I could see the yellow forsythia just starting to bloom in the garden below. There was a sweetness in the air that spoke of possibilities. Little did I know what the fates held in store for me this March morning. I stood by the doors sipping the rich French Roast brew, my mind wandering back to the memorable events of the late winter of 1982 — my discovery of an antique star ruby ring, an undiscovered painting and a secret love story in the days prior to the American Revolutionary War.

It was going to be a busy spring and summer. First would be the International Antiques Show in Charleston, South Carolina at the end of March. Then in late April the Philadelphia Antiques Show at the 33rd Street Armory and finally my favorite, The Nantucket Antiques and Design Show at Bartlett's Farm in early August. My staff, Melinda and James were planning the logistics; coordinating our furniture handlers' schedules for the coming months, my travel arrangements and helping make selections for the shows.

As I came down the stairs, I heard the business phone ring and Melinda answered the call. "Good Morning, H. R. Grasso & Daughter, this is Melinda. Hi Sarah, yes, Henrietta is coming into the showroom as we speak, please hold on. Henrietta, its Sarah Townsend from Winterthur." "Hi Sarah, how are you?" Sarah Townsend, my roommate when we were in graduate school was now making a name for herself as assistant curator of furniture at the Winterthur Museum in Delaware. Winterthur was the former estate of Henry DuPont who methodically amassed one of the finest collections of 18th and 19th century American furniture and decorative arts in the United States. Sarah and I received our graduate degrees in American Material Culture there.

"Henrietta, I have a proposition for you." Sarah always came right to the point. "Do you remember my cousin Andrew?" *Oh no, not that again.* Sarah tried relentlessly to fix me up with her cousin. "Sarah, we were never on the same continent, let alone the same state long enough to meet." Sarah had told me about her legendary cousin Andrew Townsend often enough. Andrew, a preservation architect was a graduate of the University of Virginia in Charlottesville, spent a year abroad studying at Oxford and for summer vacations went on preservation road trips in Ireland with the Irish Georgian Society. "Well, he's home for good now. In fact, he just finished renovating a townhouse he purchased at 2nd and Delancey and has set up a home office there. He's practically around the corner from you. He wants to meet you regarding a project he is working on. He has been hired by the Fairmount Park Commission to consult on the restoration of the Historic Park Houses and needs a decorative arts specialist."

I have to say I was intrigued by the prospect of working on the Park Houses, now museums. "When does he want to get started? You know I have the spring and summer antiques shows coming up." "He wants to begin right away but is flexible and you can work around the shows. He would like to stop in to discuss it with you at the shop; can he stop by around 11:30AM today?" With nothing else pressing on my schedule, I agreed and Sarah signed off with "You won't be sorry, I promise. I've been talking about my beautiful and brainy former roommate for years; he's been looking forward to meeting you for a long time."

Like a sixteen year old going out on her first date, I ran upstairs and looked in the Georgian mirror in the hallway of my apartment, tousled my pixie cut dark hair, checked my makeup and outfit – brown and ivory hound's-tooth check riding jacket, ivory turtle neck and slim khaki slacks. Low heeled brown leather laced up shoes and my ubiquitous pearl earrings and gold bangle bracelet completed the outfit — *understated elegance* as my mother used to say.

Right on time at 11:30AM, the bell over the front door jingled and in walked a very tall, dark haired man dressed in a brown tweed jacket, khaki slacks, white shirt and loafers. We were dressed almost identically and at six foot four he towered over my five foot nine frame. He looked at me with a twinkle in his eyes and said, "At long last, Ms. Grasso, I presume?" I laughed and said, "Yes and you must be Mr. Townsend or is it Mr. Stanley?" "I do confess you have been harder to track down than Dr. Livingstone on the Dark Continent." His eyes were the color of burnished gold, a lion's eyes, surrounded by long dark lashes and a dimple appeared in his cheek when he smiled. *Oh Sarah what have you gotten me into?*

I asked if he would first like a tour of the shop and he agreed. He seemed very knowledgeable about antiques and said he was looking for additional furnishings for his new home. He loved the garden and as we were leaving the second floor he asked, "What's on the third floor, more showrooms?" "No, that's my apartment." "Ah, the inner sanctum, I hope you will invite me for a visit one day, I promise I'll wear my pith helmet," he said playfully. He was not only gorgeous but charming too!

"Do you have any plans for lunch today?" asked Andrew, as he handed me his business card. "If you have some time this afternoon, I would like to take you to lunch at the Water Works Café and then a quick tour of our first house nearby — The Solitude. I can give you an overview of the project and see what you think before you commit yourself. Of course there is no *pressure*."

It was a beautiful early March day and suddenly the Charleston Antiques Show seemed far off in the distance. I ran upstairs to get my leather satchel, camera and notebook and looked one more time in the mirror — my eyes were shining, my skin glowing; now if they could only put *this elixir* in a bottle. Outside the shop parked at the curb was a 1966 Volkswagen Karmann Ghia convertible. British racing green with tan leather interior, she was a beauty. "Your carriage awaits, M' lady," said Andrew as he opened my car door.

The Fairmount Water Works sits on the eastern banks of the Schuylkill River and was the main fresh water system in its day for the city of Philadelphia. Designed by Frederick Graff and constructed in 1815 in the Classical Revival style, it was a series of classical buildings disguised to hold the pump rooms. No longer in use it was placed on the National Register of Historic Places and now restored, housed a science and environmental educational center and a romantic restaurant. At an unseasonably warm 72 degrees, we were able to sit outside and watch the sunlight sparkle on the river as the moving water spilled over the dam. At the top of the hill was a golden temple, the Philadelphia Museum of Art known for its world class collections. Andrew and I settled in to enjoy our lunch - crab cakes, sweet corn fritters and fresh coleslaw with minted ice tea – a taste of summer to come.

Not wanting to rush just yet into work mode, we talked about our travels – he about Oxford and I about my mother's home in Bath. We spoke of his work with the Irish Georgian Society and my studies at Winterthur. He'd heard of my father's passing from his cousin Sarah. He also knew about the 'amazing John Singleton Copley exhibit' I recently curated at the Historical Society of Pennsylvania and wanted to stop by to see it.

"As much as I hate to break this spell you have cast over me," he said finally, "Let me tell you about a house called The Solitude. Hidden within the oldest zoological garden in America is a house once owned by John Penn, a grandson of William Penn. Known as "The Poet", he was born in 1760, educated at Cambridge, went on the Grand Tour of Europe, returned to America in 1784 and purchased fifteen acres on a bluff overlooking the west bank of the Schuylkill River where he built a house of his own design. Today, The Solitude is considered to be one of the finest examples of the neoclassical style in Philadelphia and the last existing home owned by a member of the Penn family. The house is literally a box, twenty-nine feet square and badly in need of restoration. That's where you and I come in. After only four years, John Penn returned to England and told his agent to sell all the contents of his home. Only one piece remains, a free standing oval mahogany cabinet which Penn designed and is now in the possession of the Physick House in Society Hill. The cabinetmaker, Samuel Claphamson made a second identical piece but it has never been found. And oh, by the way, there are reports that the house is haunted. Are you ready to take a ride to see it?" *Oh no, not another haunted house* but I just smiled and said, "Absolutely, let's go."

We traveled north on East River Drive, a winding two lane road with the top down on the Karmann Ghia, pass Boathouse Row to the Girard Avenue Bridge and crossed the river to the 34th Street entrance of the Philadelphia Zoo. We walked through the whimsical Victorian gatehouse designed by Frank Furness when the zoo opened in 1874 and strolled along the path until we saw a white building. It looked like a house that children make when first learning to draw — a square with a door in the center, a window on each side and three windows across the top of the second floor with a hipped roof and two chimneys. The walls were scored stucco imitating cut stone. All it needed was a black crayon of curling smoke spewing from the chimneys.

Andrew withdrew a large iron key from his pocket and opened the door saying, "The house was last used as the zoo's administrative offices." The hall opened to a large parlor and dining room; the windows opening on to a portico with a view looking east to the river. The ceiling was ornately sculpted. An elaborate hand wrought iron balustrade attached to the staircase lead to the second floor. On that level, a large square room also with an ornate ceiling had bookcases built into the wall. "This was Penn's library; these shelves once contained fifteen hundred volumes," said Andrew. The next room was smaller. "This was Penn's bedroom." It was a simple room with an alcove where his bed must have been. On the third floor under the hip roof were several small rooms, probably servants' quarters. We then descended the stairs to the cellars. "From here there was an underground passage connecting to the kitchen building which was forty-five feet from the house. The tunnel was sealed and unfortunately the kitchen is no longer standing." I started to get a creepy feeling and was glad when we returned to the main floor. "A perfect neoclassical bachelor pad," I teased. "And a bachelor he remained his whole life, a sorry fate for any man," Andrew said with a mock sigh. He had been flirting with me all day. Was it real or was he just trying to charm me into working on the project?

"So, what did you think of the house?" Andrew asked when we were parked outside the shop on Antique Row. "I liked it very much but I don't think it's within my budget," I responded coyly. His handsome face suddenly looked crest fallen, his golden eyes clouded. "I'm only kidding - of course I'll work on the project with you as long as I also have time to attend the up-coming antiques shows. Melinda and James can handle most of the day to day business at the shop during this time." That settled, he sighed and relaxed in his seat. "I have two more questions to ask you," he said. "First, will you have dinner with me on Saturday night after a personal tour of the Copley exhibit and second...*please*, may I kiss you?" Just like his cousin Sarah, Andrew came right to the point. To both questions I answered *"Oh yes."*

We arranged to meet at the Historical Society of Pennsylvania on Saturday afternoon and then have dinner at the City Tavern at 2nd & Walnut. I hurried into H.R. Grasso & Daughter where Melinda was waiting with a pile of phone messages.

"Sarah Townsend called three times today, Pamela Stuart invited you to tea tomorrow at her apartment and Phoebe called about getting together for lunch on Friday." First, I called Pamela. "Henrietta, my dear, I've finally settled in, with your assistance I might add, I think I am going to love it here, no more stairs to climb." As a house warming present, my staff and I helped Pamela organize her antiques collection in her apartment. We agreed to meet the next afternoon for tea. I had so much to tell her. Next I called Phoebe and agreed to meet for lunch on Friday at The Garden, our favorite place. If the weather held we could sit outside in the rear garden. I told her I had great news but wanted to tell her in person.

Finally I called Sarah Townsend. "Henrietta, I've been on pins and needles all afternoon waiting to hear from you, how did it go with Cousin Andrew?" "He took me to the Water Works Café for lunch and then to see John Penn's house, The Solitude. We are going to meet at the Historical Society on Saturday to see the

Copley exhibit and then have dinner at City Tavern. I've agreed to work on the project with him." My words came out in a rush. I heard Sarah breathe a big sigh of relief and say, *"Finally,* I knew you two would be perfect together but then I've been telling you both that for years." Sarah sounded pretty pleased with herself. "Your father would have really liked him and your mother will want to marry him, herself." "Who said anything about marriage?" Ignoring my comment, she continued, "Now I can die in peace knowing that my children are happy together, just name your first daughter after me. I'm going to call Andrew and hear what he has to say about you. It's just like high school all over again, isn't it?" With Sarah's laughter still in my ears, we hung up.

I tossed and turned all night in the George III tester bed where I kept replaying the afternoon with Andrew leading up to his unexpected kiss. Giving up the fight, I rose and brewed coffee to start the day. To think, my whole life had changed in less than twenty-four hours. I remembered Pamela saying that life has a way of surprising us when we least expect it.

After a flurry of phone calls about the Charleston show and going through routine paperwork that had piled up in my absence, Melinda and I walked through the showroom and earmarked pieces for the show. While I was running around chasing down ghosts from before the Revolutionary War, Melinda and James had been very successful at the estate sales in January and February. Also, the publicity generated by the Copley Exhibit with articles in both *Art in America* and *Art & Antiques* magazines would bring additional business.

At 3PM I left the shop with a spring bouquet of salmon colored tulips and yellow daffodils from Old City Flowers and copies of the magazines and walked to Pamela's apartment on Washington Square. A bucolic six acre park, this was one of the five original squares planned by William Penn. During the 18th century the Square was used for the burial of soldiers from George Washington's Continental Army. In 1954, a monument to the Tomb of the Unknown Revolutionary War Soldier was built and Jean-Antoine Houdon's bronze statue of George Washington now stood guard overlooking an eternal flame. People say this is a haunted place but on this sunny afternoon, as I approached Pamela's new home, it was anything but haunted.

228 Washington Square West was a three story red brick townhouse built in 1809 with six over six windows, glossy black painted shutters and a matching front door. Pamela lived in the first floor apartment with a formal parlor and dining room, master bedroom, guest bedroom and kitchen with a cozy sitting area leading out to a walled garden. The parlor and dining room contained the original pair of white and black veined marble mantels and French neoclassical bronze and crystal chandeliers. I was able to find her two Axminster carpets, the patterns re-created from original 1791 designs of black, rose and yellow with a floral center medallion and Greek Key design border. The yellow damask camelback sofa and side chairs from her former home looked perfect in their new setting.

Pamela Stuart, always elegant, met me at the door. "I just returned from a stroll around the Square, the weather is so lovely today," she said as she gave me a warm hug. She was dressed in a gray blazer and ivory wool slacks with a light weight lavender mohair shawl around her shoulders and her signature south sea pearls. "I brought you the first bouquet of the season and copies of the magazines with the Copley exhibit articles." "Thank you, my dear, the flowers are lovely, come in, I think we'll have tea in the sitting room today, more intimate." The room was decorated in a Provencal style —throw pillows in yellow toile and black and ivory check on a comfortable sofa with matching tufted ottoman and two wing chairs. On the ottoman was a wooden tray with a Spode Buttercup tea service. Designed in 1885, it was a basket weave pattern with a center of yellow buttercups, perfect for an early March day.

"The apartment looks wonderful!" I commented as we sipped our tea. "I'm so glad I decided to move, too many memories in the old place. The garden will have to be done, I'm looking forward to that as soon as the ground softens, then we can sit outside and enjoy spring in Philadelphia."

I took another sip of tea and said, "Something unexpected has happened." Pamela looked at me with concern. "No, it's wonderful, really, I just can't believe it." I then went on to tell her about meeting Andrew Townsend and being asked to consult on his restoration of The Solitude. "This is the first house of the Historic Houses in Fairmount Park; we will be working on all of them. My job will be curating the furniture, silver, porcelain and art for each house. It's a dream job and with all the publicity we are receiving from the Copley exhibit, business is better than ever. I have you to thank for the donation to the Historical Society." "No my dear, you are the one who made that happen and the painting and artifacts really belonged in a museum." "There's something else…Andrew took me to lunch and to see the house yesterday. When he drove me home he asked me out to dinner for Saturday and then he kissed me." Pamela gave me a knowing smile. "I thought you looked different; there is a glow about you..and so now it begins."

Phoebe Ingersoll lived on the top floor of a Renaissance Revival townhouse at 20th and Pine. Her apartment had five arched windows overlooking a long balcony. It was the perfect home for a woman who taught a course in The Art of the Italian Renaissance and looked like Shakespeare's Juliet. Friday was her half day teaching at Penn and we tried to meet for lunch as often as possible.

Close to Phoebe's apartment was the Garden, an elegant 19th century townhouse on Spruce Street near 16th - dark paneling with botanical prints on the wall, intimate lighting, fresh floral arrangements and a hidden garden for outdoor dining, hence the name. I arrived at the restaurant at the same time as Phoebe and received a warm hug. "It's a little cooler today so perhaps we should sit inside," she said. The hostess seated us at a table for two in the corner; we ordered glasses of Chardonnay and shrimp salad and settled in for a long chat. I hadn't seen her since the Copley exhibit opening a few weeks before but she had been invaluable in researching Copley's body of work and working with Dr. Spiller to authenticate the portrait of Caroline Blackburn Stuart.

"I have something to tell you," she said. "I received a call from Jamie Cadwalader yesterday." Jamie Cadwalader was an assistant curator of American Painting at the Philadelphia Museum of Art and a friend of Phoebe's brother, Stephen. I was introduced to him at a First City Troop event at the 23rd Street Armory and dated him for about a year. As a member of this elite military group going back to the days of protecting George Washington, Jamie was tall with black hair and ice blue eyes and looked dashing in his military uniform on horseback. He was witty and sophisticated, taking me to the Pennsylvania Ballet and the opera at the Academy of Music and dinner at the Fountain Room at the Four Seasons. After about six months it was as if a switch had been turned off and he started to belittle me in front of my friends and was emotionally abusive when we were alone.

The final straw was the night of the Philadelphia Charity Ball. After the ball, Jamie dressed in white tie and tails and I in an emerald green satin gown were alone in the limousine having just dropped off Phoebe and Stephen and their dates. All night he had been acting strangely, constantly disappearing into the men's room. In the car, he started to kiss me and became increasingly aggressive. He pulled me down on the long seat and pushed up my gown; I thought he was going to rape me when the driver finally pulled up in front of my father's home on Clinton Street. I was confused and feeling vulnerable, my father had just been diagnosed with heart disease. I broke it off but Jamie continued to harass me with threatening letters and phone calls. With the help of Stephen, Jamie was reprimanded and given a warning of a dishonorable discharge from the First City Troop. I hadn't seen or spoken to him in two years.

"What did he want?" I asked nervously. "He's angry that the Copley painting was offered to the Historical Society and not to the Art Museum." "But that was Pamela's choice to make, not mine." "I told him that you had nothing to do with her decision but of course he didn't believe me. That would have been a real feather in his cap if he had been able to procure a never before seen portrait by John Singleton Copley, one of the greatest American artists in the 18th century. And of course he would have taken all the credit," Phoebe said knowingly. "The closest I *ever* want to get to a Cadwalader again is a piece of Chippendale furniture," I said heatedly. The Cadwalader family had commissioned one of the finest furniture collections of the 18th century and an antiques dealer's dream was to find a piece. Most were in museum collections. "I called my brother Stephen to put him on the alert. Don't worry; I just wanted you to know about his phone call. Now, on to happier topics, you said you had great news…"

I told Phoebe about finally meeting Sarah Townsend's cousin, Andrew and that he asked me to curate the decorative arts collection in The Solitude, the first of the Fairmount Park House restorations. "Oh Henrietta, that is great news!" "There's more…he asked me to go to dinner on Saturday and then he kissed me. Oh Phoebe, I'm scared, especially now that Jamie has resurfaced." Sweet and gentle Phoebe could be a lioness when provoked and said, "I won't let Jamie do anything to mar your happiness, Henrietta. One phone call from Dr. Spiller to the Director of the Art Museum and he'll find himself looking for a new job. Let's order another glass of wine to celebrate your great news. By the way, you didn't tell me if Andrew is a good kisser…"

I was a nervous wreck all day Saturday and must have changed my clothes three times. I finally settled on the outfit I wore to the opening of the exhibit - a simple bateau neck black dress with long tight fitting lace sleeves and a claret red cashmere shawl. I wore my grandmother's pearl necklace and matching ruby and pearl earrings. I was happy I could wear my three inch black leather pumps. Andrew said he would meet me at the Historical Society at 4PM. I called a cab and was just getting out of the car when I saw him enter the building. I hurried to catch up to him. In his hand was a miniature bouquet of ruby red roses. "These are for Caroline, you look beautiful." He hadn't yet seen the show and had no way of knowing about the ruby red rose I found on Caroline's grave after the opening of the exhibit. I had told no one about it, it was to be our secret – mine and Caroline's.

"Well, well, look who it is; please don't let me interrupt, I would hate to break up this cozy tête à tête." Recognizing that voice, I quickly turned. It was Jamie Cadwalader. "Congratulations, Henrietta on the Copley exhibit. I just got back into town or I would have attended the opening. Pretty impressive to have not one but two featured articles - *Art in America* and *Art & Antiques*. However it would have made a far more prestigious showing at the Art Museum and so much better for your reputation…" Andrew could see I was visibly upset and moved to stand between me and Jamie. "The name's Andrew Townsend and you are?" "An old friend," answered Jamie. "I was just leaving." I heard him laughing as he walked out the door. *"Who was that?"* asked Andrew.

I wanted to believe that Jamie was not going to ruin my date with Andrew but my heart wasn't in it. As we toured the exhibit, I gave him the abbreviated version of how I and my friends found the painting and amazing artifacts. "The exhibit, as well as the design, is exquisite," he said. "It was a team effort and I'm so lucky to have these people in my life," I replied. Andrew stopped in the middle of the exhibit and as if he could read my mind, looked at me and said, "Henrietta, don't let one bad apple ruin it for you, you are an amazing person and I'm looking forward to getting to know you better, if you'll let me. Besides, my cousin Sarah would kill me if I ever did anything to upset you."

We left the Historical Society as they were closing for the day and walked west on Locust to Broad Street. "Would you like to have a drink at the Union League before dinner?" asked Andrew. "I've been consulting with them about a future restoration project." The Union League at 140 South Broad Street was a private club built in 1865 and the oldest loyalty league to support the Union and the policies of President Abraham Lincoln. Designed in the Second Empire style by John Fraser with later Beaux Arts additions by Horace Trumbauer, it was made of brick and brownstone and had dramatic twin circular staircases leading to the main entrance.

My father had been a member of the Union League and Mother and I always looked forward to their New Year's Day Open House to view the Mummers Parade within the warm confines of the building. The club was for men only but women could be invited as guests or take lunch in the ladies lounge before Friday afternoon concerts of the Philadelphia Orchestra at the Academy of Music. It was still very Victorian and a vote to admit women members in January had been defeated.

Once seated, we ordered our drinks and I told Andrew about Jamie Cadwalader. He listened intently to my story and when I was finished looked at me with those golden eyes, now a dark amber and said, "He will never hurt you again, I promise." In the future, I thought, I would be able to read Andrew's emotions by the color change in his eyes. He would not be able to hide his feelings from me.

The evening improved and soon we were seated in the Long Room at City Tavern at 2nd and Walnut. Faithfully reconstructed in 1976 in time for the Bicentennial, City Tavern was originally built in 1773 and quickly became the favorite meeting place of the Founding Fathers and members of the First Continental Congress. John Adams called it the "most genteel tavern in America." The restaurant was one of my father's favorites. With a harpist playing standards from the 18th Century, we started our meal with a glass of Dry Sack and appetizers of cornmeal fried oysters, cups of West Indies pepper pot soup and Tavern lobster pie. For dessert, we shared a single serving of Martha Washington's chocolate mousse. Andrew was impressed with my hearty appetite. We learned we had much in common – we both loved history and architecture and were born one day apart – I on May 5th and he on May 6th. "Ah, emeralds are the birth stone of May, I'll have to remember that," he said teasingly. Lingering over coffee, all thoughts of Jamie Cadwalader had vanished.

Later, we found ourselves in front of the antiques shop, not wanting the evening to end. "Do you have time to stop by my house tomorrow for Sunday brunch?" he asked. "I make a pretty decent spinach and mushroom omelet, we can go over our schedules and I will give you a set of floor plans. I have a tentative budget for the interior furnishings but you can give me a more realistic number after you review the plans. Our target completion date is December - ten months from now. The Park Commission would like to plan an open house for Christmas." "I can work with that time frame; I may even find items we can use when I travel to the antiques shows coming up this spring and summer. I wonder if we could hire the harpist from the City Tavern for that evening?" "I think I'm going to enjoy working with you, Ms. Grasso *very, very much*." And with that, this time without asking permission, he leaned in and kissed me and then he did it again.

Sunday afternoon I was at Andrew's door at 126 Delancey Street. He came to the door barefooted, wearing faded jeans and a rumpled white shirt with the sleeves rolled up. His dark brown hair was wet from the shower and his skin gave off a fresh, citrusy scent. "Good afternoon Sir, can I interest you in a slightly used set of encyclopedia?" "*You interest me*, but I'll keep those bad thoughts to myself, it is the

Lord's Day," he said as he took my hand and lead me inside. "First, brunch, young lady and then work, I always feed my women first."

Delicious smells of sautéed spinach, onions and mushrooms, mixed with freshly brewed coffee, emanated from the kitchen. *Spring* from Vivaldi's Four Seasons was playing softly in the background. The kitchen housed a large white marble counter over an ebony wood work station with a set of four black Italian leather swivel bar chairs, shaker style white wooden cabinets, a matching wood paneled refrigerator and a black six burner Aga stove in an alcove. The floor was black and white checkerboard tile. Afternoon sunlight streamed through French doors leading to the garden beyond.

"Well, if the rest of the house is as nice as the kitchen, I'll take it," I joked. "I wish you would and I'll give you a good price - but there is one slight problem…" "Oh, and what might that be?" "I come with the house - package deal." We looked at each other for a long moment until he broke the uncomfortable silence. "M'lady, please forgive my impertinence, your omelet is served, would you like a glass of orange juice?" Thankfully the awkward moment passed.

After brunch he showed me the house built in 1810 in the Federal style. On the second floor I saw that the master bedroom had an inviting unmade king sized bed and a fireplace. Then up a flight - the whole top floor was Andrew's studio with northern light coming in from the two front windows and a skylight. "Let me get a set of plans for you and then we can go back to the kitchen," he said. We worked well together and several hours later, after a few more cups of coffee, we had hammered out a schedule to meet our deadline. He gave me a duplicate key to The Solitude. "They will have your name at the front gate at the zoo and you can come and go as you please." "I'll start right away and will have my presentation ready before I leave for the Charleston show." "Great, I'll set up a meeting with the Commission."

It was time to go. At the door, he looked at me and gently folded me in his arms. I could hear his heart beating when he said, "Henrietta, what am I going to do with you?" As I walked home on Pine Street I knew one thing; yet another sleepless night awaited me in the George III tester bed.

After an emotional several days, I decided to make Sunday an early night, so, after a light supper, I went to bed.

I was sound asleep when the phone rang. I answered it and Andrew was saying "Henrietta, I'm at The Solitude, you must come right away, I have something amazing to show you." "But Andrew the zoo is closed at night." "No, you can come in through the back entrance; I'll leave the gate open for you." I hurried to get dressed and left the shop just in time to see a yellow cab come down the street. East River Drive was shrouded in heavy fog; I couldn't see where we were going. Finally we arrived at the back entrance to the zoo. I walked through the open gate, the fog thickening; I could smell the animals. As I approached The Solitude, I saw candles burning in the windows. The front door opened to my touch and I called Andrew's name. "I'm down here in the cellars, come see what I've found," he answered. I slowly descended the stairs and I saw him standing there with his back to me. There were more candles all around the room. "Andrew, what is it?" My words dried in my throat as he slowly turned and in the flickering candlelight I saw the face of - Jamie Cadwalader. "You'll never get away from me, Henrietta, don't even try."

The ringing of the phone woke me from my nightmare. It was only 10PM according to the clock on my bedside table. Andrew was on the line just like in my dream. "I wanted to say goodnight, I really enjoyed our day today and last night." "Oh, Andrew…" "What's wrong, you sound upset." I told him about my frightening dream. "Do you want me to come over?" "Yes, please." "I'll be there in ten minutes." He arrived and as we walked up the stairs to my apartment, he gently placed his hand on my back. We sat in the red sitting room and he turned on the gas fire. Without saying a word, he went into the Pullman kitchen and found the tea things. And after all the tea was gone, he took me by the hand and we walked into my bedroom to the waiting George III tester bed.

Since my father died, I had difficulty sleeping but the next morning I awoke feeling a sense of peacefulness. As I looked over, I saw Andrew, sound asleep, still dressed n his jeans and shirt from the night before. Things were happening so fast that it scared me but I knew one thing – I could trust him.

I was in the kitchen making coffee when he came into the room. "Chief Dragon Slayer, at your service, M'lady," he said as he kissed my hand. I handed him a cup of coffee and he looked around the red sitting room spotting the Chippendale secretary. "So this must be where you found the star ruby ring." I nodded in agreement. "What a story to tell our grandchildren." With that comment, he laid his cup down. "I don't want to say or do anything to upset you and we can take it as slow as you like but I must tell you - I'm falling in love with you."

I had three weeks to prepare my presentation to the Fairmount Park Commission on The Solitude before Andrew was leaving for his alma mater, the University of Virginia in Charlottesville. He was invited as a guest lecturer to discuss his work with the Irish Georgian Society. Luckily, he was going to be gone the same week Sarah Townsend and I were attending the Charleston Antiques show. Sarah had been helping me at the Charleston show for the last few years. The furniture, mirrors, sconces, sterling pieces and porcelains were selected and I always borrowed a collection of framed antique prints from Washington Square Gallery. This year I would also have on display the spring issues of Art in America and Art & Antiques magazines featuring the articles on the John Singleton Copley exhibit.

I unrolled The Solitude floor plans and anchored them on my work table in the back of the shop and started to make a list: custom draperies, carpeting, mirrors, paintings, prints, furniture for the parlor, dining room, library and bedroom, upholstering for chairs and sofas, bedding for the bedroom, books for the library, tea and dinner service, sterling candlesticks and bowls and decorative porcelain. I placed a general value by each item and came up with a rough estimate, then factored in my consulting fees and estimated reimbursable expenses. Next I looked through my reference books and photocopied examples from 1780 to 1815. I could rely on my sources at Winterthur for period fabric, carpet and paint reproductions and upholsterers. There were antiquarian book stores I wanted to visit to select books for John Penn's library. I also needed to make an appointment at the Physick

House to examine the oval mahogany cabinet that had come from The Solitude. Perhaps I would have some luck tracking down its twin.

It felt good to be busy, my mind occupied with work but my thoughts kept returning to Andrew, this amazing man who had come into my life. No matter what the future held, I was lucky to have met him and to now have him in my life. I silently agreed with Sarah that my father would have liked him very much.

With these thoughts still in my head, I picked up the phone and called the Physick House. Even though the museum was closed on Mondays, I was able to get an appointment for that very afternoon and headed out to 321 S. 4th Street. The Physick House, the only free-standing Federal mansion remaining from Colonial Philadelphia was impressive. Built in 1786 by wealthy Madeira wine importer Henry Hill, it became the residence of Dr. Philip Syng Physick, known as the father of American surgery, in 1815. Managed by the Philadelphia Society for the Preservation of Landmarks, I was welcomed at the door by education coordinator, Emily Miller. As a member of the Society, I knew Emily well. "Henrietta, I'm glad you called, your project sounds so intriguing." Emily led me into the breakfast room to see John Penn's oval mahogany cabinet. "You know we normally don't allow photographs to be taken but, for you, we'll make the exception." "Thank you Emily, this shouldn't take long," I said as I took out my camera, tape measure and notebook from my leather satchel.

Displayed in the cabinet was a collection of Tucker porcelain. In 1826 William Ellis Tucker founded a porcelain factory in Philadelphia, considered the first in America to compete with European imports. By 1838 the factory closed making the existing pieces quite valuable. "You know, the Philadelphia Museum owns a large collection of Tucker porcelain. Now that I think of it, I remember seeing a vase with a painting of The Solitude when we were researching our collection" she said. "Maybe they would donate it or lend it to the Fairmount Park Commission for the house. We might also be able to lend the cabinet for your open house if you don't find the mate to it in time." "Emily, that would be wonderful, thank you!" We spoke for a few more minutes then said goodbye at the door. As I walked out I thought the project was getting off to a great start in more ways than one. I was curious to see this Solitude vase; maybe I should plan a trip to the Art Museum next.

When I returned to the shop I called Sarah. "Well, how did Saturday night go with Andrew?" "We had a wonderful time and then he invited me for brunch on Sunday to go over our work schedule." I didn't want to tell her about seeing Jamie Cadwalader or that Andrew stayed over in my apartment Sunday night. "Sarah, I was told that the Art Museum has a piece of Tucker porcelain – a vase with a painting of The Solitude on it. I would like to see it, who should I speak to there?" "You remember William Becker; he took a seminar at Winterthur with us on Chinese blue & white export porcelain. He's now the assistant curator of ceramics at the museum. I can call him and tell him to expect your call regarding the vase." A few minutes later Sarah called back and gave me William's phone number. I immediately called him and he agreed to see me the next morning.

That night my bed felt strange without Andrew. Oh, I had my share of flirtations in high school and college but this was different. Then my phone rang and I heard his rich, deep voice say, "Just checking to see if you need a dragon slayed tonight, I must admit, it *was* kind of fun last night. Don't get much of a chance these days, more's the pity, and my armor's a bit rusty. I've been sitting here in my kitchen surrounded by cans of Rustoleum and WD-40." The image of Andrew in his elegant white kitchen dressed in a suit of rusty armor made me laugh so hard I could barely catch my breath. "I love to hear you laugh, Henrietta, get a good night's sleep. Call me if you need me."

I arrived at the Art Museum the next morning for my appointment with William Becker. "I was happy to hear from Sarah that you are working on The Solitude, Henrietta. Fortunately, that particular Tucker vase is not on exhibit at the moment and we can go to the storage room and take a good look at it." In the storage room, William retrieved two pairs of white cotton gloves and led me to a work table. A few minutes later he returned with The Solitude vase. "William Tucker painted images on porcelain copied from prints of Philadelphia landmarks by local artists like Thomas Birch. The portrait of The Solitude is a particularly good one."

William turned it around for me then showed me the hallmarks underneath the base. "You're not allowed to photograph the vase but I can give you a picture of it. Sarah asked about a loan or donation of the vase to The Solitude and I will look into that for you – no promises but I'll try."

I thanked William for showing me the vase and the possibility of having it for the Solitude collection. It was quiet this morning, hardly anyone in the museum, so I decided to view the decorative arts and furniture galleries for inspiration. But first, I was drawn to the museum's dramatic armor collection at the top of the Great Stair Hall. As I walked into the gallery, I was thinking about Andrew's phone call from last night and still smiling about his rusty armor when I felt someone come up behind me and roughly grab my right arm - *it was Jamie Cadwalader.*

We were all alone in the dark gallery as he pulled me against him and whispered, "I heard that the *celebrated* Ms. Grasso was here but I think I could *feel you* as soon as you entered the building." As he pressed me into him, I could feel his arousal and I tried to break away but he tightened his grip – his whisper turning into a low growl - "You think you can try to get me discharged from the First City Troop and now fired from my job? Well think again, *Madam* because this time I won't be so *gentle*…" Just then a man and woman walked into the gallery and he let go of my arm. I ran down the stairs and out the back entrance to the taxi cab stand where a line of cabs was waiting and jumped in the first one. I didn't know where to go when I suddenly told the cab driver to take me to 126 Delancey Street.

I saw the Karmann Ghia parked at the curb - I told the driver to wait and knocked hard on his door, hoping he could hear me from his third floor studio. He answered right away. "What a pleasant surprise…" he stopped midsentence when he saw the look on my face, ran to the cab, paid the driver and ushered me into the house. "What happened?" I broke down in sobs and couldn't speak. He led me to the sofa where we sat with his arms around me until my crying subsided. He handed me a white handkerchief from his pocket and rose to get me a glass of water. When he returned I told him of my visit to the art museum and my horrible encounter with Jamie. He removed my jacket and rolled up my sleeve to reveal red welts on my skin. "Oh sweetheart, *this* is what he did to you? I'll kill the bastard!" "No Andrew, it was partly my fault, he's still angry about the reprimand from the First City Troop and now - losing his job at the museum if I report him. I'm afraid of what he might do. He seems to be spiraling out of control!"

"Henrietta, I have to get something from my office upstairs, I'll be right back." He returned with a Polaroid camera and said, "I know you don't want to go to the police but we have to document the bruises on your arm." After he took the photographs we sat together on the sofa and he outlined his plan:

"Use my phone to call Melinda and James, tell them you will be working at my home for the next few days but will check in with them. Give them my number for emergencies. If anyone calls, they can say you're away on business. We'll go back to your apartment after the shop has closed to get extra clothes and you can stay in one of my guest rooms. Do you have Phoebe's brother's phone number at work?" Stephen Ingersoll was a lawyer with Ballard Spahr Andrews and Ingersoll. "We need to speak to him and Phoebe and then make an appointment to meet with Jamie's father." General Thomas Cadwalader was retired and living in Haverford on the Main Line. I had been there several times to visit when I was dating Jamie. Andrew spoke to Stephen on the phone and I called Phoebe. Stephen called back with a meeting scheduled with the senior Cadwalader for the next afternoon.

That evening, Andrew fixed a simple meal of chicken soup and fresh bread from Sarcone's Bakery. I didn't have much of an appetite and decided to retire early. Tomorrow was going to be a stressful day. In my haste to pack my clothes, I had forgotten my nightgown and robe. Andrew handed me one of his soft white shirts and led me to the guestroom door. "I'm going upstairs to do some work for awhile, call me if you need anything. Try to get a good night's sleep, I'll check in on you before I go to bed."

I woke up in the dark room not knowing where I was – then I remembered - I was in Andrew's guest room. The house was quiet; he must be asleep in bed. I got up and slowly walked down the hall. His door was open and I found him sound asleep, lightly snoring. I whispered his name and he awoke. "Can I sleep with you?" I asked. His chest was bare and I could see a line of dark hair receding into his pale blue boxer shorts as he lifted the white comforter. I lay down and he held me against his chest. "Does your arm still hurt?" he asked. "Just a little." Then I looked into his eyes and said, "Make love to me Andrew, please." "Are you sure you want to do this, I can wait." I answered, "But I can't."

The next morning I awoke to the aroma of fresh coffee drifting up from the kitchen. Andrew entered the bedroom, smiling. "Good morning sleepy head, did you have a good night's sleep?" I smiled back and nodded as he handed me a cup of coffee. I took a few sips and then he placed the cup on the bedside table and took both my hands in his. "I want you to know how much last night meant to me, how much *you* mean to me. I love you, Henrietta."

After breakfast, we drove to Stephen's office and then to the Cadwalader home with Stephen and Phoebe. General Thomas Cadwalader, still vigorous at 73 stood up as we entered the room. "Welcome to my home, although I wish it was under better circumstances. Henrietta, how are you, my dear?" Stephen introduced Andrew to the General and he asked us to be seated.

"Jamie was my last child; I was 41 when he was born. I blame myself in a way, I indulged him. When he received his degrees in Art History I felt he had finally found his niche and with my family's recent donation of the Charles Willson Peale portraits to the Art Museum, I hoped his position there was secure. The problem continues to be his cocaine addiction. He's been to rehabilitation but the problem persists. I'm so sorry for what he's done to you Henrietta, both in the past and from what I hear, more recently. His behavior is abominable."

Stephen then spoke. "General, here is an envelope with copies of signed and notarized affidavits from all of us as witnesses to Jamie's behavior, his reprimand from the First City Troop, the threatening letters he sent to Henrietta, her account of his sexual assault in the past and more recently yesterday at the museum and photographs of her bruises. If Jamie ever attempts to contact Henrietta again, we shall go to the police and he will be prosecuted, I assure you." "Thank you Stephen, for giving him this last chance. He resigned from his position at the museum today citing health reasons. I have secured a position for him in London at Sotheby's only *if* he undergoes successful treatment. He has agreed to this arrangement, he has no choice, and will be in a facility in London where he can't leave. They are going to hold his passport. I have colleagues there who will report to me. I've notified his brothers and they are going to personally escort him to London on the 6PM flight tonight." Stephen said, "I will also be at the airport tonight to make sure he gets on the plane." The General looked at me and said, "He won't bother you again, Henrietta, you have my word and that of my sons."

Once all danger from Jamie was safely in the past, we were back on Delancey Street. His eyes filling with emotion, Andrew said, "I promised you he would never hurt you again and yet it still happened. I'm so sorry for what he did to you. I want to string him up by his balls." I hugged him tightly. "Andrew, you are an amazing man; I'm safe now, thanks to you, Stephen and Phoebe but there is a much more important issue." "What is it Henrietta?" "I would be remiss, for not thanking you properly for slaying yet another dragon." A dimple appeared in his cheek when he finally smiled. "Well, since you brought it up what would be a proper token, M'lady?" And on that note, I grabbed his hand and my knight and I hurried up the stairs to his room with the king-sized bed where I gave him a few tokens of my affection.

Life back at H.R. Grasso & Daughter seemed suddenly dull since I met Andrew but we both agreed we needed to spend a few days apart just to get some work done. Could it be only a week had gone by since I agreed to work on The Solitude and we had gone on our first date? So much had happened since then. Now I really had to focus on the presentation and the upcoming Charleston Antiques Show.

Finally my presentation was polished and ready to deliver to the Fairmount Park Commission. We planned to meet at the Fairmount Park Conservancy offices— the funding organizational arm of the project. After Andrew's slide show highlighting images of The Solitude and an update of the restoration work in progress he proudly introduced me to the group, citing my credentials: BFA in Art History, University of Pennsylvania, MFA in American Material Culture at Winterthur, University of Delaware, owner of a well established family antiques business in Philadelphia since 1955 and most recently, curator of the John Singleton Copley exhibit at the Historical Society of Pennsylvania. He then handed out copies of *Art in America* and *Art & Antiques* magazines flagged with the Copley articles and the itemized budget and time-line for completion. I continued the slide show with images of furniture and decorative art suggestions for The Solitude. After answering questions from the group, we received an enthusiastic thumbs *up* to proceed.

As we left the meeting Andrew said, "This is a cause for celebration; I'm taking you to lunch at Le Bec Fin." Le Bec Fin at 15th and Walnut was the premier eatery in Philadelphia. With its superb French menu, gilt mirrors and crystal chandeliers, it was a jewel box of a restaurant. "It's impossible to get a reservation this quickly," I replied. "Never fear my sweet, I have connections; actually I reserved it as soon as I set up the meeting almost three weeks ago. I just knew your presentation would knock them off their feet."

December 1983

Philadelphia

As I approached The Solitude in the darkness, candles were burning in the windows. The strings of a harp, playing the music of Handel, floated on the night air. The front door opened to my touch and the co-mingled scents of balsam, citrus and cloves permeated the room. Greenery entwined the ornamental ironwork balustrade going up the staircase. In the dining room under the exquisitely carved ceiling, a Federal mahogany pedestal table was laden with food lit from above by candles in a gilt chandelier. John Penn's oval cabinet created by Samuel Claphamson stood on the right side of the fireplace with the Tucker Solitude vase proudly displayed within, over the mantel was James Reid Lambdin's portrait of John Penn, and on the left side, a sterling silver punch bowl sat on a Hepplewhite serpentine sideboard filled with Philadelphia Fish House Punch.

The restoration of The Solitude was complete. At the end of the evening, Andrew and I stood in John Penn's library on the second floor, which once empty, was now filled with volumes of Dante, Petrarch, Chaucer and Shakespeare. He took me by the hand and led me into Penn's bedroom where a solitary bed stood in the alcove and said, "John Penn never married although he was a firm believer in matrimony. He even created the Outinian Society whose purpose was to encourage young men and women to marry." He put his hand in his pocket and withdrew a small leather case. Inside was an antique cabochon emerald ring.

"I think I loved you from the first moment," he said as he looked at me; his golden eyes warmed by a fire lit from within. "Henrietta, will you marry me?" And I responded as I had the first time he asked to kiss me and said, "Oh yes."

On Christmas Eve a special delivery arrived at H.R. Grasso & Daughter. Wrapped with a large red satin bow was a pair of antique Chippendale arm chairs with an attached card that read:

Henrietta - Congratulations on your engagement - We sincerely wish you and Andrew much happiness - The Cadwalader Family.

New Year's Eve 1983
Philadelphia

To celebrate my engagement to Andrew Townsend and to welcome in the New Year, Pamela Stuart invited us to a formal midnight supper at her home on Washington Square. Phoebe and Stephen Ingersoll, Sarah Townsend, Samuel Jacobson, Pamela, Andrew and I sat around the mahogany table in her dining room, the men in black tie, the women in black gowns, a fire blazing in the grate and the crystal and gilt chandelier aglow in candlelight. One of the most beautiful pieces in classical music, Mozart's *Requiem in D Minor* was playing softly; Pamela's dry sense of humor heralding the demise of the old year. The table was laid with the Haviland Limoges in the Symphonie pattern, white with a thin black and gold border.

At my place setting was a miniature bouquet of white roses tied with a white satin ribbon and a small square gift box. Nestled inside was an exquisite tea cup. Pamela looked at Andrew and me and said, "I wanted it to be a surprise but I think this occasion calls for it – I want you to have Caroline's china for your new life together." The Chelsea Darby china was Caroline Blackburn Stuart's 1769 wedding set – English porcelain with a robin's egg blue scalloped and roped border on a white ground with a floral bouquet in the center. Tears came to my eyes as I looked at Pamela and then Andrew – they both knew what this meant to me. "I don't know what to say, Pamela." Andrew answered for us both when he stood and took Pamela's hand, gently kissed it and said, "Pamela, Henrietta and I thank you for your most loving and generous gift and promise we will be good stewards, no pun intended." His humor broke the tension and we all laughed.

The eighth place at the head of the table was left empty. "This is for your father whom I'm sure would have loved to be with us tonight," she said. "I think we should now make a toast to Henry Richard Grasso, an exceptional man and a wonderful father." "To Henry Richard Grasso," we answered as we raised our glasses. The evening progressed merrily from there and at the stroke of midnight we hugged and kissed and said, "Happy New Year." Then Andrew reminded everyone that they were his guests at the Union League open house on New Year's Day.

As we opened the door to take our leave, standing at the curb was a driver with a top hat, a chestnut horse and a gleaming black carriage with brass lanterns. "Your carriage awaits, M'lady," said Andrew. On the seat was a fur blanket which he tucked around us and said, "Happy New Year my love," and kissed me. He then voiced instructions to the driver, "Once around the square *very slowly* and then home to 126 Delancey Street." And so we did.

The Royal Crescent

June 1984
Philadelphia

I woke up the first of June in Andrew's arms in his house on Delancey Street and *Summer* from Vivaldi's Four Seasons was playing on WFLN, a good omen. With the Charleston and Philadelphia antiques shows behind me, I accepted my mother's invitation to spend the month of June at her home in Bath, England. I had not been to visit in over seven years. I called her and my step-father, Arthur on Christmas Day and told them of my engagement to Andrew Townsend. "Darling, once you're married, you'll be too busy to visit," she said. She was determined to have me come.

Anxious to get going, I still had packing to do before Andrew drove me to the air-port for an early afternoon flight to Heathrow. My plan was to stay in London the first two days and then travel to Bath for the remainder of June. I wanted to visit certain places in London first; John Singleton Copley's paintings at the National Portrait Gallery, Hanover Square - the site of his former home at Nos. 25-26 George Street and his grave at Highgate Cemetery. Shopping at Liberty of London and Harrods, then afternoon tea at Fortnum & Mason was also on the agenda.

I bid goodbye to Melinda and James knowing I was leaving H.R. Grasso & Daughter in capable hands. On the drive to the airport, Andrew assured me that our second Fairmount Park House restoration, Woodford was on schedule and to try not to think about work while I was gone. "Call me when you arrive at

Dukes Hotel." *"I will."* "Enjoy London and Bath, I wish I was coming with you." *"Me too."* "Don't let your mother and Arthur drive you crazy." *"I won't."* When we arrived at the British Airways terminal, he took me in his arms and gave me a proper American goodbye. "I love you Henrietta; don't fall in love with the lord of the manor while you're there and forget all about me." I laughed and said, "Fat chance of that ever happening, my love. You will always be my first knight in rusty armor."

June 1984

London

The seven hour flight from Philadelphia to London was uneventful and soon the taxi was pulling up to Dukes Hotel on St. James Place, a quiet street off Piccadilly Circus. I checked in at the reception desk and was escorted to my room. There waiting for me was an exquisite Victorian bouquet of ruby red roses and lily of the valley. The card attached said:

"Lily of the Valley symbolizes the return of happiness, sweetness and a feeling of contentment – all these things you have given me, Love, Andrew."

I hurriedly called the Old Rectory to let my mother and Arthur know I had arrived and would see them in two days. I was going to take the 10AM train from Paddington Station and would arrive in Bath by 11:30. I checked the time; it was 7PM in Philadelphia and midnight here in London then called Andrew. "I've arrived at Dukes and just received your flowers and card," my voice started to break… "they're beautiful, thank you." "Philadelphia feels so lonely without you, particularly my bed," he sighed. "You've ruined it for me you know, I don't think I can go back to my nefarious bachelor ways." "I love you Andrew." "Sweetheart, I love you too, get a good night's sleep – I know I won't." We both laughed and said good night.

I was able to get a running start on my jet lag and had a restful night's sleep. Awaking late the next morning and starving, I ordered a hearty English breakfast from room service — Freshly squeezed Valencia orange juice, Burford brown eggs, Middlewhite sausage, grilled tomato, field mushroom, toast and coffee. After that, I had a hot shower and dressed for the day.

My first stop was the National Portrait Gallery. I was eager to see the John Singleton Copley portraits from his later period and compare them to the Caroline Blackburn Stuart portrait. As I walked into the gallery, there was a man standing in front of one of the Copley paintings. He happened to turn around as I approached. I thought - *Mount Olympus must be missing one of their gods* - dressed in a dark blue pinstriped three piece suit; he was tall with blond hair and blue eyes and extraordinarily handsome. He had been gazing at one of Copley's monumental historic paintings — *The Collapse of the Earl of Chatham in the House of Lords.* It was said Copley was ahead of his time, working in the style of the Romantic Movement as witnessed in this dramatic painting. Nearby was his portrait of George John Spencer, 2nd Earl Spencer, the ancestor of Princess Diana.

"You are an admirer of Copley too, I see," he said. "Yes, I am." "You're an American — I've heard you have a fine collection of Copley paintings in your museums. Of course the family sold off most of the good ones to American collectors." "Well, he was an American," I replied. "Yes, but he did defect to the other side," he said teasingly. "I'm Harry Atherton, at you service, Madam and may I know *your* name?" "My name is Henrietta Grasso; do you work here at the National?" There was a fleeting look of recognition in his eyes upon hearing my name. "No, but I am in the art business." "Well, Mr. Atherton it was nice meeting you," and turned to leave. "Could I interest you in a cup of tea, Ms. Grasso? I've gotten quite thirsty with all this art talk." "No, I must go but thank you." I walked out of the gallery and turned back just in time to see him looking at me.

I went to the museum store and purchased a few books; gifts for Dr. Spiller and Phoebe and for my reference library and requested they be shipped to Philadelphia. Now in full shopping mode, I left the museum and headed to Liberty of London. The Tudor design of the flagship store at 210-220 Regent Street was actually constructed in 1924 from timbers salvaged from two ships — HMS Impregnable and

HMS Hindustan. There I had fun selecting colorful silk ties and scarves in classic Liberty prints for the men and women in my life and asked the sales staff to also ship them home.

After browsing through Harrods, I strolled along the Old Brompton Road and noticed a tiny shop with a sign saying Cavendish Estate Jewellers. I went inside; the interior looked like nothing had changed since the Victorian era. A man came out and said, "Madam may I assist you?" He wore an old fashioned three piece suit with a high collar and tie and long bushy sideburns - mutton chops. "Just looking, thank you," I replied. "Are you looking for yourself or perhaps a gentleman?" As he was speaking I gazed into the display case and saw a pair of gold cufflinks. "Ah, for a gentleman then. May I suggest these cufflinks made of 22 karat gold English sovereigns depicting St George and the Dragon? They are of recent mintage – 1910." The cufflinks would be the perfect present for Andrew, my dragon slayer and also reflect my half British heritage. "There is also a bracelet to match for Madam." He opened the drawer behind him and removed a gold link bracelet with a gold sovereign in the center and a small heart locket dangling from the clasp. It was beautiful. "I think I shall take the cufflinks for now and think about the bracelet."

It had been a very satisfying day of shopping and I finally worked my way back to Piccadilly to Fortnum & Mason for a well deserved afternoon tea. Started as a grocery store in 1707, they became purveyors to the Crown. It was now a department store known for elegant food hampers and a delightful tearoom. I arrived just in time to see the mechanical clock strike the hour. In 1965 Fortnum and Mason added the ornate clock over their front entrance. The eighteen bells chimed every 15 minutes and on the hour, to the tune of the Eton School anthem, doors opened and four foot high figures of Mr. Fortnum and Mr. Mason in 18th century powdered wigs and attire emerged. They bowed to each other, turned around and then returned to their business. Once inside, before taking my tea, I purchased one more collection of gifts to ship home: F & M's "Rubies in the Rubble", a specialty chutney made from fruits obtained in the London markets and honey from their own bee hives. I saved the sample tea menu as a souvenir for Pamela.

Returning to the hotel after tea, I filled the bathtub with lavender salts and took a long hot soak. Relaxing in the tub, my mind wandered back to the events of the day. I decided to return to the little jewelry shop tomorrow and purchase the bracelet. Wrapped in one of the hotel's white fluffy robes, I turned on the lamp by my bed and inhaled the sweetness of the lily of the valley and roses on the bedside table. Then I pulled the covers back and climbed into bed and fell fast asleep dreaming of Mount Olympus and a tall blonde Greek god.

In the morning I made my way to Hanover Square in Mayfair, once the site of the Copley home. While a few of the 18th-century houses remained, most of the square was now almost entirely occupied by offices. As I walked around the square I envisioned what life must have been like for the Copley family in 1775, to think - they walked these same streets. On St. George Street, near the square, stood St. George's Anglican Church. This must have been the church where the Copley family worshipped. I stepped inside and picked up a pamphlet and read: "The church was designed by John James and built in 1721. The classical portico is supported by six Corinthian columns...George Friderick Handel was one of the church's most famous parishioners. It was in his house on Brook Street that he composed some of his greatest works, including *Messiah*." Dad would have enjoyed seeing all this.

Leaving Hanover Square I headed back to Piccadilly returning to Fortnum & Mason to pick up a bouquet of roses to take to John Singleton Copley's grave. Highgate Cemetery was in North London, about five miles away, so I took a taxi to the entrance of the cemetery and asked the driver to wait. I had called ahead to gain access and directions to Copley's grave. He was buried in the East cemetery in a grave belonging to the Hutchinson family. At the gate I received a pamphlet and a map.

It was a glorious place - otherworldly. I finally came to the Hutchinson family mausoleum and laid the red roses on the grave of John Singleton Copley, silently thanking him for remembering Caroline Blackburn Stuart. I still believed, in some mystical way, that it was he who placed the red rose on Caroline's grave in St. Peter's churchyard last year. The sky suddenly darkened threatening rain; the overgrowth of trees and gloomy statuary adding to the spooky atmosphere. I was relieved to see the amber glow of the taxi headlights as I hurried back to the entrance.

I asked the driver to take me back to the Old Brompton Road to Cavendish Estate Jewellers; I wanted to pick up the sovereign coin bracelet. "Do you have an address, Madam?" "I don't, but the shop is right down the road from Harrods." When we arrived he said, "Are you sure this is the correct location, Madam?" "Yes, I was here yesterday and purchased a pair of cufflinks. Wait, I may still have the receipt in my purse - here it is - Cavendish Estate Jewellers, 159 Old Brompton Road. The driver pulled up to the address but it was an *empty* store front. I got out of the taxi and peered through the glass. There was nothing there. Still, I knocked on the door hoping that Mr. Cavendish was inside. There was a sign on the window – *To Let* and a phone number. I wrote it down and would call as soon as I returned to the hotel

The phone number belonged to a real estate office and I asked them about the former tenant and how I could reach him. "Hold on, let me get the file for that property," a pleasant young man responded. "159 Old Brompton Road was last rented to a confectionery but they moved a year ago." "That's impossible, I was there yesterday and purchased a pair of cufflinks from Cavendish Estate Jewellers, I have the receipt with the address." "I'm afraid not Madam. Did you say Cavendish? Let me check the rest of the file. Oh, yes, here it is, Mr. Henry Cavendish rented the shop until *1910*. I'm sorry I could not be of more help." I thanked him for his time and hung up. I had the cufflinks as tangible proof I was there!

Mr. Cavendish did seem out of place in his Victorian attire and his shop looked like something out of a museum but I thought this was just part of the charm of London. Had I entered a rift in time just by walking down the Old Brompton Road? Since my discovery of the star ruby ring, I'd been having these experiences. I would have to tell Phoebe and Dr. Wendt when I returned to Philadelphia and I had so wanted that bracelet.

The Royal Crescent

June 1984

Bath

The following morning after checking out of the hotel, I took a taxi to Paddington Station and boarded the train to Bath. Set in the Avon Valley in the county of Somerset, Bath was considered one of the most elegant cities in England. The Romans were the first to arrive in 43A.D. to discover a series of hot springs. In the 18th century the city of Bath was completely rebuilt in the local honey colored limestone as a Georgian spa town. Bath was one of the settings of Jane Austen's novels and the location of my mother's antiques shop, H.R. Grasso & Daughter, Bath.

I arrived at Bath Spa Station and looked to see if my mother or Arthur was waiting for me. I heard a man call my name and when I turned around it was *the Greek god* - Harry Atherton. "May I give you a lift Ms. Grasso?" he asked as he climbed out of a dark green Range Rover. "No thank you Mr. Atherton, I'm waiting for someone to pick me up." "And that someone would be me," he said grinning sheepishly. "I don't think so." "No really, your mother, Charlotte was busy with clients in the shop and asked me to do the honours. I am also a client of your mother's; she's going to help me select pieces for my new flat in Bath. You can call her, if you like, to verify my integrity." He was as handsome as when I first saw him. Dressed casually now in jeans and a navy blue vee neck sweater over a white collared shirt, his blonde hair mixed with sunlight, his blue eyes smiling mischievously. "I believe you but I have a feeling it's going to cost me in the end," I replied. "You *wound* me Madam, the only price I wish to extract is the pleasure of your company. Shall we go?"

We pulled up in front of H.R. Grasso & Daughter at No. 3 Quiet Street in less than ten minutes. Mother came out and embraced me saying, "Darling, are you eating enough? You look so thin and pale." "I'm fine Mother, really." "I see you've met Lord Atherton. Thank you, Harry for picking up my daughter." "It was my pleasure, Charlotte but we actually met in London two days ago, at the museum. I was trying to entice her to have tea with me but she turned me down." "Now Henrietta, you must be especially nice to Lord Atherton, he is going to be one of our best clients." "Then may I extend my invitation again?" asked Harry. "Ms. Grasso, may I call you Henrietta, will you do me the honour of having tea with me tomorrow at the Pump Room?" My mother looked at me expectantly and Harry was trying not to laugh. They both had me cornered. "Yes, I will have tea with you," I reluctantly replied.

The next day I was waiting at the shop when Harry came by to take me to tea. "I have to stop at Bath Abbey for a moment and then we can have our tea," he said. We walked down the street to the church. The Abbey Church of Saint Peter and Saint Paul, Bath, commonly known as Bath Abbey was an Anglican parish church and a former Benedictine monastery. Originally founded in the 7th century and rebuilt in the 12th and 16th centuries, it was one of the largest examples of Perpendicular Gothic architecture and the last of the great medieval churches. As my eyes adjusted to the darkness inside the church, Harry led me to a seated figure in one of the pews. As we approached, a man stood up and faced us. Tall with black hair and those ice blue eyes, I couldn't believe who was standing before me. It was Jamie Cadwalader.

"Henrietta, Jamie has something to say, please just hear him out. I will be sitting right here with you the whole time." We sat in the pew and Jamie started to speak. "Henrietta, I know this must seem very strange but let me try to explain. Harry has been my sponsor since I entered rehab last year. I am in recovery now and working with Harry at Sotheby's. When he met you at the museum two days ago, he immediately knew who you were. I have talked about you to him. He knows everything about what happened between us. I want you to know how deeply sorry I am for the way I treated you. I realize now how much I hurt you. I know you don't want to have anything to do with me and I will always have to live with that. But I want you to know that I am sober now, thanks, in no small part, to you."

I could barely look at Jamie. The memory of the pain I had experienced with him came rushing back. He was just sitting there with his head down, looking so vulnerable, that tears came to my eyes. Harry stood and took my hand. "Henrietta, we're going now. Jamie, I'll call you later and see you at the office tomorrow."

Harry continued to hold my hand as we walked back to the Pump Room. Once seated, he ordered our tea and said, "We knew you would never agree to see him and I'm sorry if it all seemed a bit under-handed. Your mother and Arthur knew of this meeting with Jamie today and I promised them I would take every precaution to let nothing happen to you. This was one of the reasons your mother wanted you to come to Bath. I hope you can forgive us."

Harry then went on to tell me that he first started working as a counselor in 1982 with addicted veterans returning home from the Falklands. Harry's father, Lord William Atherton served in the Second World War with Jamie's father, General Cadwalader and they had remained good friends. It was Harry and his father who made the arrangements for Jamie to come to London for rehab and then take the job at Sotheby's.

"Harry, I don't know what to say, except thank you for doing this for Jamie and me and for all the work you do in helping people who are suffering. Then I leaned over and kissed him on the cheek. "And I have Jamie to thank for finally meeting you," he said.

That night, in the drawing room overlooking the garden at the Old Rectory, Mother, Arthur, Harry and I were having pre-dinner drinks, the dogs, Naomi and Isabella sleeping peacefully at their feet. Bach's *Violin Concerto in A Minor* was playing in the background. Mother had invited Harry to dinner to thank him for helping Jamie and me. "Mother and Arthur, it means so much what you did for me, thank you," I said. Never one for showing emotion my mother responded, "Darling, it's all behind us now, we were glad we could help." But I knew what it had cost her and how worried she and Arthur had been.

"Now we can move on to other things. I suggest you stop by the Museum of Costume on Bennett Street first thing tomorrow to get inspired. I've already made an appointment for you after lunch at Farthingale's to be fitted for your costume." I gave her a puzzled look. "Didn't I mention it to you? We're all going to the Netherfield Ball at the Guildhall on the 23rd. You're going to need a Regency ball gown." I looked at Harry who said, "Yes I'm going as well and thanks to my mother who forced me to take dancing lessons at a tender age, I actually know how to do the period dances." Harry then stood and bowed from the waist and said, "Ms. Grasso would you do me the honour of escorting you to the Ball?" It was as if my mother had conjured Jane Austen and we were acting out a scene from one of her novels. "M' lord, it would be my pleasure to attend the Ball with you," I replied and curtsied.

At the end of the evening we were finishing our dessert and coffee when Mother made another announcement. "Henrietta, now that you're here, I wish you to lend your expertise to a very special client. Lord Atherton is in great need of a decorative arts specialist. As he may have mentioned, I have agreed to help him acquire items for his new flat at No. 28 Royal Crescent. But he needs someone who has the time to work with him and that's you, my dear." "But I thought you worked at Sotheby's?" "I do, in the Asian Arts Department but I'm hopeless when it comes to decorating a flat with English antiques and I need someone who can incorporate my Asian art collection. I collect dragons, by the way. I'll be back from London late in the afternoon tomorrow. Can you stop by the flat around 4PM?"

I decided on a simple high waisted white silk organza gown with shear elbow length sleeves after visiting the Costume Museum the next morning and getting fitted at Farthingale's. Mother was going to let me borrow her emerald and diamond necklace and matching earrings. At 4PM I stood on the doorstep of No. 28 Royal Crescent. The Royal Crescent built of the local honey colored Bath stone was a street of 30 terraced houses laid out in a sweeping crescent. Designed by the architect John Wood the Younger and built between 1767 and 1774, it was among the greatest examples of Georgian architecture to be found in the United Kingdom. In more recent times, some of the houses had been divided up into flats. It was in a word – magnificent!

I knocked on the door and waited, then knocked again. I was about to leave when the door flew open and there was Harry, hair sopping wet, wearing only long gray drawstring pants. "Sorry, I was in the shower." I looked at his chest. On his right breast was a small tattoo of a dragon. I couldn't take my eyes off it. I suddenly had this great urge to kiss it.

"Henrietta, welcome to my humble abode. Let me put on proper clothes and I'll be right with you." He came back, hair combed, light blue oxford cloth shirt tucked into khaki slacks and loafers without socks. His eyes were deeper blue against the color of his shirt and his blonde hair was darkened from the shower. I was fascinated. I kept staring at his chest expecting the dragon to spring to life breathing fire at any moment.

"I see you noticed my dragon tattoo. As I mentioned I work in the Asian Arts Department at Sotheby's. More than any other image, the dragon is associated with the Orient. A symbol of the emperor himself, it can take many forms and can be victorious in any circumstance. I got the dragon tattoo when I started working with the vets. It reminds me of our determination to protect and defend against all odds. "That's why you collect dragons," I said. "Yes, that's why and they're great for picking up damsels, in distress or *otherwise*. Let me give you a tour," he said with a wink.

At less than 1800 square feet it was perfect for a man who spent a good portion of his time in London. The sitting room was large with a fireplace; there was a smaller dining room and a good size kitchen, a master bedroom with a fireplace and private bath and a guest room and bath. The flat was on the first level and had access to a private courtyard off the kitchen and master bedroom.

"I just bought it last month and also rent a furnished flat in London so I'll need furnishings for every room." I was quickly gaining admiration for this man and said, "I'll help you as much as I can for the time I'm here in Bath. We may be able to pick up some pieces from estate sales and may even find a few dragons to add to your collection." "Great news, I'm taking a much needed vacation and plan to spend it here in Bath for the month of June. When do you want to get started? Will tomorrow be too soon?"

Harry liked my suggestions for decorating the flat and we got to work immediately. He had the sitting room walls painted in Farrow & Ball Drawing Room Blue, a dark navy, with the molding and trim painted in white gloss enamel, the better to set off the collection of blue and white Chinese porcelain he collected. We found a chesterfield sofa, matching tufted ottoman and a pair of club chairs in cobalt blue velvet. We used antique Chinese silk embroidered fabrics with dragon motifs for pillow covers and an antique Chinese dragon carpet, gray blue with gold dragons for in front of the white marble fireplace mantel. To the right of the fireplace we hung a dramatic Chinese ceremonial armor robe with brass metal work, embroidered with dragons from Harry's personal collection. The dining room was painted Yellow Ground No. 218, a butterscotch yellow with white gloss enamel molding and trim. We were able to fine a regency round mahogany dining table, able to seat 12 when extended and a regency side board by Honore Lannuier circa 1840. Harry's bedroom was painted in Borrowed Light, a pale gray blue. His king bed's headboard was upholstered in a button-tufted midnight blue suede with a matching bench at the foot of the bed and dark blue and white bedding. The basics were now in position. It was time for the fun part of filling in with accessories; antique prints, mirrors, lamps, candlesticks and china. I found a tea service in the Mottahedeh Blue Dragon pattern which I planned to give Harry as a thank you gift and the classic Mottahedeh Blue Canton dinner service as a nod to my American roots. The most fashionable tables in the early American Republic were set with blue and white "Canton" ware.

June 1984
Oxford

Harry asked if we could visit an estate sale in Oxford, an hour and a half drive from Bath and make a day of it. I had only been to Oxford once and was looking forward to seeing it again. Driving in his Range Rover, Bach's *Brandenburg Concertos* playing on the car stereo, we chatted like old friends about his job at Sotheby's and my antiques business. He had been to the states to visit Sotheby's in New York several times but had never been to Philadelphia.

Arriving at the estate sale, we browsed around but didn't find anything of interest until we were getting ready to leave. On the wall was a striking Regency gilt-wood convex mirror circa 1810. It had a reeded circular frame topped with a hand carved, ebonized winged dragon with an arrow tail and tongue flanked by eagle heads with foliate tails. At 46" high by 27" wide it was spectacular and perfect for Harry's entrance hall.

We were exclaiming our good fortune over a hamper lunch, lying on a blanket in Christ Church Meadow as we watched the punters on the River Cherwell. Harry told me he and his older brother William, as well as his father and grandfather had all attended Christ Church. "Christ Church has produced thirteen British prime ministers, I don't know if that's a good thing or not," he joked. "It looks like you turned out pretty well, M'lord." "Well, Lord Byron went to Trinity College in Cambridge where legend has it he used to bathe naked in the Great Court's fountain with his pet *bear*. Trinity always seemed like a more fun place to be than around a bunch of boring aristocrats at Christ Church but now that you're here, looking so seductive lying next to me, things may be about to get more interesting." "Dream on, M'lord," I laughingly replied. "Oh, but I do..." he said.

Late in the afternoon after taking in the classic sights of Oxford – Christopher Wren's Sheldonian Theatre, the Bodleian Library, the circular Radcliffe Camera; the repository for scientific books and the beautiful Queen's College, distinguished by its neoclassical architecture, we stopped at the Cotswold Lodge Hotel for tea. Sitting in a Mediterranean inspired courtyard, surrounded by olive and lemon trees and water trickling in a central fountain, the sky was just beginning to turn a rosy hue. Harry said, "Thank you for coming with me to Oxford today, I really enjoy being with you, Henrietta. These last few weeks have been wonderful." "I've enjoyed being with you too, Harry, it's been fun and we work so well together." "I have a confession to make. When Jamie talked about you, I hoped we might meet someday. Then I bought the flat in Bath and purely by chance found your mother's shop. She mentioned she had a daughter in Philadelphia who also owned an antiques shop and I knew there could be only one Henrietta Grasso. She said you were coming for a visit. That day, when I first saw you at the National

Portrait Gallery, I'm embarrassed to admit, I had gone to brush up on my knowledge of Mr. Copley, hoping to impress you when we met and then you appeared, as if by magic."

We were both quiet on the drive home, deep in our own thoughts, as we listened to Beethoven's *Moonlight Sonata*. This man was stirring strong emotions in me the more I spent time with him. Then I remembered Andrew's joking plea not to fall in love with the lord of the manor and forget about him.

June 1984
Bath

We arrived back at the Old Rectory and Harry walked me to the door. I could smell the perfume of my mother's roses in the garden. I turned to say good night and Harry took me in his arms and kissed me. Both breathless when we finally pulled apart he looked at me and said, "I wanted so much to just carry you upstairs when we were at the hotel..." "Harry ..." "I know." His blue eyes, now dark with emotion, he searched my face and saw the same in mine.

When I came through the front door, Mother and Arthur were still awake. "Andrew called and asked you to return the call if you didn't get home too late. I told him you had gone to Oxford to an estate sale with Lord Atherton. Did you find anything at the sale?" I told them about the extraordinary regency mirror with the ebonized dragon. "I think we can use the George Smith six foot demilune table under it with the gilded lion heads and brass paw feet. The proportion is right to balance the mirror above it and we have a pair of gilt and ebonized bronze candle sticks to go on the table." "Excellent work, Darling, we can't wait to see it all come together. You may have to start dividing your time between Bath and Philadelphia in future. There will be increased demand for your services once everyone hears about your work with Lord Atherton and you know Arthur and I would love to have you here with us in Bath." I didn't know what to say so I thanked them, said good night and then went to my room to call Andrew.

"Sweetheart it's so good to hear your voice! I miss you terribly. How was Oxford?" "Very educational," I tried to joke. "If I had known you when I was there I never would have passed my courses," he joked back. "And how is Lord Atherton? I hope to meet him one day to thank him personally for his amazing help to Jamie and you. By the way, have you heard from Jamie since you saw him at Bath Abbey?" "No, but according to Harry, he is doing very well in recovery and making a name for himself at Sotheby's." "Henrietta, I meant to ask you, is there a *Lady* Atherton?" "Yes." "Oh good, I was afraid I might have some competition." "Lady Atherton is his mother." "Henrietta, what's wrong? I can always tell when you're upset." I didn't want to lie to him. "It's just that he kissed me at the door tonight and I…I felt something."

He was quiet for a long moment on the phone and then spoke. "My love, you are the dearest person in the world to me and I'm so lucky to have you in my life. I think you know how much I love you and if you changed your mind, for whatever reason, I would never want to hold you to a commitment. I want and will always want what's best for you. Do you understand?" "Yes, Andrew I do." "You have been through emotionally trying times these last few years and I don't want to put more pressure on you. Your father's death hit you hard." Andrew knew what it meant to lose a parent. He lost both of his from cancer after he graduated from college. Being an only child, like me, it was his cousin Sarah and her parents who helped him through those difficult times. "You've had a prickly relationship with your mother since your parents' divorce but from what I hear things are improving. I appreciate what Charlotte and Arthur did to help you with Jamie. Jamie is no longer a threat to you, thanks to Harry Atherton. I could even understand why you feel a certain attachment to him. It seems you now have two knights wanting to be your champion. Say the word M'lady and I'll pack my rusty armor and challenge Lord Atherton to a joust, or if you prefer, a duel with broadswords to the death." At that last comment he made me laugh. "Thank you Sir Andrew, but I think I prefer a joust, we Brits have a thing for pageantry." And with that our good humor was restored.

The next morning I left for Harry's flat at the Royal Crescent with a lighter heart. We were going to take the mirror out of the Range Rover and drive back to the shop to pick up the demilune table. Harry answered the door at No. 28 and led me to the kitchen where a French press of hot coffee, orange juice and fresh scones with marmalade from Sally Lunn's bakery were waiting.

We had found an antique French chestnut farmhouse table with eight ladder back chairs with rush seats for the kitchen and a Welsh cupboard to display the china. There was a black enameled Aga in an alcove and a pumpkin and black checkerboard tile floor. When we were seated opposite each other, he said, "Henrietta, I must apologize for my behavior last night, I never meant for it to get out of hand. We Brits usually have better control over our emotions." I smiled at Harry and said, "You forget I'm half British and you could see how in control *I* was..." "From now on, I shall act like a gentleman." "And what fun would that be?" Happily, with the sound of our laughter, the tension from the night before was broken and we enjoyed our breakfast.

The dragon mirror was finally in place over the demilune table. Harry gave me a hug and said, "My parents are having a fund raising garden party on Saturday at Bathampton Hall. The proceeds are going toward the addiction recovery program. I've told them all about you and they are looking forward to meeting you. Can you come? Your mother and Arthur will be there as well." William Atherton, 3rd Earl of Bath and his wife Frances lived at Bathampton Hall, a Georgian manor house built in 1727 across the River Avon. "I would be honored to attend, M'lord, thank you."

After the installation of the mirror, we planned to go to George Bayntun on Manvers Street near the Bath train station to look at antique prints. The shop had a large selection relating to Bath, along with other topographical maps and views. There was also an extensive stock of engraved portraits and natural history prints. We might even find a dragon or two.

And a few dragons we did find and some special views of Bath. From the 1675 volume of Historia Naturalis we found three hand colored copper engravings of *de serpentibus et draconibus*, wonderful engravings of dragons and three 1829 steel engravings drawn By Thos. H. Shepherd of the Royal Crescent, Guildhall and Bath Abbey. Harry loved the one of the Royal Crescent; you could see his flat in the drawing. Bath Abbey held special meaning to both of us because of our meeting with Jamie and Guildhall was the site of the Netherfield Ball on mid-summer's night next week. We selected a simple frame profile in gilded wood for all the prints. The scenes of Bath were going to hang in the sitting room and the dragons, more appropriately, were for the master bedroom.

We arrived at Bathampton Hall on Saturday afternoon and Harry took me over to where his parents were greeting their guests. "Father and Mother, I would like you to meet Ms. Henrietta Grasso." "Lord and Countess Atherton, it's a pleasure to meet you." "Henrietta, it's our pleasure, please call us William and Frances. We hear you are doing fine work at our son's home. We've been trying to get him to return to Bath and it looks like you succeeded where all others have failed," said Harry's father. "Why, she is lovely Harry, where on earth did you find her?" asked Harry's mother. "At the National Portrait Gallery in London, we were admiring the John Singleton Copley portraits." "We've known your mother and Arthur for some time," said Frances. "Your mother said she had a daughter in Philadelphia who also owned an antiques business and told us of your discovery of the Copley portrait. She is so proud of you, my dear."

"Father and Mother, I'm going to borrow Henrietta and give her a tour of the gardens," said Harry. "Henrietta, I have to get something from my car, I'll be right back." Harry returned with a package wrapped with Liberty of London paper and ribbons and led me to a quiet, secluded corner of the garden. "This is for you." I unwrapped the package and inside was the most beautiful silk scarf in shades of emerald greens and royal blues with a coin motif of golden dragons. "We joined with Liberty of London to create a limited edition of one thousand scarves with the dragon design as part of our fund raising efforts for our program. They are all numbered and signed. Yours is the first of this series - 1/1000. We hope to do a new design every year. This year's scarf was created by Catherine Walker, one of Princess Diana's designers. "It's beautiful Harry; will you help me put it on?" "It would be my pleasure," he said as he removed the scarf from the box, folded it into a blind fold and playfully tied it over my eyes.

He leaned in close and whispered in my ear, "Blind Man's Bluff is an ancient game originated in the late Zhou Dynasty in China. It is played in a spacious area, ideally in a garden such as this one, in which one player, designated as "It", is blindfolded and attempts to touch the other players without being able to see them. I reached out to touch Harry but he was gone. I turned in a circle with my hands in front of me but there was nothing but thin air. I started to laugh - "Harry, where are you?" I could hear his laughter a distance away then nothing but bird song. After a few moments, I was feeling a little foolish and was about to remove the blind fold when suddenly I felt someone's lips on mine. "Don't…not yet," he said huskily as he deepened the kiss.

Harry slowly removed my blind fold, his blue eyes darkening and said, "You know, in medieval times there was a tradition known as courtly love whereby a knight would pledge his allegiance to his lady and she would give him a favor, usually a scarf, to wear in battle and then return to her. Courtly love was considered a platonic form of love, but not always, as it contained a goodly amount of sexual attraction."

It was late at night when I arrived at No. 28 Royal Crescent. Wearing my sheer white regency gown, I walked into the entrance hall and stood in front of the dragon mirror which seemed to dimly glow from within. The mirror then slowly cleared and I saw Henry Cavendish holding the gold sovereign coin bracelet and saying, "The man who returns this bracelet to you is the man who is your destiny." Then the scene changed and Jamie Cadwalader was standing behind me in his First City Troop black military jacket with the silver braid and white breeches, his hands caressing my breasts. "It's not over, you know, until I say it is." Then the scene changed again and there was Andrew in his white shirt and jeans kissing me and unlacing my dress. "I want you in my bed, you've been away too long." And at last there was Harry, his chest bare, wearing only his gray strawstring pants. I turned to him and placed my mouth on the dragon tattoo on his right breast. He put his hands on my hips and pulled me closer. "I've wanted you from the first moment; I don't want to wait any longer." He picked me up and carried me to his bed and I could feel the dragon's tail moving slowly inside me and then faster until I cried out.

My cries woke me; I was back in my bed at the Old Rectory. I could feel soreness between my thighs and my mouth and breasts were tender. Just then the phone rang and I answered it. It was Harry. "I had the strangest dream last night; I'm almost embarrassed to tell you. We were standing in front of the dragon mirror one moment and the next we were making love in my bed." "I know…I had the same dream." There was a silent pause and then he said, "Perhaps we are under some form of enchantment, I already know I am."

It was the evening of the Netherfield Ball at the Guildhall on High Street. Harry had a last minute emergency in London; a client under his sponsorship suffered a relapse. He promised he would meet us at the ball. "You look lovely, darling," said my mother. "The white gown is perfection and the emeralds match the sparkle in your eyes. A sparkle placed there by one Lord Atherton, no doubt." "Henrietta, you look just like your mother tonight, I have the privilege of escorting two of the most beautiful women in Bath to the ball," exclaimed Arthur. We arrived just as the first strains of a quadrille were being played. I had taken advantage of the dance workshop earlier that day. The quadrille was a lively dance with four couples, arranged in the shape of a square, with each couple facing the center of that square. One pair was called the head couple, the other pairs the side couples. A dance figure was often performed first by the head couple and then repeated by the side couples. The next tune was a sauteuse. The sauteuse was a turning dance for couples in 2/4 time with small leaping steps; *sauter* means to leap in French.

I was dancing The Patriot's Waltz with a colleague of Arthur's when Harry arrived. His blonde hair glowing in the candlelight, he looked like Captain Wentworth in Jane Austen's *Persuasion*, dressed in a black fitted jacket and breeches, white stockings, white damask waistcoat and white linen cravat. As the dance ended, he walked up to me and bowed. The classic trio of flute, violin and piano started to play the Sussex Waltz and we danced for the first time together. "You take my breath away," he whispered in my ear. After glasses of champagne and dinner, then more dancing, the evening flew by and before we knew it, the Netherfield Ball was over. The last dance was appropriately called the Finishing Dance, a precursor to the American dance, the Virginia Reel.

Wishing my parents a good night, Harry helped me into the Range Rover. "I want to take you to a very special place." We drove two miles to Prior Park, an 18th-century garden designed by the poet Alexander Pope and the landscape gardener Capability Brown in 1734. This garden was influential in defining the style known as the English garden. From here, we could see the skyline of the city of Bath. The centerpiece was a dramatic Palladian bridge, designed in 1755 by Richard Jones, one of only 4 left in the world. Made of limestone with a slate roof it had stairs leading up on both sides to a temple like structure with ionic columns and pedimented arches. The sky held the last remnants of daylight on this midsummer's night as Venus, the Evening Star made her appearance in the sky.

Harry held my hand as we walked up the stairs onto the bridge. Dressed as we were, I found it hard to believe we were in the year 1984. The whole evening had been pure magic as had every moment of my stay here in Bath. How was I ever going to return home to Philadelphia? We stood in silence for a long time just looking out from the bridge at the water below, Harry's arm securely around my waist. Then he turned and looked at me, his eyes two blue embers and said, "I was going to ask you not to leave and just stay here with me forever. You must know I've fallen in love with you. But that would be very selfish on my part. You have a life back in Philadelphia, I know of a man there who also loves you, dear friends, and a business. But now you have all of us here in Bath too. I'm asking you to consider the possibility." With that, he removed a slim leather case from his pocket, opened it and withdrew a bracelet with a gold sovereign coin in the center. *It was the bracelet from Mr. Cavendish's shop.* "This bracelet belonged to my grandmother. It was given to her by her father on the occasion of the coronation of George V in 1910. It shows St. George and the Dragon. Whatever you finally decide, I want you to know if you ever need me, I'll be there." And with that, he took me in his arms and no more words needed to be spoken.

July 1984
Philadelphia

Back on Antique Row at H.R. Grasso & Daughter the gift packages I shipped from London had safely arrived - the books from the National Portrait Gallery, the Liberty of London ties and scarves and the treats from Fortnum & Mason. And among the packages was one from Lord Harry Atherton – an antique Grainger Worcester green & gilt porcelain plaque with an exquisite hand painted view of the Royal Crescent circa 1820. A white card with a small embossed gold dragon was enclosed and in Harry's handwriting were the words of Jane Austen –

" I can listen no longer in silence. I must speak to you by such means as are within my reach. You pierce my soul. I am half agony, half hope. Tell me not that I am too late, that such precious feelings are gone for ever...You alone have brought me to Bath..."

I Love You,

Harry

The Knights' Tale

July 1984
Philadelphia

Returning to Philadelphia after that unforgettable month of June in England was one of the most difficult trips I've ever had to make. As I exited the British Airways gate at the airport I saw a familiar figure standing there. It was Andrew. "Welcome home, Henrietta." "Hi Andrew, thanks for meeting me," I said as I hugged him. "I'm actually here waiting for my flight to Ireland but I wanted to see you before I left. I have time for a cup of coffee before I leave. Let's get your luggage first." After picking up my luggage we took a seat at a cafe table and ordered coffee. Neither of us spoke for a moment, we just looked at each other. There was a new sadness in Andrew, a sadness I had put there. Those golden eyes had lost their luster. He reached for my hand across the table and noticed the absence of the emerald engagement ring from my finger. He made no comment. Then he told me his plans.

"I'm going to work on a new restoration project in Ireland with the Irish Georgian Society and will be gone for the rest of the summer. Fortunately, the Woodford project is on hold, they need to raise additional funds. I've also been asked to be a guest lecturer at the University of Virginia for the fall semester. I wasn't going to accept it; I didn't want to be away so long from Philadelphia. But now I think I should. It will add teaching credentials to my resume and will also give us time to decide what we want to do. I know how I feel about you, that hasn't changed but I think you need more time and this will give it to us. Here's my contact information in Ireland if you need to reach me. They can get a phone message to me and you can write if you want." I didn't know what to say, my heart was breaking. "Andrew, I didn't plan for any of this to happen, I love you, I do." "…But you love Harry too; I know you and he didn't cross that line but you both wanted to. I can see it in your face; you used to look at me that way."

Soon his flight departure on Aer Lingus was called. He gave me one last hug, kissed me softly and said, "I hope you find what you are looking for my love; I know I found it in you." And then he was gone.

H.R. Grasso & Daughter was no longer the safe haven it once was. There was an ache deep inside me, a longing. I was restless upon my return and James and Melinda could sense the change in me. We were in preparation for the August Nantucket Antiques show less than five weeks away. During July and August I let them leave early on Fridays for a long weekend and in August we were open by appointment only so they could take their much needed vacations. I was also looking forward to spending time on Nantucket with Phoebe.

After the packages from England arrived, I gave James and Melinda their presents. They loved the tie and scarf from Liberty of London and the chutney and honey from Fortnum & Mason. Harry's surprise gift of the painting of the Royal Crescent just made me miss him more and I wanted to take the next flight back to England. Instead I called Pamela Stuart and invited myself to her home under the guise of bringing her presents.

She opened the door of her apartment on Washington Square and my mind instantly returned to the night of our engagement party on New Year's Eve when Andrew had rented a horse and carriage to drive us around the Square and home to Delancey Street.

Pamela embraced me in a warm hug. "Henrietta, I've missed you so, how was England?" "Wonderful and I've returned with a few mementos for you." "Let's go into the sitting room, I have tea and sandwiches waiting…" We sat together drinking Darjeeling tea as she opened her presents. She loved the Liberty scarf in tones of deep amethyst, rose and lavender, the "Rubies in the Rubble" chutney and honey and the sample afternoon tea menu from Fortnum & Mason.

"Henrietta, I can see you are deeply troubled, please tell me what's happened. You are as close to me as if you were my own daughter…perhaps I can help." I told her the whole story of going to England and meeting Harry; how he, with my mother and Arthur's help, arranged a conciliatory meeting with Jamie Cadwalader, about his work with addicted vets and his job in the Asian Arts department at Sotheby's in London. I told her about helping him furnish his flat in Bath, going to the Netherfield Ball and that we had fallen in love. I then told her about meeting Andrew at the airport and that he was going to be gone for the rest of the summer in Ireland and the following fall semester in Virginia.

Pamela was silent for a moment and then spoke. "Harry sounds like a very special, caring and dedicated man; I hope you'll bring him to meet me when he comes to visit you. Andrew is also a wonderful man, one of the finest I've met and he loves you dearly, of that I have no doubt. He reminds me of a man I once knew before I married Peter. Carl and Peter were students at Haverford College. The truth is I loved them both." "How did you decide?" "Well, I met them in 1937 when I was 18. I was getting ready to enter Bryn Mawr College in the fall. No one knew that war was going to break out in 1939. In the end, Carl had to return to Germany. I never heard from him again. I still think about him and wonder if he survived." She looked at me and smiled. "I loved them both deeply, always will. In the end it was life's circumstances that made the decision for me because I could never have chosen one over the other."

It was early afternoon on Friday and I had been home less than a week. Melinda and James left for the weekend and I was alone in the shop catching up on some paperwork, very now and then looking at the gold sovereign bracelet on my wrist when I heard the bell over the front door jingle. I looked up to see Harry standing there. He was wearing jeans and a white polo shirt, his blonde hair mussed, his face unshaven. "I took the first flight I could get on." As I ran over to him he dropped his luggage and took me in his arms. "How I've missed you," he said. "I can't believe you're really here." "Let me prove it to you," he replied and kissed me.

Upstairs in the red sitting room, we sat together on the blue velvet camelback sofa. "How long can you stay?" "Until next Sunday, I need to find a hotel and check in with the London office. I told Sotheby's I had urgent business in New York. Luckily they didn't question it - surprisingly so, considering I had just returned to the office after being in Bath all month." "Can I fix you something to eat and drink? It will only take a minute and then you can take a long nap." "Thanks, Henrietta I would like that and am also in great need of a bath."

After lunch, I showed Harry the bedroom and bath, gave him some fluffy white towels, a bar of soap and a wash cloth and I told him to make himself at home. I closed the bedroom door and went back downstairs. I still couldn't believe he was here and upstairs at this very moment sleeping in my bed. It was impossible to concentrate on paperwork so I locked up the shop and went to the market to buy fixings for supper.

In the garden the summer sky was slowly turning to twilight. It was going to be a beautiful night, we could have supper outside. As I came back upstairs the only sound to be heard was the faint hum of the air conditioner. I decided to take a quick shower and change my clothes. Afterwards I quietly opened the bedroom door to find Harry sound asleep on his stomach, his clothes neatly folded on the Queen Anne bench at the foot of the bed. In repose he looked like a sleeping angel. I walked up to the bed, leaned over and gently placed a kiss between his shoulder blades. His skin smelled of verbena, my bath soap, a citrus blend from Caswell-Massey. He stirred, opened his eyes and smiled.

"I must still be dreaming…" "Afraid not, M'lord, you're no longer in London or even Bath for that matter but here in Philadelphia." "Thank God," he said as he raised himself up on one elbow, the dragon tattoo now visible on his chest, a fateful talisman. "I was afraid I might never see you again." He looked at me a long moment and said, "Henrietta, please forgive me if the timing is inappropriate…but I *must* know. May I ask about your relationship with Andrew?" "Yes, he was at the airport when I arrived home. He was on his way to Ireland for the summer and then on to Virginia in September until the end of the year. He knows Harry…that you and I have feelings for each other and has given us time to explore those feelings…to see if they're real." "Oh, they're very real, at least on my part; I've never felt this way about anyone…I love you…how do *you* feel…do you love me, Henrietta?" I couldn't wait any longer to show him how much, to touch him. I slowly removed my jeans and blouse. He got out of bed, stood before me and said, "I'd like to do that" and gently removed my bra and panties. He kissed me and then I put my lips to his chest and kissed his dragon tattoo. It was just like our dream in Bath but this time it was real. And slowly the ache and longing deep inside me was eased and filled with a deeper, richer warmth until I and the golden dragon finally slept.

I rose early on Saturday to make coffee while Harry was still sleeping. I brought his coffee to the bedroom as he was waking. "I was just dreaming about you," he smiled as I kissed him and handed him his cup. After taking a few sips, he rose to use the bathroom. As I looked at his body I thought what a beautiful man he was; both in the physical sense and in his loving, caring ways. When he returned, he asked, "What would you like to do this morning?" "You are my guest, M'lord what would be your pleasure?" "My pleasure, if I may be so bold, would be to do what we have been doing all night." And so we did.

By the time we left my apartment it was early afternoon and we were famished. I took Harry to the Italian Market to introduce him to the classic Philly cheese steak sandwich at Pat's Steaks and a Sicilian treat, ricotta cannoli with candied citrus peel at Isgro Pastries. Philadelphia's Italian Market on Ninth Street in South Philadelphia, was one of the oldest and largest open-air markets in America. Always a lively scene, vendors lined the street, selling the freshest fruits, vegetables, fish, meats, cheeses and spices from their stalls and store fronts. We stopped in DiBruno's House of Cheese to taste a sampling of exotic cheeses and buy fresh mozzarella and then on to Giordano's for New Jersey tomatoes and peaches.

That night we had dinner at Ralph's Italian Restaurant at 9th and Christian at the northern end of the Market. Ralph's was the first restaurant my father brought me to as a child. I introduced Harry to the Italian half of my heritage and he was more than enthusiastic. We ate mussels in a garlicky red sauce soaked up with fresh bread from Sarcone's Bakery and a salad of Italian salami, provolone and olives washed down with a California Zinfandel. For dessert, we had fresh lemon favored Italian water ice at a stand nearby. Afterwards, contented in each other's company, we strolled home hand in hand to my apartment where we made love again in the George III tester bed.

On Sunday afternoon we took a trip to the Philadelphia Museum of Art to see the Asian Arts collection. The collection spanned from 2500 B.C. to the present day, including paintings and sculptures from China, Japan, India, and Tibet; furniture and decorative arts, major collections of Chinese, Japanese, and Korean ceramics; a large and distinguished group of Persian and Turkish carpets; and rare and authentic architectural assemblages such as a Japanese teahouse, a Chinese palace hall, and a sixteenth-century Indian temple hall. He was impressed with it all especially the ceremonial teahouse from Japan named Sunkaraku. Harry said, "Sunkaraku means Evanescent Joys. The word evanescent means lasting only for a short time, beauty that is as evanescent as a rainbow, ephemeral, fleeting…I don't want what we have to be evanescent, I want it forever."

Monday through Thursday Harry took the Metroliner to work in New York at Sotheby's to arrange a series of upcoming Asian art auctions. On Tuesday night we went to the Mann Music Center in Fairmount Park to listen to an all Mozart concert by the Philadelphia Orchestra as we lay on a blanket under the stars. The rest of the week our evenings were spent having dinner in my garden watching the fireflies come out and strolling around Society Hill. One night we went to St. Peter's churchyard and I showed him my father's grave and the one belonging to Caroline Blackburn Stuart and her family.

I called Pamela and told her Harry was visiting. She didn't sound surprised and invited us for tea on Friday afternoon. I told Harry all about Pamela, how she had owned the John Singleton Copley portrait and the star ruby ring and he was looking forward to meeting her. After a visit to the Historical Society to see the portrait and artifacts, we arrived at Pamela's apartment and she greeted us warmly. "Mrs. Stuart, it is such an honour to finally meet you." "It is my pleasure, Harry; please call me Pamela. Henrietta has told me so much about you. Let's go back to the garden." Pamela's garden was in full bloom with purple and white impatiens, lavender geraniums, summer iris and ivy covering the brick of the walled garden. We sat on the flagstone terrace around her black cast iron table.

"Pamela, I see you have wisteria vines," commented Harry. "Yes, they were glorious in the spring this year." "You know, wisteria is used frequently in Chinese art and symbolizes playfulness and adventure. It is also believed to bring love; legend has it that the fairy of love holds a bunch of wisteria in her hand sending blessings to lovers all around." "That's an interesting legend, Harry, especially considering the conversation I had with Henrietta earlier in the week about my old friend Carl. It may be time to see if I can find him, perhaps the fairy of love can help."

After tea with Pamela, we strolled across the street and sat on a bench in Washington Square, the late afternoon sun slanting through the trees. All was quiet except for the distant laughter of children playing.

"Pamela is quite charming and I can see she adores you." "Yes, she is a very special woman and has been like a mother to me." "Speaking of mothers, it seems yours and mine are getting quite chummy and already talking about grandchildren. If you agree, I think we could accommodate them given all the practice we've had lately..." He looked at me lovingly with those royal blue eyes and golden hair and for the first time I considered the possibility of having a family with Harry. "My mother does want me to spend more time in Bath to help run the business I will inherit one day." "Well, you've made one *very* satisfied client thus far," he said as he leaned in to kiss me.

Saturday night arrived and Harry had a special evening planned. We were going to have dinner at The Fountain Room at the Four Seasons Hotel. He looked handsome in his dark blue Savile Row suit and yellow Hermes tie. I wore a blue sleeveless sheath dress with the emerald green and blue silk scarf with the gold dragon coin design he gave me in Bath, blue sapphire earrings and the gold sovereign bracelet. We were seated at a table near the window overlooking the fountain across the street. A miniature bouquet of peach and cream roses was at my place setting. The wine steward brought an iced bottle of Perrier Jouet champagne, popped the cork and poured the effervescence into two crystal flutes. Harry raised his glass to me and said, "Dearest Henrietta, this is a very special night being here with you, thank you for the profound happiness you give me," and reached across the table to kiss my hand.

After dinner we walked to the Swann Memorial Fountain at Logan Circle across from the hotel. Designed by Alexander Stirling Calder, it featured three dramatic reclining Native American figures symbolizing the Delaware, the Schuylkill and the Wissahickon waterways and sculpted frogs and turtles spouting water sprays toward a 50-foot geyser in the center. The fountain was beautiful tonight lit with underwater lighting and a full moon overhead. As we approached I heard the opening strains of *La Vie en Rose* played live on an accordion. "The hotel helped me with the arrangements…may I have this dance?" And so we danced around and around the fountain as the music played and all the stars came out to listen.

Afterwards, in the yellow cab, Harry instructed the driver to take us to 3rd and Pine. "Just a slight detour, my love, before we go home." I liked the sound of him saying the word *home.* We arrived at St. Peter's and he escorted me through the churchyard to my father's grave. He turned to me smiling and then started to speak. "Good evening Mr. Grasso, my name is Harry Atherton. Sir, I have come to ask you for your daughter's hand in marriage. I love her very much you see and will do everything in my power to protect her and care for her…and make you a grandfather. I hope that's not being too personal." Suddenly a breeze blew up and caressed our cheeks and we could hear soft laughter. I looked at Harry and whispered, "I think he approves." "Oh good, I was worried there for a moment." Then he got down on one knee and removed a small case from his pocket. Inside was a round blue sapphire ring surrounded by diamonds. "This ring, like the bracelet, belonged to my grandmother. Henrietta, I love you, will you marry me?" There was only one answer. "Yes, Harry, I love you, I would be honored to marry you."

Monday morning came too soon at H.R. Grasso & Daughter. On Sunday night Harry flew back to London. Before he left we agreed to keep our engagement private out of respect for Andrew until I had the opportunity to tell him in person. Now that we were engaged, Harry planned to spend more time at Sotheby's New York office and I was going to revise my schedule to include trips to Bath. I knew my mother would be thrilled.

We had two more weeks to finalize arrangements for the Nantucket antiques show the first week of August. James and Melinda were finishing the last of the details and looking forward to their vacations. Phoebe was teaching summer school at Penn and anticipating a much needed break in August before school started again in September. Sarah Townsend was away on vacation at her family's home on Martha's Vineyard. I thought of Andrew and hoped he was enjoying his stay in Ireland.

With everyone else busy with their lives I decided to call Dr. Frederick Wendt for a long overdue and much needed consultation. Dr. Wendt had helped me in the study of Psychometry and was an expert in past life regression. Luckily, he was in his office at the university. "Henrietta, how are you? I haven't spoken to you since your success with the Copley experiment. You are going to have your own chapter in my next book." "Dr. Wendt, I would like to come and see you as soon as possible to discuss my most recent experiences." "Why don't you come to my office tomorrow at 1PM? I'm very interested to hear all about it."

I arrived at Dr. Wendt's office the next afternoon. "Welcome Henrietta, have a seat, how can I help?" I started by telling him of my experience on my first day in London at Cavendish Estate Jewellers when I purchased the cuff links and first saw the bracelet. I told him when I returned the next day to purchase the bracelet, the shop was empty and that the real estate agent said Mr. Cavendish hadn't rented the shop since 1910. I went on to describe the antique regency mirror Harry and I purchased at an estate sale in Oxford for his home in Bath and the strange nightmare like dream I had about the mirror – how Mr. Cavendish appeared in the mirror telling me that the man who returned the bracelet to me was my destiny and the subsequent appearances of Jamie, Andrew and Harry. I also described my love making with Harry in the dream, how real it was and that Harry called me the next morning and described the same dream. I finally told him that Harry gave me the exact bracelet I saw in the shop and said it belonged to his grandmother.

"Well, you *have* had a lot going on since I last saw you. Perhaps the star ruby opened the channels for everything else to come through. What I think is happening may have originated in past lives that you and these three men experienced together and are still experiencing in your present lives. I think we should do a series of past life regressions through hypnosis to better understand your present day relationships. Are you willing to try this? We can do the first session today." "Yes, Dr. Wendt I really want to understand why this is happening." "Good, then let's get started. With your permission I would like to record these sessions." I agreed. He led me to a high back wing chair and I settled in.

"Let's start by getting comfortable in your chair and closing your eyes. Next take a series of deep breaths – inhale and exhale slowly...

Now that you are totally relaxed, let your mind roam free and allow whatever feelings, thoughts, images, or impressions you have go through your mind.

Imagine finding yourself out in the country on a beautiful summer's day. You are standing on a path, going through the forest. As you walk down the path you notice that just up ahead is a small bridge shrouded in fog. Wherever you choose to go from here, you will be safe and will not experience anything first hand, it will be as if you are watching your journey unfold in front of you, as if you were sitting in a theater watching yourself on a movie screen.

As you emerge on the other side of the fog, you find yourself in a past life. I will be asking the questions to help you with your journey, and the first thought or impression that comes to mind is the right one. Don't try to analyze it or think critically of it, just let it happen. So get an idea of where you are now, your surroundings. Take in all the feelings, the sensations. Do you recognize anyone you might know in your present life?"

The Knights' Tale

Dr. Wendt's voice started to fade and I was in a great hall with cold stone walls dripping with damp, a castle. Torches were burning and the scene was colored as if in a golden light. I could hear music playing; fiddles, drums and flutes. I was seated on a dais next to a man and a woman watching groups of people dancing. I looked at my shoes of soft brown suede and my gown of dark green velvet with gold embroidery around the bell shaped long sleeves and hem. I had long blonde hair woven in a single plait down my back. Two knights approached my father, bowed to us and asked his permission to dance with me. One was dark haired and the other fair. I danced with the first knight a stately line dance with other couples. The next dance was with the fair-haired knight, a lively, leaping dance. "Kind Knight, pray what is the name of this dance?" "My Lady, it is called "Dance with Dragons." "Kind Dragon you dance very well indeed." A third knight approached, one with hair as black as night and cold blue eyes. "Such beauty should be shared...Lady may I have the next dance?" He frightened me and I replied, "No Sir, I must take my leave for I am thirsty and tired." "I shall have you another time, never doubt it," he said and walked away.

Then the scene changed, my father was sending the knights into battle. Both men came to me and asked for a token. I gave them each a scarf in my family's standard colors of green and blue with a gold dragon design and a pair of gauntlets with a star ruby imbedded in each right handed glove to protect them in battle. Then the black-haired knight approached and asked, "Lady, may I also have a token to take with me into battle?" "Alas, Sir, I have none left to give." He looked at me, his eyes filled with anger and said, "One day, my Lady you shall give of your last measure to me."

In the next scene the castle was under siege; I could hear men, women and children screaming and a strong acrid smell filled my nostrils. I knew my parents were dead. I was desperate as I ran blindly towards the woods. Immediately I could hear a horse's hooves fast approaching from behind, my heart racing as I ran. I turned and saw a knight pursuing me on horseback; he swiftly grabbed me by the hair and thrust his sword into my chest. I could feel the cold earth rise up and the metallic taste of my own warm blood in my mouth as the voice of my murderer started to fade. "Lady, you shall join your parents in Hell before this day is over."

The soothing voice of Dr. Wendt returned. "...Take a deep breath and exhale and imagine a large door of warm, comfortable, inviting light right in front of you. Go ahead and step through the light now leaving that life behind. Go down the path back to the bridge. As you cross the bridge you come out on the other side and you feel yourself coming back to the present day and time, to the present date, feeling wonderful and refreshed from the journey."

"Henrietta, how do you feel?" "As though I've been far away…" "I'm impressed with your clarity of vision and how easily you were able to go back." "They were all there Dr. Wendt; my father, Pamela, Andrew, Harry and even Jamie." "And now you are in love with both knights in the present day and suffered abuse at the hands of the third." "Yes, that's true." "I would like to schedule the second session tomorrow. Will that work for you?" "Yes, and Dr. Wendt, thank you for everything." "No Henrietta, it is I who thank you. Your psychic abilities are exceptional and getting stronger all the time. My advice is to keep following your instincts, they are very powerful."

I went home feeling somewhat relieved about my feelings toward Andrew, Harry and even Jamie. It was all starting to make sense. I was looking forward to learning more tomorrow.

Pamela called me the next morning with good news of her own. "Henrietta, I felt so inspired after you brought Harry to meet me last Friday. I decided to search for Carl and on the first try I found him. He's still in Heidelberg, Germany and just retired from his position as a history professor at the university. He is a widower and was so happy to hear from me. He wants to come and visit, we have a lot of catching up to do." "Oh Pamela, I am so happy for you, this is wonderful news. I can't wait to meet him." "You and I seem to have had a very special connection from the beginning," she replied. With her comment, I felt I had to tell her about my first past life regression session with Dr. Wendt back to medieval times when she was my mother, the roles the three men played in my life and the first appearance of the star ruby.

"That explains everything that is happening now in your life, doesn't it?" "Yes, and I don't feel as conflicted about my deep feelings for both Andrew and Harry or Jamie for that matter." "Well I hope you will look upon me as your mother in this life as well. I love you very much Henrietta and want only what's in your best interest. I also think Harry will play a big part." "Thank you Pamela, I love you too. I only hope Andrew will understand when the time comes to tell him." "He loves you, my dear and will also want what's best for you. Besides, you may someday see him back in your life as Carl is returning to mine."

I couldn't wait to return to Dr. Wendt's office that afternoon and soon I was sitting in the high back wing chair once again going through the hypnosis process.

Dr. Wendt began the second session as he had the day before – "Let's start by getting comfortable in your chair and closing your eyes. Next take a series of deep breaths – inhale and exhale slowly…

Now that you are totally relaxed, let your mind roam free and allow whatever feelings, thoughts, images, or impressions you have go through your mind…"

I was in a ballroom, lit with chandeliers, wearing a damask blue gown embroidered with flowers, my auburn hair piled on my head with a single curl trailing down my neck. I could feel the heat and the smell of hot wax coming from the profusion of candles. A man approached, very handsome with blonde hair and blue eyes. I recognized him immediately. He bowed and said "Do you know the new dance from France, the Allemande, Miss Blackburn?" "Why yes, Mr. Copley." It was a lively dance of turns and close embraces. "You dance very well, Sir, how did you come to learn?" "You remember my step-father was a dance master among his many talents and gave me instructions starting at a young age." As the dance ended he bowed and we were approached by another man. "Miss Blackburn, allow me to introduce to you Mr. Charles Stuart from Philadelphia." He was very tall with dark hair and golden eyes. "Miss Blackburn, it is my pleasure to know you, would you also honor me with a dance?" The musicians started playing music for La Bourgogne, a slower courtly dance. "Yes Mr. Stuart, I will".

Then the scene changed and I was sitting in a room in a claret red satin gown. I could smell the strong odors of oil and turpentine and leather. Outside the window, the church bells were ringing and inside the room a clock was slowly ticking on the fireplace mantel. I could taste oranges and sherry. Mr. Copley was sitting opposite me behind a painter's easel. He abruptly stood and came over to me and took the book from my hands. "Caroline, I can hold back no longer, I must declare my feelings. I have loved you since the first day you came into your uncle's studio here in Boston." He took my hand and kissed it and then removed a maroon leather heart shaped case from his waistcoat. Inside was a star ruby ring surrounded by seed pearls. "I give you this ring with my eternal love to guard and protect you always." Inside the band was the inscription *Far Above Rubies JSC to CCB 1768*. As I rose from my chair he caught me in a long awaited embrace.

The scene changed again and I was now in Mayor Powel's House in Philadelphia. My husband Charles was introducing me to Captain Cadwalader of the Light Horse of the City of Philadelphia, General Washington's cavalry. He was an extraordinary figure of a man, tall with black hair and piercing ice blue eyes. "It is my pleasure to meet you Mrs. Stuart," he said and bowed. "It is my honor, Captain to meet someone who is protecting our esteemed General, you humble us, Sir." "May I call on you Mrs. Stuart when you are at home?" "Yes, Captain, you may." At that very moment, in walked John Singleton Copley. "John, we didn't know you were going to be in Philadelphia" said Charles. "My wife and I were in New York where I was working on portrait commissions and we were invited to Philadelphia to see Justice Allen's collection of Titians and Correggios. She would have come with me but is feeling tired from the journey. Mrs. Stuart it is a pleasure to see you again." He bowed and kissed my hand. "Mr. Copley," I said, "You have been away from us for too long."

Later that evening I was standing alone in the back parlor on the second floor of Mayor Powel's home when John came to me. "Caroline, my love, I have something to tell you. I am leaving soon. I have the opportunity to travel to Europe to study and then will settle in London. My wife and children will follow me there. The situation in America is deteriorating and war is very likely. There will no longer be work for me here. My only hope now is England where my friend Benjamin West has secured an introduction for me to the Royal Academy. Perhaps after the war is over, we will be able to return." I was overcome with emotion and started to cry knowing I would never see him again. He took out his lace handkerchief and wiped my eyes. He kissed my hand and I brought his hand to my lips. He looked at me with eyes filled with longing and said "I shall always love you and when this life is over I shall find you again in the next, this I promise."

"…Take a deep breath and exhale," said Dr. Wendt and I was back in his office in the high back wing chair. "So in this life you *were Caroline Blackburn*…fascinating." "Yes and Harry was John Singleton Copley and Andrew was Charles Stuart. Jamie was a member of the cavalry which he still is today." "We don't require a third session unless you feel you need to, I think we found the answers you were looking for," replied Dr. Wendt. "This is an amazing story and I have a feeling it's not over yet…"

August 1984
Philadelphia

The Nantucket antiques show was successful and Phoebe and I were able to relax before returning home to school and work. It was hard not being able to tell her the full story about Andrew and Harry. I was glad Sarah Townsend, Andrew's cousin, was still away. I was going to have trouble facing her with the truth after I told Andrew. At this point only Pamela had met Harry and Dr. Wendt was sworn to patient confidentiality. And no one knew I had accepted Harry's proposal of marriage while still technically being engaged to Andrew. Phoebe knew Andrew was in Ireland for the summer but didn't know he was going to be teaching in Virginia all fall semester. She was very pleased to hear that Jamie and I had finally made peace with each other and that my mother and I were getting along better. I told her of my mother's wish that I begin traveling to Bath more frequently. "I think your mother's right, Henrietta. It's time to bury the hatchet and I would love to go over with you during school holidays."

The last week in August came too soon. Andrew wrote to me and said he would be home for a few days before he had to be at the University of Virginia to report for classes. It was just as hard to face him now as it had been in July. The truth was I still loved him and since my sessions with Dr. Wendt, I understood how powerful my connection was with all three men. Yet in this life I felt very strongly I was supposed to marry Harry and have a family with him as I had done with Andrew in 1769. I missed my opportunity with Harry back then and didn't want to miss it again. In a sense, Harry had been my first love all along.

Andrew arrived home as planned and called me at the shop. "I'm home and would like to see you. Can we meet somewhere?" I decided to meet him half way between my home and his. "Let's meet at Washington Square, I'll bring lunch," I replied and then said, "I'm glad you're home safe, Andrew." I was waiting on a park bench when he arrived looking handsome, tanned and healthy in his white shirt and jeans. I rose, gave him a hug and said, "Welcome home Andrew."

"How is everyone?" "Everyone is fine; Sarah sent me a post card from Martha's Vineyard, your aunt and uncle are both well." "How was Nantucket?" "We had a very successful show and Phoebe and I had a relaxing time together...how was Ireland?" "It was great this year; we worked on a 1790 manor house outside Dublin." We both knew we were running out of small talk but were trying to find the courage to say what needed to be said.

He looked at me for a long moment and finally asked, "And how are *you*?" "...I, I'm the same as the last time you saw me at the airport." "I see, so nothing has changed." I didn't want to prolong our suffering, I had to tell him. "Andrew...I'm going to marry Harry." With that said I withdrew the antique emerald engagement ring he had given me from my pocket. He looked at the ring with mixed emotions; hurt and disbelief and shook his head. "Keep it, it belongs to you." One day I would write to him and tell him about my sessions with Dr. Wendt but now was not the time. Instead I said, "I love you both very much and always will. There is a big part of you that I will carry with me until the end of my days. You have enriched my life; I never expected to meet anyone like you but I wasn't ready to get married." We both had tears in our eyes when he took out his handkerchief and gently wiped my face.

"Henrietta, I'm a selfish bastard, I may have pushed too hard because I wanted you so much..." "No Andrew, I wanted it too, wanted you...can you ever forgive me?" "There is nothing to forgive, I love you and always will. This is just not our time, maybe in our next life..." He didn't know how prophetic his words were.

Andrew stopped by the shop before he left for the University of Virginia in Charlottesville. "Here is my contact information if you need to reach me. I realize Harry's in London, so if you need a knight to come to the rescue…in other words, call me if you need me for any reason. After all I was your first knight." "And you still are…thank you Andrew. You don't know how much it means to me to hear you say this." "Oh, and before I forget, please tell Harry I *cede the field* and what a very lucky man he is." Then he held me for a long moment, kissed my hair and was gone.

That night I called Harry at his Royal Crescent flat in Bath. "Henrietta, good evening my love, I was just sitting here looking around, everywhere I look I can't help thinking of you and remembering… How I miss you, everything alright? "Everything is better than alright. I spoke to Andrew and he said to tell you he was *ceding the field* and left for Virginia today. I must say he handled it very well." "That's because he loves you and is a gentleman. I hope someday we can be friends." I thought *that's because you were good friends in your past lives but didn't say it*. There would be a time to tell both men the stories of our lives together. "I do too my love, that would be wonderful." "So when shall we tell our families and friends? I think it would be appropriate if we told our parents in person, don't you?" "Yes, I can book a flight on the 6th and spend a long weekend, will that work?" "Fantastic, I'll pick you up at Heathrow and we can drive to Bath together, I think we should surprise them, just let me know your flight arrival time. "I will, I love you Harry and can't wait to see you, good night." "Good night, my love, I love you too, sweet dreams."

It was official. I called Pamela the next morning and asked if I could stop by with some important news. I wanted to show her Harry's grandmother's sapphire and diamond ring and tell her about the amazing night when he proposed in St. Peter's churchyard. I also wanted to tell her about my final session with Dr. Wendt when it was revealed I had been Caroline Blackburn, Harry had been John Singleton

Copley and Andrew had been Charles Stuart. We were really related to each other and the star ruby brought us back together again.

"So you and Harry are to be married, how wonderful!" she said as she hugged me. "Not that I'm surprised, I saw the way he looks at you, he can't take his eyes away…" "You are the first person we've told; he took me to St. Peter's churchyard after dinner that Saturday night in July, and asked my father for his permission. I swear we could feel his presence and then he got down on one knee and presented me with his grandmother's ring." "This blue sapphire ring is exceptionally beautiful and I love the Victorian setting. Are you going to share the good news with your mother and Arthur?" "I'm leaving for London on Thursday for a long weekend so we can tell both our parents in person. We are working on a plan where Harry will work in Sotheby's New York office part of the time and I will divide my time between my business here and the shop in Bath." "Until the babies start to arrive…" Pamela said with a smile. "Yes, until the babies arrive…" "My dear, I think they will be here before you know it."

The Promise Fulfilled

September 1984
London and Bath

Heathrow was bustling on this Thursday evening in early September; the weather still mild coming on the heels of tourist season. It was wonderful to be back; the air felt electric as though a live current was running through it. Harry was waiting for me at the international terminal when I emerged from customs. He didn't say a word at first, just swept me into his arms and kissed me. "Welcome home, my love. Let's get your luggage so we can escape to more comfortable quarters." Once we were in the Range Rover, he kissed me more intimately and whispered, "I don't know if I can wait until we get to the flat in Bath, but then again, we do have the christening of my new bed to look forward to..." "M'lord, I seem to remember we christened it fairly well in our dreams last June..." "And I've been fantasizing about that particular dream and the ones we had in Philadelphia in July ever since," he replied with a devilish grin.

It was exciting to be in London again and my thoughts returned to the first time I saw Harry at the National Portrait Gallery staring at the John Singleton Copley painting. As if he could read my mind, he said, "I was thinking about that first day when we met at the National and you practically ran away from me. That really wounded my *manly pride*, I must say." "But I did turn and look back at you..." "By that time I was already planning my next strategic advance. You don't think your mother came up with all those ploys to throw us together without a little help on my part, do you?" "Why you flatter me Lord Atherton." "And that's not all I'm going to do to you once we get to Bath. Can't this damn traffic go any faster?" I couldn't wait to stay at No. 28 Royal Crescent in Bath, the home he and I designed together. Little had I known all that was to unfold when we made the purchase of the dragon mirror in Oxford in June.

After a ninety mile drive which Harry made in record time under an hour, we finally arrived at No. 28 Royal Crescent and Harry carried my luggage to the master bedroom. "First I'm going to draw you a warm bath, then chamomile tea and sandwiches and then to bed, my sweet. I want you to get plenty of rest so I can have my way with you in the morning." Once I was in the lavender scented bathwater, he gently washed my back. After tea, he wrapped me in a warm towel and tucked me into the king sized bed with a kiss. "I'm going to take a quick shower and then come to bed. Try to get some rest." I was asleep by the time my head touched the pillow.

I walked down the candlelit corridor to the foyer where the dragon mirror was mounted on the wall. As I gazed deeply into it, it emitted a warm amber glow and then it cleared. I saw Pamela; she was holding two babies in her arms, a boy and a girl. "Until the babies start to arrive... My dear, I think they will be here before you know it."

I awoke to the smell of fresh coffee and instinctively touched my abdomen. It was a lovely dream. I would have to tell Pamela about it when I returned to Philadelphia.

Harry came into the bedroom carrying two cups of coffee; wearing only his gray drawstring pants. "Oh good, you're awake...sleep well, my love?" "Wonderfully, thanks to you." "I just want to get a bit of business out of the way first...I thought we might tell our parents our good news over dinner on Saturday night at the Bath Priory Hotel. This way we can spend the rest of the weekend just enjoying Bath. We don't even have to go out; I have a well stocked kitchen." "But what will we do to keep ourselves busy for all those hours?" "Allow me to come over there and show you..."

Saturday night both sets of parents were sitting at a round table in the center of the elegant dining room of the Bath Priory Hotel, a former private manor house built in 1835. "Darling, we didn't even know you were coming," said my mother. "Charlotte, please blame me, I wanted it to be a surprise for everyone," declared Harry. "Our son Harry is full of surprises tonight," teased his mother, Frances. Harry's father, William and my step-father, Arthur just looked on indulgently, not saying a word. Harry nodded his head to the maître d and several bottles of Dom Perignon magically appeared. When the champagne was poured Harry smiled at everyone around the table then took my hand and kissed it. "Mother and Father, Charlotte and Arthur, Henrietta and I are going to be married and we wanted you to be the first to know."

Usually the British are a reserved group but you would have thought we were six overly emotional Italians the way everyone carried on. "Does this mean you will be moving to Bath full time?" asked my mother, a hopeful gleam in her eyes. Harry answered for both of us and replied, "For now, we are going to try and do both; I will be working out of Sotheby's New York office about one week a month and Henrietta is going to come to Bath once a month for long weekends." "Have you set a date for the wedding?" asked Frances. Harry looked to me for a response and I said, "We haven't had time to discuss it yet." Frances replied, "It would be lovely if you could be married in Bath, we can accommodate your guests from Philadelphia at Bathampton Hall." "Thank you Mother, that's very kind of you," replied Harry "Henrietta and I will consider it and let you know what we decide."

September 1984
Philadelphia

Before I knew it I was back at H.R. Grasso & Daughter in Philadelphia. On Monday morning I awoke in the blue bedroom in the George III tester bed with *Autumn* from Vivaldi's Four Seasons playing on WFLN. The weekend had been a memorable one; our parents were thrilled with our engagement and Harry and I had plenty of time to get reacquainted in his king sized bed in Bath. Now we could tell our friends the good news. I rose to brew a pot of French Roast when a wave of nausea hit me. *I must be coming down with something,* I thought. I probably picked up a bug from the recent air travel. I hoped I wasn't getting the flu; it was too early in the season. My breasts also felt tender. Instead, I made a cup of English Breakfast tea and had some toast to calm my stomach then took a shower and got dressed.

James and Melinda were both back from their vacations, well rested and looking forward to the fall estate sales and updating the furniture displays in the showrooms. I told them of my engagement to Harry and my planned long weekends in Bath. They were thrilled to hear the good news and also that our shop would be collaborating more frequently with my mother's business in Bath. We were still getting referrals and inquiries from the Nantucket antiques show in August and the phone and the shop were busy with our customers returning to the city from their summer homes.

Late morning I called Samuel Jacobson to see if he was available for lunch. Sam was my mentor and surrogate father since my own father died. We had a standing date at the Saloon in South Philly at 7th and Fitzwater not far from his estate jewelry business on Jewelers' Row. We had missed July and August since we were both away and had a lot of catching up to do. "My sweet Henrietta how was your trip to England in June?" he asked as he gave me a warm hug. I could smell the comforting aroma of his pipe tobacco. "Oh Sam, I have so much to tell you, I don't know where to begin." I took out my gifts for Sam - the silk tie from Liberty of London and the goodies from Fortnum & Mason. "These are wonderful, thank you for thinking of me," he said and kissed my cheek.

As we placed our lunch order, my stomach was still a bit queasy, so I ordered chicken soup with Italian bread and sparkling water. Then I showed him my blue sapphire and diamond engagement ring and told him I had ended my engagement to Andrew and was going to marry Harry. "Sam, the ring belonged to Harry's grandmother." "This is a Kashmir blue faceted natural sapphire; about five karats surrounded by one karat of European cut diamonds in an 18K yellow gold Victorian setting. It's a very special ring Henrietta; the Kashmirs are highly desirable especially in this karat weight." I showed him the gold sovereign bracelet and told him about Henry Cavendish and his vanishing estate jewelry shop in London. "My dear, I've lived long enough now not to question anything. I know there are certain things that we can never explain. Your stories are fascinating. My only concern is that you are happy with your choices, I will always want what is best for you." I told Sam how Harry had taken me to St. Peter's churchyard to ask Dad for permission to marry me. "I'm *very* happy, Sam and can't wait for you to meet Harry when he comes to Philadelphia. I'll bring him along for our next lunch." "I'm looking forward to that, my dear, very much."

The next morning the nausea returned. September was going to be a busy month and I didn't have time to get sick. With all the traveling I was planning to do it might be a good idea to see my doctor for a quick check up. I called Dr. Lowenberg's office and spoke with his assistant, Agnes. They had a concellation and I was able to get an appointment for that afternoon at his office at Jefferson Hospital.

After my examination, Dr. Lowenberg invited me back to his private office. "Henrietta, you're in excellent health and I hope this will be good news – you're 8-10 weeks pregnant. It looks like you will be having the baby at the end of March or early April. *I didn't know what to say, my emotions were fast forwarding from disbelief to anxiety to happiness all at the same time.* "Do you have any questions for me?" I was still too much in a state of shock to speak. Dr. Lowenberg smiled and said, "That's usually the reaction I get from first time mothers, I don't take it personally. Let's get you a prescription for pre-natal vitamins, schedule an ultrasound and I would like to see you in one month for a follow up visit." "...Doctor, I do have a few questions. I was planning to travel to England monthy for short stays. Will I still be able to do that?" "Absolutely, the best time for air travel during pregnancy is between 14-28 weeks as long as there are no complications." "And what about...sexual intercourse?" "Henrietta, you can continue as you have been...just relax and enjoy this time, it's very special. Call me if you think of anything else. And, by the way, congratulations and my best to you both...see you next month."

After I left the doctor's office I walked around Society Hill in a daze. I wasn't ready to go back to the shop just yet. Somehow I found my way to St. Peter's churchyard and my father's grave. "Dad, I don't know what you and Harry cooked up together but you're going to be a grandfather." I felt the breeze caress my cheek and the soft sound of laughter. "I guess you're feeling pretty pleased with yourself...I love him so much, Dad and he's going to be a great father just like you were to me."

When I arrived back at the shop it was late in the day and James and Melinda were closing up. It was a warm afternoon so I made a cup of tea and took some biscotti and went to sit in the garden. The dahlias were magnificent this fall. Known as the queen of the autumn garden, the dahlia signifies dignity and elegance. Pamela had given me some bulbs from her garden to plant in mine. Thinking of Pamela, I wanted so much to call her and tell her about the baby. I thought of Harry and counted back the weeks. It happened the first time we made love when he arrived that Friday in July. That first time I felt something deep inside me, it was hard to describe it, a spark, a connection that I had never felt before. He was coming on Friday and I couldn't wait to tell him the news.

Harry arrived in the late afternoon on Friday. We were going to have the whole weekend together before he had to report to work in New York on Monday morning. I was trying to decide how best to tell him, how to find the right moment and then it just happened. We were in bed Friday night lying in each other's arms. His hand was softly caressing my breast and trailed down to rest on my abdomen. "I can't get enough of you my love; I want you all the time." He started kissing my neck and then my mouth. "Harry?" "Hmmm?" I'd like to re-decorate the guest room at No 28 Royal Crescent. "Anything you want, my love...now where were we?" "You see I have a very special purpose for that room." He rolled on top of me and touched his fingers to my lips, "Hush, my darling, you'll make me lose my... concentration." "We will need to re-decorate the room as a...nursery." I let the word just hang in the air; he was so preoccupied I didn't think he heard me. Then all movement stopped and he looked at me.

"What did you just say?" I had his full attention now. "M'lord, we are going to have a baby."

"Henrietta, did you just say we are going to have a baby?" "Yes, Harry, you and I are going to have a little lord or lady, whichever the case may be." "How...when did you find out?" "Well, I wasn't feeling up to par so I went to the doctor's on Tuesday, turns out it was a case of morning sickness and the rest I just told you," I smiled back at him. "How…when did it happen?" "Well you already know how it happened. I assume your father has informed you of the proper procedure. Do you remember that Friday in July when you arrived from London?" "You mean when we made love for the first time?" "Exactly, you were quite diligent, if I remember correctly." "When is the baby due?" "The doctor said at the end of March, early April." "Can we continue to make love until then?" "As much as we want…"

The next morning we awoke in the George III tester bed. Harry got up to use the bathroom. I didn't think I would ever get tired of looking at his body. He came back into the bedroom and just stood there in all his glorious maleness. "We have to get married," he said suddenly looking like a little boy. "Yes we do unless you want me to become a fallen woman," I replied. "No, I mean we have to get married *soon*. I think our parents will want to know that particular piece of information after we tell them about the baby, don't you?" "Harry, come back to bed so we can discuss it properly…" And so he did.

Sunday afternoon it was another warm September day and we went to Valley Green Inn for brunch and to stroll through Wissahickon Creek Park, a part of Fairmount Park. A picturesque inn built in 1850 as the Valley Green Hotel, the land went back to 1685 and William Penn. Over brunch we worked out a plan that we hoped would work for everyone. We would get married in Bath on Christmas Eve and invite my friends from Philadelphia to stay at Bathampton Hall, Harry's parents' home. We both wanted a small, intimate wedding. Harry's older brother, William who would inherit the title of 4th Earl of Bath and the manor house already had the big society wedding along with two children, the heir and the spare. Until then we would keep to our travel schedules and when I was in Bath on the weekends, we would plan our wedding. I would move to Bath full time at the end of January since constant air travel would not be advisable for the last eight weeks of my pregnancy. When it came time to have the baby in the spring, we would stay in London to be near St. Mary's Hospital. Then we would set up housekeeping at No. 28 Royal Crescent with the baby in residence. We would still maintain the business and apartment on Pine Street for when we had to be in Philadelphia and New York but our main base would be London and Bath.

We decided to wait to tell our parents until after the ultrasound. The ultrasound was scheduled for the following Friday and Harry was going with me. As the technician rubbed the gel on my abdomen she asked us if we wanted to know if we were having a boy or a girl. We both said, "Yes!" Harry said, "We have already agreed on names — John Henry if it's a boy and Caroline Charlotte if a girl. He looked at me and said, "That will make your mother very happy since my mother already has two grandsons — William and Francis."

"Well you're in for a treat today," said the technician with a big smile. It looks like you'll be able to use both names. You're having twins, a boy and a girl, congratulations!"

That night in the red sitting room in my apartment, we called Bath and spoke to our parents.

Both mothers said they suspected as much when we announced our engagement at dinner two weeks earlier — there was a special glow about both of us, they said. Then they focused on the wedding arrangements. Harry's father and Arthur congratulated us on having twins. "Excellent form, Harry, first set of twins in the Atherton clan." "Thank you Father, I did my best."

After the call, we had a toast of chamomile tea to celebrate our upcoming wedding and the birth of the twins. "That was a bit of *macho* male bonding with your father," I teased. "What he doesn't know is that I did it on the first try," said Harry, pretty pleased with himself.

"Now that the pressure is off I think we should retire to the bedroom. Watching the technician rub that gel on your tummy really turned me on." "You're incorrigible M'lord," I said laughing as he grabbed my hand and led me to the George III tester bed. Hours later as we drifted off to sleep I remembered the dream I had in Bath of the vision in the dragon mirror where Pamela was holding two babies – John and Caroline after John Singleton Copley and Caroline Blackburn. I would have to remember to tell her.

Harry flew back to London on Sunday night but this time he was even more reluctant to go. "How can I just leave the three of you behind? I want to put you in my pocket and carry you around with me wherever I go until next March." "Now that would look a little silly, don't you think?" "When will you be able to fly to Bath?" Once I'm safely past the first trimester, two or three weeks from now." "Better make it two, I don't think I can last that long," he said trying to smile. "Take good care of John and Caroline for me, my love. They're not even here yet and I miss them almost as much as I do their mother." "It sounds strange to hear you call me that." "And soon I shall be able to call you my wife, I love you Henrietta, don't ever forget how much." He then took me in his arms and held on tight, to all three of us.

The morning sickness eased and I started to feel more energetic, thanks to the prenatal vitamins. Dr. Lowenberg was going to oversee my pregnancy in Philadelphia and then refer me to a colleague in London for the babies' delivery. I planned to set up an appointment with Dr. Winthrop the next time I was in London. Now I had the luxury of telling my friends the wonderful news. First on the list was Pamela. I called her and she had news of her own.

"Carl is coming for a visit this weekend; I would love for you to meet him." I could hear the excitement in her voice. "That's wonderful, Pamela. Perhaps you can bring him to Bath for Christmas. Harry's parents have invited my friends to stay at their home for our wedding. We set the date for Christmas Eve. It's going to be just family and friends. Harry and I are going to book your flights so we can spend Christmas Day together." "Oh Henrietta, I'm so happy for you, of course I'll be there and you can invite Carl in person." "I also want you to set aside some time at the end of March or early April. Harry and I are having twins, a boy and a girl." "Oh my dear girl, my heart is bursting, I don't think I can take any more good news, congratulations!" "Well, you did tell me they were coming and their names are going to be John and Caroline after John Singleton Copley and Caroline

Blackburn." "It seems we all have come full circle – our future has finally come to meet our past," she said knowingly.

The next person I needed to speak to was Phoebe. I called her and we arranged to meet at The Garden, our usual place, for lunch on Friday. We hugged at the entrance of the restaurant. I requested a private table at the back. "I think I'll have a glass of Chardonnay," she told the waitress, "what about you?" "I'll have a glass of sparkling water with lime." "You're not drinking, are you okay?" "Better than okay...I have a lot to tell you and I hope you'll forgive me for not saying anything sooner..."

I told her the whole story about meeting Harry in London in June and that Andrew and I had ended our engagement but remained friends. I told her I was pregnant with twins and that Harry and I were to be married in Bath at Christmas. "And you and your brother Stephen are invited to the wedding." She looked at me in amazement. "You couldn't have written a better soap opera for television," she laughed. "How did you manage all this? It sounds like something out of a fairy tale." "Believe me I know and you don't even know the *half* of it." I then told her about my two past life regressions with Dr. Wendt and how all three men; Jamie, Andrew and Harry appeared in each life. "And it all started with the star ruby ring." "There definitely is a book in your future, Henrietta." "Oh, Dr. Wendt is already on it," I said laughing.

December 1984

Bath

On Sunday, December 23rd the guests from Philadelphia arrived for our wedding. There were Pamela Stuart and Carl Eckhart who flew in from Heidelberg, Germany, Samuel Jacobson, Phoebe and Stephen Ingersoll, Sarah and Andrew Townsend and General Thomas Cadwalader. I had written to Andrew and he, the gentleman that he was, graciously accepted our wedding invitation. Jamie Cadwalader was also invited and driving in from London. Jamie and I might never be close friends but he had once been an important part of my life. He was sober now, more like the man I once knew and looking forward to seeing his father. Harry hired a limousine and driver to pick up everyone from Heathrow and drive them to Bath. Waiting for them was Bathampton Hall, the 18th century Georgian manor house decorated for Christmas with fresh greenery, fruits and berries and a magnificent Christmas tree in the entrance hall.

Harry & Henrietta's Wedding Day
Christmas Eve, December 24, 1984
Bath

The white regency gown I wore to the Netherfield Ball was to be my wedding dress. It reminded me of that special night and accommodated my expanding waistline with only a slight alteration. Sown into the hem of my gown, instead of the traditional silver horseshoe charm, was a 1984 St. George and the Dragon gold sovereign from Harry for good luck. For something borrowed, Harry's mother Frances lent me the Edwardian diamond tiara she wore when she was presented to Queen Elizabeth. For something blue, I was going to wear Pamela's blue sapphire and diamond necklace and matching earrings. My engagement ring, which once belonged to Harry's grandmother, was something old and Farthingales designed a velvet floor length hooded cloak the color of sapphires for something new.

At dusk the guests gathered at the 13th century church of Saint Nicholas in Bathampton; the men in formal white tie and the women in jewel toned gowns of ruby, emerald and amethyst. The church was simply decorated for Christmas with fresh greens and red velvet ribbons. Traces of Incense scented the old pews and a profusion of ivory candles on the altar cast a halo in the growing dark. The first notes of Bach's *Air on a G String* started to play on a single violin. I felt the spirit of my father, by my side, as I slowly walked down the aisle toward my future husband, his hair golden in the candlelight. At the altar he took my hand and soon we were pronouncing our wedding vows from the Book of Common Prayer written in 1662:

I, Henry William Atherton take thee, Henrietta Charlotte Grasso, to my wedded wife.
To have and to hold from this day forward, for better for worse,
for richer for poorer, in sickness and in health.
To love and to cherish, till death us do part.
According to God's holy ordinance, and thereto I plight thee my troth

I, Henrietta Charlotte Grasso take thee, Henry William Atherton, to my wedded husband.
To have and to hold from this day forward, for better for worse,
for richer for poorer, in sickness and in health.
To love and to cherish, till death us do part.
According to God's holy ordinance, and thereto I plight thee my troth

We exchanged simple gold wedding bands. As we exited the church to the sound of Bach's *Jesu Joy of Man's Desiring*, Harry placed the velvet cloak on my shoulders and kissed me as the first snowflakes started to fall and said, "I love you, Lady Atherton, you have made me the happiest man tonight."

Welcoming us back to Bathampton Hall was a roaring fire in the hearth in the Great Hall. There were seventeen for dinner around the large banquet table set with the Wedgwood and Bentley Anthemion Blue; a cobalt blue, gold and white dinner service of neoclassical design, cream roses in antique blue and white porcelain, ivory candles in George II sterling candlesticks and the music of Albinoni, Pachebel and Bach playing softly in the background. We celebrated with an English Christmas dinner of mulled wine, turkey with stuffing, roast beef, potatoes and seasonal vegetables. For dessert instead of plum pudding, we cut the traditional wedding cake, a round three tier fruitcake with raisins, ground almonds and cherries decorated in fondant icing to replicate Wedgwood blue jasperware with white neo-classical designs. The top layer, called the "Christening Cake" was to be saved for the christening of our twins after their arrival in the spring.

The Promise Fulfilled

Christmas, December 25, 1984

Bath

After our guests retired for the evening, Harry and I left the Hall. It was after midnight, Christmas Day. We took a short drive to Prior Park to the Palladian Bridge. On the bridge where he first declared his love, he gave me a Christmas present; our initials carved into one of the ionic columns with the dates 1768 and 1984 in memory of our past lives as John Singleton Copley and Caroline Blackburn and now our present one.

Early on Christmas morning, Lord Henry Atherton carried his new bride of less than eight hours over the threshold of No. 28 Royal Crescent.

He removed my velvet cloak and wrapped his arms around me as we stared into the dragon mirror and slowly whispered the words of the poet Robert Herrick, *"... Whenas in silks my Julia goes, then, then, methinks, how sweetly flows the liquefaction of her clothes, next, when I cast mine eyes, and see that brave vibration, each way free, oh, how that glittering taketh me!"* As if on cue, I felt the first fluttering, like butterfly wings in my abdomen. Harry felt it too and cradled the soft mound with his hands. We looked at each other in wonder and then he grinned and said, "Well, my love, look who's awake just in time for Christmas. Do you think they will mind if their father makes love to their mother? It is our wedding night after all..."

In the master bedroom Harry lit the fire and the candles on the mantel. A slow piano version of Bach's *Air on a G String*, started to play. In silence he removed his jacket and white waistcoat, loosened his white tie and removed the pearl studs from his shirt. He smiled as he removed the gold sovereign cufflinks I had given him for his wedding present. He came to me and removed the diamond tiara from my hair and Pamela's sapphire and diamond necklace from around my neck and took a jewelry case from his pocket. Inside was a very fine chain of platinum with two round diamonds. He placed the chain around my neck and kissed the hollow of my throat where the stones lay and then both my breasts as he slowly removed my wedding dress. He carried me to the bed and lay me down. I watched the fire light reflected on his body as he removed first his white shirt, then his trousers until nothing was left but the dragon tattoo on his right breast. Then he came and lay beside me and stroked my abdomen and reached further down between my thighs where it was warm and moist. I kissed the dragon tattoo as he gently placed his body on mine and entered me. We started to move ever so slowly in silence, the only sound that of the music and our breathing. As in our dream, I could feel the dragon's tail once again moving deeper inside me and then faster all night until the fire was dying embers and, finally sated, we slept.

The Sweetest Song

January 1985
Philadelphia

On a snowy morning in the second week of January, Harry had reluctantly risen and taken the Metroliner to New York to work at Sotheby's. We returned to Philadelphia after our wedding to finalize my business arrangements and prepare for my move to Bath. With our busy schedules over the next three months and frequent flying out of the question in my last trimester, we decided to forgo a formal honeymoon and instead take long weekend road trips closer to home. I lingered in the blue bedroom in the George III tester bed, playing with my diamond necklace and blushed as I remembered our wedding night. With the twins kicking away, I listened to *Winter* from Vivaldi's Four Seasons playing on WFLN and remembered another snowy December morning in 1982 when I first met Pamela. As she had predicted, how quickly our lives can change. I met Carl Eckhart, her old love in September and again at our wedding and had gotten to know him; he was a fine man. I wouldn't be surprised if he and Pamela had a wedding of their own in the near future. I had never seen her happier. As for Andrew Townsend, he was dating a fellow architect, Jessica Moran from Dublin, a colleague from the Irish Georgian Society and she was visiting him in Charlottesville, Virginia where he had been asked to extend his guest professorship. I was happy for him and he and Harry really hit it off. Harry even extended an open invitation for Andrew to visit us in Bath when he was over in Dublin next summer. Phoebe Ingersoll had been offered a full art history professorship at Penn and Sarah Townsend was moving up the ladder at Winterthur as Curator of Furniture. Phoebe and Sarah both wanted to visit me in Bath during school holidays and vacations and Pamela was coming over for the birth of our twins.

Among other things I needed to hire a third employee for H.R. Grasso & Daughter to work as my replacement and to cover the antiques shows in Charleston, Philadelphia and Nantucket. Business decisions had to be made given my permanent move to Bath at the end of January, a mere two weeks away. The Chippendale secretary which had belonged to Caroline Blackburn Stuart and where I discovered the star ruby ring had already been shipped and was on its way to Bath to reside in the blue sitting room. Harry and I still planned to visit Philadelphia for business and to see our friends and would stay in my apartment over the shop. I was excited and looking forward to my new life with Harry and yet, a little sad for all I was leaving behind. Philadelphia would always be a big part of my life and my first home. Perhaps our children would return one day to H.R. Grasso & Daughter on Antique Row on Pine Street.

When Phoebe and I were in Nantucket in August, we met Jonah Coffin who expressed interest in coming to Philadelphia. A descendant of one of Nantucket's original families, Jonah graduated from Harvard with a master's degree in history and was now working on his thesis. He had been offered a part time teaching position at Penn and was available to work in the shop and travel for the antiques shows. Phoebe had a little crush on him and offered to show him around campus and the city of Philadelphia. I called him and asked him to stop by to meet with James, Melinda and me.

In the afternoon, after his classes, Jonah came to the shop. He was tall with auburn hair and a closely trimmed beard and piercing blue eyes. He looked exactly like an 18th century sea captain. Handsome in a rugged way, with his New England accent, good looks and brains he was sure to hold the attention of his female students and break a few hearts in the process.

"Good afternoon, Ms. Grasso or should I say Lady Atherton now? Phoebe told me congratulations are in order." "Jonah, you can call me Henrietta and this is James and Melinda, my staff. James and Melinda, I'd like you to meet Jonah Coffin from Nantucket.

James, why don't you show him around and then we can all sit down with a pot of tea and discuss the schedule for this year." Melinda went to prepare the tea, set it up in the library and turned on the gas fireplace as I looked over my notes. After about an hour we had a workable schedule that covered our needs for the year. I explained to Jonah that I was moving to Bath at the end of January and that Harry and I were expecting twins at the end of March so, although not physically available, I would still be as close as a phone call. I also told him about my mother's shop in Bath and how we would be working together. "This will work very well with my teaching schedule and in the summer Phoebe can stay at my family's home on Nantucket for the August antiques show." I smiled to myself; Phoebe would like that arrangement very much and they might even be able to fit in a summer romance… if it didn't happen sooner.

After Jonah left I went upstairs to the red sitting room, turned on the gas fireplace and called Phoebe at home. "I must say, Jonah is *quite the dreamboat* in a rugged sea captain sort of way. I like his name too, Jonah, something quite biblical about it." "I know," sighed Phoebe. "I think I'd like to get "biblical" with him. He asked me out for coffee and I told him he could call anytime if he needed help navigating his way around the city." "He mentioned you could stay at his family's home on Nantucket when you two do the antiques show in August together." "Really?" "Perhaps he will be the sea captain who hears the siren call of a beautiful blonde-haired mermaid." "Henrietta, you and your romantic notions, that's what got you into trouble in the first place." "Double trouble, you mean," I said patting my swelling belly and we both laughed.

That night, Harry returned from New York and as part of his continuing education in all things Italian, I took a more than willing Lord Atherton to dinner at the romantic Victor's Café at 13th and Dickinson in South Philly. A unique restaurant, Victor's started as a gramophone shop in 1918 where friends and neighbors could drop in for a cup of espresso to listen to the latest operatic recordings. It evolved to become the restaurant of choice for famous and up and coming opera stars passing through Philadelphia. Signed photographs and operatic memorabilia covered the walls above the ubiquitous red and white checkered table cloths. You never knew who was in town and might stop by. They would be encouraged to sing for their supper with an aria or two. The wait staff consisted of opera students studying at the Curtis Institute of Music or the Academy of Vocal Arts who were encouraged to sing between serving patrons. If you were lucky enough to be celebrating a birthday, they were happy to perform an operatic rendition of *Happy Birthday* in three part harmony. In between solos, Victor's played many of the original 78 rpm recordings. On any given night you could hear the voice of Enrico Caruso singing *vesti la giubba* from Leoncavallo's Pagliaccio.

We were lingering over our espresso and tiramisu when our waiter, a young tenor from Cincinnati, sang *e lucevan le stelle* from Puccini's Tosca:

> The stars were shining,
> And the earth was scented.
> The gate of the garden creaked
> And a footstep touched the sand...
> Fragrant, she entered
> And fell into my arms.
> Oh, sweet kisses and languorous caresses,
> While feverishly I stripped the beautiful form of its veils!
> Forever, my dream of love has vanished.
> That moment has fled, and I die in desperation.
> And I die in desperation!
> And I never before loved life so much,
> Loved life so much!

Mario Cavarradossi singing about his memories of nights of love with Floria Tosca, now gone forever, always made me sad. After the applause and shouts of *"Bravo"* faded in the dining room, I sighed and said, "Sometimes I think we *are* living in an opera...Phoebe called it a soap opera and today on the phone said my romantic notions are what got me into trouble in the first place." I was feeling nostalgic and my hormones must have been working overtime, making me emotional. Harry, sensing my mood, kissed my hand, called for the check and said, "Henrietta, your romantic notions are what make you this unique, loving, creative and passionate woman I fell in love with. Don't let anyone take that away from you...and while we're on the subject of *passione, Amore Mia*, I think its way past our bedtime, don't you?" And with that, we ran off into the night back to the George III tester bed, where, thanks to my passionate husband, my good mood was restored.

The end of January had arrived and Harry returned to take me home to England. We said our goodbyes to our friends and my staff. It was hardest leaving Pamela but she promised she would see me when the babies were born. Harry and I had a final lunch with Sam Jacobson at the Saloon. Sam also had a standing invitation to come and visit us in Bath. "Take good care of my girl, Harry, I promised her dad I would look after her. I've known her all her life and you will never find a sweeter person." "I know what a lucky man I am Sam and I shall treasure her always." We took a cab back to Jewelers' Row and we both hugged him goodbye. As we turned away from Sam's shop I started to cry and Harry held me in his arms in the middle of the sidewalk. "Let's go see your Dad," he whispered and directed the cab to St. Peter's.

We arrived at St. Peter's churchyard and told the cab to wait. We walked past the graves of the famous Philadelphians until we arrived at my father's grave.

"Hi Dad, we came to say goodbye for now. We will come back to see you when we're in town again although we know you are with us wherever we are. Don't forget our new address; No. 28 Royal Crescent, Bath. I think you'll like it there." "Mr. Grasso...Dad, I promise I will love and cherish your daughter and our children, your grandchildren, for as long as I live." In response we felt a warm caressing breeze on our cheeks even though the temperature was well below 30 degrees, but this time, we could hear no laughter.

That night was the last night we would spend in the blue bedroom in the George III tester bed in my apartment over the shop until after the birth of the twins. This was a special place for Harry and me where we first expressed our love for each other and where the twins were conceived. I looked around the room and tried to memorize all the details to take back with me to Bath. I thought of Andrew and how he came to stay with me in this room when I had the nightmare about Jamie. I thought of the red sitting room where I first discovered the star ruby ring in the secretary and where Phoebe and I discussed John Singleton Copley's painting on Christmas Eve two years ago.

Harry stirred and opened his eyes. "Love, is everything alright?" "I was just remembering..." "Try and get some rest, we have a long day tomorrow." He reached down under the covers to rub my abdomen. "The twins are growing so much we are going to have to find more creative ways to make love...but I think I may know how to help you relax so you can fall asleep." And then he kissed me and we settled in for a long winter's nap.

February 1985
Bath

It felt good to finally be settled in at No. 28 Royal Crescent and have a new project to concentrate on. We were re-decorating the guest room, bath and office into a suite for the twins and the nurse who was going to stay with us when they were born – a generous gift from Harry's parents and mine. We selected two matching English walnut cribs and a changing table, A warm yellow velvet loveseat and matching wing chair, a painted satinwood bookcase, an area rug with a fleur de lis pattern of yellow, gray and beige, yellow and gray patterned linens for the cribs and a Farrow & Ball wallpaper, Ringwold Yellow, a white and yellow floral pattern.

Harry was taking the train into London everyday during the week to Sotheby's. He still leased his furnished flat in London where we were to stay the last week in March pending the babies' births but was planning to give it up after I came home from the hospital. Dr. Winthrop reserved a private room for March 27th in the Lindo wing at St. Mary's hospital in Paddington. At the end of February we were in the babies' room admiring my efforts. With only a month to go before the twins arrived we finished just in time. "This room looks wonderful, my love. You did an excellent job; I think John and Caroline will really enjoy living here." "Thank you M'lord, I'm glad you're pleased." "You always please me but…hmmm, something is missing and I'll have to rectify that when I come home tonight," he said with an enigmatic smile as he kissed me goodbye.

That night, I was preparing our supper when there was a knock on the front door. As I opened it, a six foot giraffe poked his head through the door, followed by a lion, two rabbits, a teddy bear and a yellow baby dragon. "I stopped at Harrods today and somehow found myself in the toy department. These happy chaps seem to have followed me home. You should have seen the looks on people's faces on the train. Can they come and live here with us?" "Well, if they promise not to make too much noise when the babies are sleeping and not eat too much, I think they can stay." "I can't speak for the others but lions are nocturnal and like to roar at night." "Just like someone else I know." "Speaking of eating, this lion is quite hungry and has been thinking about you all day." And with that our menagerie was left to fend for themselves for the night.

John Henry and Caroline Charlotte Atherton's Birthday
March 27, 1985
London

Harry and I welcomed John Henry and Caroline Charlotte Atherton to the world on March 27th, 1985 at 11:30AM. John, the spitting image of Harry, arrived with blonde peach fuzz hair and Caroline had a shock of dark hair just like her mother. Our parents and Pamela Stuart were in attendance to welcome these two wonderful additions to our family. Harry and his father William were beaming to have a son and another grandson and my mother, Charlotte and his mother Frances were already making plans for their first granddaughter's social calendar. This day was especially meaningful to my mother to be able to hold her first grandchildren in her arms.

After everyone left the hospital for the night and the babies were sleeping peacefully, Harry climbed into bed with me and held me in his arms. I asked him to open the bedside table and remove a small leather case. Inside was a pair of platinum and mother of pearl cufflinks with a dragon etched in the center. In China, mother of pearl was connected to family and particularly motherhood. Worn as an amulet, it attracted good fortune and happiness. "Thank you my love, I will treasure them always and remember this day, this moment."

Then he reached into his pocket and removed a small gift box wrapped in silver paper. Inside was a pair of pearl earrings with platinum and diamond butterflies. "I wanted to give you butterflies to remind you of our wedding night when we first felt the babies move, that fluttering, like butterfly wings. In China the butterfly symbolizes marital bliss and joy and in Greek mythology it is seen as the symbol of the soul's undying love; Psyche takes the form of a butterfly and is forever bound to Eros and they share a passion that transcends time. See, I did pay attention during my Greek studies at Oxford," he said with a smile and kissed me. "Thank you Harry, they're beautiful and I shall always remember that night and today as the two happiest days of my life."

"There is something else I have to tell you," he said more seriously. "I wanted to wait until after the twins were born. Remember that day last month when I was at Harrods and picked up the toys for the children's room? Before I went to Harrods, I decided to stroll down Old Brompton Road. I was curious about Mr. Cavendish's vanishing estate jewellery shop at No. 159 where you purchased my sovereign cufflinks and first saw my grandmother's sovereign bracelet. Henrietta, I can tell you now, he was *there* again in his shop, exactly as you described it to me. He seemed to recognize me and asked if I liked my cufflinks and how did you like the bracelet. He congratulated us on our wedding and the coming birth of the twins. These earrings are from his shop..."

June 1985
Bath

it was the month of the Netherfield Ball and John and Caroline's christening. I dozed in Prior Park with Harry and the twins on a blanket after a hamper lunch enjoying the warm sunshine.

The twins were growing rapidly and thanks to our parents, our nurse Mrs. Thompson, and their doting parents, they never lacked for attention. Their christening was planned for the Sunday after the Netherfield Ball at the Church of St. Nicholas. Harry's mother Frances presented us with the Atherton family christening gowns and Mother and Arthur were hosting the luncheon afterwards at the Old Rectory where we were going to cut the "Christening Cake", the top layer from our wedding cake. We were all going to the Netherfield Ball. I remembered the year before when Harry and I danced to the Sussex Waltz. "Lady Atherton, may I have the first dance?" asked Harry as he bowed before me. I curtsied and replied, "With pleasure, M'lord." After the ball we left the Guildhall to make our way to the Palladian Bridge and as the Evening Star rose in the sky, we held each other and sent a special prayer of thanksgiving for all the blessings we had received.

The Lovers' Tale

Carl and Pamela Eckhart's Wedding Day
September 29, 1985
Philadelphia

The organist was playing Schubert's Ave Maria as we gathered at St. Peter's church at 3rd and Pine for the afternoon wedding of Pamela Stuart to Carl Eckhart. It was an Indian summer day, warm with just a hint of fall in the air. Carl, standing at the altar, tall, silver haired and handsome in a three piece gray suit and tie, wore a lavender rose in his lapel. As the soloist started to sing Walter Scott's immortal words, Pamela, wearing a long sleeved fitted dove gray lace dress with her gray south sea pearls and carrying a bouquet of lavender roses slowly walked up the aisle. Harry and I held hands as we listened to them take their vows, remembering our own less than a year ago. After the ceremony, we walked to the churchyard where Pamela placed a single lavender rose from her bouquet on the grave of her ancestor, Caroline Blackburn Stuart and looked up at me and smiled. She remembered. Harry and I lingered in the churchyard to visit my father's grave then walked to the Powel House nearby for the wedding reception.

At the reception in the garden we could hear the first chords of Bach's *Harpsichord Prelude and Fugue in C Major* drifting from the ballroom on the second floor. We were all together again; Pamela and Carl, Harry and I, Sam Jacobson, Phoebe and Jonah, her brother Stephen, Sarah Townsend and her cousin Andrew. Dear, sweet Andrew had come to Bath in August on his way back from Dublin to see us and meet the twins. I was in the Powel House with the two most important men in my life who were last with me, in this very house more than two hundred years ago. I didn't see any ghosts this time, they were all dispelled and at peace as we celebrated with only joyful emotions on this very special day.

It was wonderful to be back in Philadelphia for Pamela's wedding. Carl moved here from Germany to live with her in her apartment on Washington Square. Phoebe and Jonah Coffin, as I predicted, had fallen in love and were making wedding plans. Jonah finished his thesis and was offered a full time position teaching history at Penn starting in January, much to Phoebe's delight. I would have to find another employee for H.R. Grasso & Daughter but I was so happy for them. The twins, now six months old, were safe and sound back in Bath with Mrs. Thompson and their grandparents and Harry and I took this opportunity to have some time alone together.

After the wedding reception, we slowly strolled up Pine Street, hand in hand savoring the moment toward our apartment over the shop. "Seeing Andrew tonight made me wonder what would have happened if I hadn't shown up on your doorstep in Philadelphia last year in July," Harry mused. "I would have returned to Bath," I replied, "But I'm so glad you did show up." "Not more than I, my love…" When we reached our apartment, we climbed the stairs to the familiar blue bedroom and the waiting George III tester bed where our reunion was savory and sweet and continued well into the autumn night.

October 1985
Philadelphia

Harry and I stayed the first week of October in Philadelphia and decided to make this an annual event. Philadelphia, like Bath, was a city for strolling leisurely and admiring the architecture. The climate was temperate; warm in the day and cooler at night. The trees were dressed in russet and gold and the aroma from wood burning fireplaces scented the air as we strolled along the streets of Society Hill. It also was the perfect time of year for antiques shopping. The morning after Carl and Pamela's wedding Harry kissed me goodbye and took the Metroliner to Sotheby's in New York. *Autumn* from Vivaldi's Four Seasons was playing on WFLN as I finished my cup of French Roast and looked out the French doors to the garden below where the last of Pamela's dahlias were blooming. I had a meeting with my staff, James, Melinda and Jonah. I hadn't seen them since the end of January. We sat together at the round George IV mahogany table in the library drinking Darjeeling tea from the Coalport Indian Tree Coral tea cups.

"It's so good to have you back," they all exclaimed. "I'm thrilled to be back. Jonah, I hear congratulations are in order for being offered a full time teaching position at Penn. We are going to miss having you here, come January." "Thank you, Henrietta, I am looking forward to it but will miss working with these two." He smiled as he looked at James and Melinda. "We were very successful at the shows this year, particularly Nantucket and Phoebe and I enjoyed the rest of August on the island." I was planning to have lunch with Phoebe on Friday at the Garden and get an in-depth report of her sea captain's proposal and her introduction to his family. I wondered if Harry and I would be flying into Nantucket next summer for their wedding. I couldn't wait to show him the island known as "The Gray Lady". Melinda interrupted my romantic musings and said, "The Nantucket show went very well this year and we're still getting calls and referrals. James and I need to refresh our inventory and get ready for the upcoming holidays." This time of year was always busy; our customers would be redecorating and selecting items for gift giving at Christmas.

In addition to attending the private estate sales, we regularly frequented Freeman's Auction House on 18th and Chestnut established in 1805. Freeman's was a treasure trove with over 30 in-house auctions a year including our special areas of 18th and 19th century American & English Furniture and Decorative Arts. I hadn't been to Freeman's in a long time so I invited Jonah to the auction and to lunch afterwards to get to know him better. H.R. Grasso & Daughter was registered and received all the catalogues. There was an Asian Arts auction scheduled for 11AM. I thought I might find a dragon or two for Harry's collection. Recently, to make even

Sotheby's sit up and take notice, a Qing Dynasty imperial white jade double dragon seal sold at Freeman's for an impressive $3.5 million, a price 8-10 times the original estimate of $30,000-50,000. Harry was very impressed with my home town and all the treasures it held. "One treasure in particular," he said, "Is priceless…"

I bid on two items made by Wang Hing & Co - a Chinese repousse silver vase circa 1900 with an undulating rim of cherry blossoms, decorated with a continuous band of dragons and a Chinese silver dragon bowl circa 1907, the dragon encircling the bowl in high relief. Wang Hing was a maker and retailer of quality Chinese export silver from 1875 to 1925 in Hong Kong. The company was patronised by Tiffany's, Indian Maharajas, and other notables. These would be the first silver dragon pieces in Harry's collection, one to give him at Christmas and the other on his birthday, August 3rd. I requested they be shipped to me in Bath.

Feeling rather pleased with myself for not one but two successful bids, I took Jonah to lunch at the Philadelphia Art Alliance at 18th and Walnut across from Rittenhouse Square. The weather was mild and the restaurant garden was still open for lunch. After we ordered, we sat and relaxed taking in the atmosphere. "There's something special about eating outside," remarked Jonah." "Yes there is… so how do you like Philadelphia?" "I love it, so much to see and do, all the cultural venues and the university is a great place to work. Now I know why Phoebe loves it so much," he said with a shy smile. "Well, I think Nantucket is a pretty fantastic place as well." "We'll try to go back during school vacations and in the summer. It's pretty spectacular at Christmas, you and Harry should come and bring the little ones one year. We have plenty of room." "We just may take you up on that." We talked about Carl Eckhart, Pamela's husband and how impressed Jonah was with the retired history professor from Heidelberg University. "Now that Carl has moved here I hope to spend more time with him, he's a brilliant guy. I'd like to have him come to my classes as a guest lecturer."

After lunch we strolled through Rittenhouse Square, one of the five original squares planned by William Penn surrounded by luxury high rises and cultural institutions such as the Curtis Institute of Music and the beautiful neo-Romanesque Church of the Holy Trinity designed by John Notman in 1859. One of the rectors, The Rev. Phillips Brooks, a young man destined to become one of the most prominent preachers of the age, in 1868 wrote the Christmas carol, *Oh Little Town of Bethlehem*. It was also the church that hosted the Handel's Messiah sing-a-long which my father and I attended faithfully every year. "Phoebe and I spend a lot of our free time in the Square since we live close by. It's a great place to just lie on a blanket, have a picnic and relax." Jonah moved into Phoebe's apartment on 20th and Pine at the beginning of September. I was glad she had found someone who truly loved her. I didn't feel so guilty now about leaving my friends and returning to Bath. I hadn't lost Philadelphia but gained London and Bath and now Nantucket.

On Friday Phoebe and I had lunch at the Garden and it was just like old times. We sipped our Chardonnay as she told me about Jonah's courtship. "I was feeling kind of lonely, it was Valentine's Day and I was remembering the opening of the exhibition at the Historical Society, the great love story between John Singleton Copley and Caroline Blackburn and missing you. He appeared on the street in front of my apartment and tossed pebbles up at my balcony. When I came out he quoted from the balcony scene in Shakespeare's Romeo & Juliet. He had a bottle of red wine and a *pizza* in his hands. So of course I had to invite him in, what else could I do?" she said with a giggle. "That was quite romantic and a very creative way to get your attention." "Wait it gets better…he also brought two chocolate covered strawberries for dessert which he fed me ever so *slowly* by the fire as he read from his tattered copy of Dante's Inferno the story of Paolo and Francesca. And then he kissed me, it was very sensual…" "Sounds like quite a seduction." "You have no idea…" We both giggled like the schoolgirls we used to be and I squeezed her hand in remembrance, dear, sweet Phoebe.

"So, how did things go on Nantucket in August when you met his family?" "Well, he has a large extended family on the island and I met *all* of them. Both his parents are history professors at Harvard; he's the eldest and has a brother and sister, Elijah and Mariah. They were great! They told me Jonah could not stop talking about me and they couldn't wait to meet me. Our last night on the island he took me to dinner at Chanticleer in 'Sconset. After dinner, the waiter brought us a plate of chocolate covered strawberries and in the center was an antique aquamarine and diamond ring. Jonah placed the ring on my finger and said, "Phoebe, I will always remember our first Valentine's Day when you made my life the sweetest it's ever been…will you marry me?" Then she showed me the ring for the first time. It was a round three karat baby blue aquamarine surrounded by diamonds in an Edwardian platinum setting. The stone was the color of Phoebe's eyes and was also her birthstone for the month of March. "We just got it back from Sam Jacobson; he had to adjust the size." "Oh Phoebe, congratulations …it's beautiful, I'm so happy for you both." "Henrietta, he's everything I've always wanted, smart, funny, sensitive… and a great kisser. We're thinking about an August wedding on Nantucket when everyone is off from school." "First Pamela and now you, of course Harry and I will be there."

July 1986
Dublin, Ireland

Harry and I were surprised and pleased to receive an invitation to Andrew Townsend's and Jessica Moran's wedding in Dublin on July 12th. Having sold his house on Delancey Street in Philadelphia, they were living in Charlottesville, Virginia. Andrew was teaching architecture at his alma mater, the University of Virginia part time and working on preservation projects with Jessica, a graduate of Trinity College, Dublin. Every summer they returned to Ireland to see Jessica's family and continue their preservation work with the Irish Georgian Society.

The Irish Georgian Society, headquartered in Dublin, was founded in 1958 by the Hon. Desmond Guiness to conserve, protect and foster an interest and a respect for Ireland's architectural heritage and decorative arts. The Society also supported scholarly research through its journal, Bulletin of the Irish Georgian Society. Andrew presented multiple papers to the Bulletin over the years and lectured at the Society's annual conferences. Through this group he had made lasting friendships and had found love as well.

I was happy for Andrew. There would always be that connection with him; I was thankful that they would be in Ireland in the summers and we would be able to see them in Bath or Dublin. The marriage ceremony on Saturday was going to be at the Chapel at Trinity College and the afternoon reception at the Shelbourne Hotel at No. 27 St. Stephen's Green where we were staying with Sarah Townsend, Andrew's cousin and her parents.

Sarah and her parents flew in from Martha's Vineyard on Friday morning and Harry and I arrived from London to spend a long weekend. Jessica, Sarah, her mother Marjorie and I reserved a day at the hotel's spa and afternoon tea in the Lord Mayor's Lounge while the men spent time together. Andrew was hosting a pre-wedding party on Friday night at O'Neill's on Suffolk Street where bands from all over Ireland came to perform.

After a relaxing day, we were enjoying our tea when Sarah and Marjorie excused themselves to take a much needed nap. I took the opportunity to get to know Jessica. She was a classic Irish beauty with pale skin and rosy cheeks, light chestnut hair and warm brown eyes. She reminded me of Andrew's cousin Sarah. "Thank you for inviting us, it's going to be a beautiful day tomorrow and Harry and I look forward to your visits to Bath when you and Andrew are in Dublin in the summers. "We do too; I miss my family and Ireland terribly when we are in Virginia but knowing we can visit at Christmas and the summer makes it more bearable. Andrew loves Virginia and the university but I know they would be thrilled to have him here at Trinity. He's been approached several times but always turned down the offer. Although I think that had more to do with his relationship with you... maybe now he'll reconsider."

She looked at me with those brown eyes and said, "You must know, Henrietta you were the love of his life. I've also loved him a long time...from the moment I saw him when he first started coming to Ireland in the summers as a college student." "I didn't know..." "When he came to Dublin the summer of 1984, he was heartbroken. The last we heard, he was engaged to marry you. He called me from Virginia that September and told me you were going to marry Harry. I saw this as my last opportunity and went to visit him in Charlottesville. I think I can make him happy, I know I am going to try..." We both had tears in our eyes as we hugged each other and at that moment I knew Andrew's bride and I would be friends.

O' Neill's Pub and Restaurant at No. 2 Suffolk Street in Dublin was a public house for over three hundred years, the current owners in residence there since 1927. Live traditional Irish music was played nightly during the summer. Friday night the pub was packed and the party was going strong with Andrew and Jessica's friends from the Irish Georgian Society adding to the merriment. Sarah, her parents, Harry and I joined in the fun, dancing and singing and ordering draughts of Guinness. In between musical sets, we were introduced to Andrew and Jessica's friends.

"Uncle Joe, Aunt Marjorie, Sarah, Harry and Henrietta, here is someone I want you all to meet," said Andrew, "My good friend and Best Man, Luke Gardiner. Luke, *this...* is my cousin Sarah. Luke is working on the Henrietta Street project here in Dublin." Luke Gardiner was tall and very good looking with brown hair and intelligent grey blue eyes. When he smiled I noticed his lips and the defined philtrum, the groove above his upper lip. *According to folklore, God sent an angel to a woman's womb so that the angel could teach the baby all of the wisdom of the world. Then the angel pressed its finger, leaving an indentation above the baby's mouth to shush the baby from telling the secrets.* The word philtrum is from the Greek which means "to love; to kiss".

"Handsome devil, isn't he?" said Andrew. "The women on the team can't keep their minds on their work when he's around." Even in the darkened pub I could see Luke blush. Sarah's eyes were sparkling as she looked at him. "It's a pleasure to meet you and I'll deal with Andrew later, he is the groom after all..." laughed Luke. "Sarah, your cousin has told me about your promotion at Winterthur, very impressive." Now it was Sarah who was blushing. I think it was payback time; it was Sarah who first introduced me to Andrew and now he was engaging in a little matchmaking of his own.

Andrew and Jessica Townsend's Wedding Day
July 12, 1986
Dublin, Ireland

Founded in 1592 by Queen Elizabeth I, Trinity College was Ireland's oldest college. Jonathan Swift, Oscar Wilde, Bram Stoker, and Samuel Beckett were among the college's literary alumni. The library housed the famous Book of Kells painted in extraordinary colors, some of which were derived from shellfish, beetles' wings, and crushed pearls. The Chapel designed by Sir William Chambers in 1798 had a classical temple front and an interior lit by semi-circular windows set into the ceiling and ornate plasterwork on the ceiling by Michael Stapleton.

The Chapel pews were simply adorned with white roses tied with white satin ribbons. Andrew, with his dark hair and golden eyes, looked handsome in his light gray suit and tie, a white rose in his lapel, as he stood at the altar with Luke Gardiner by his side. The 18th century music of Turlough O'Carolan, *Carolan's Dream* started to play on a celtic harp as Jessica's niece, four year old Meghan Moran, walked up the aisle tossing white rose petals. Jessica followed in a fitted strapless white dress with a ballerina waltz length tulle skirt. The afternoon sun shone through the ceiling windows setting her chestnut hair aglow. As they said their vows I started to tear up. Harry looked at me, handed me his handkerchief and leaned in to kiss me. All too soon it was over. After the ceremony, the harpist played a lively *O'Carolan's Concerto* as we all left the Chapel and walked back to St. Stephen's Green and the reception at the hotel.

I was looking forward to the opportunity to dance with Andrew at the reception; we hadn't had a moment to talk since Harry and I arrived. "Andrew, thank you for inviting us, the ceremony was lovely and Jessica is a wonderful woman. I had a chance to get to know her better over tea yesterday. You are a lucky man." Andrew smiled. "I could say the same for Harry." "Thank you. I hope we will always be friends, you will always be welcome to our home in Bath." "Henrietta, I'll remember." Then he took my hand and placed it over his heart, his golden eyes shining.

July 1986
Dublin, Ireland,
Bath, England

The next day was Sunday and we said goodbye to Sarah and her parents before they left for Martha's Vineyard. I noticed Luke Gardiner occupied most of her dances at the wedding reception and he came this morning to say goodbye and exchange phone numbers and addresses. Harry and I had a flight back to London that afternoon. We ate our breakfast in the hotel dining room and planned to do a little shopping before we left. Andrew and Jessica had already departed on their honeymoon for a tour of the chateaux of the Loire Valley in France.

It had been a wonderful but emotional weekend and I needed to get back to our twins, John and Caroline - I missed them. I was feeling a little let down, all my friends were married or about to be – Pamela, Andrew, Phoebe, maybe Sarah in the future. I was happy for them and at the same time I knew our relationships would change. Sensing my unsettled mood, Harry said, "Let's go see the Powerscourt Centre. I went through the building on Friday with Andrew. It would make a great location for a Dublin branch of H.R. Grasso & Daughter." Now he had my attention! As we strolled over to No. 59 South William Street, Harry told me the history of the Georgian townhouse, one of the finest in Dublin, designed in 1774 by Robert Mack for Richard Wingfield, 3rd Viscount Powerscourt. It was now a shopping centre for antiques, jewelry and fashion with a sky lit food court. It was a beautiful building and as we walked around, I *could envision* our antiques shop here. I grabbed him and kissed him in the middle of the food court. "Lady Atherton, my, my, such public displays of affection…" he laughed and kissed me back. "I've spoken to the letting agent and gotten all the information for you. We can talk about it on the plane and the drive home." "Oh Harry, it sounds like a wonderful idea, thank you for giving me a new project to think about." "I *know* how much you like your projects. Don't forget my love; I was your first one in Bath and look how well that turned out."

Soon we were home at No. 28 Royal Crescent in Bath and played with the twins after dinner until it was their bedtime. "I think we need a nice soak in the bath, I'll wash your back, what do you say?" asked Harry. "Only if I can wash your dragon, M'lord..." I said laughing, pointing to the dragon tattoo on his chest. M'lady you can wash me *anywhere* you prefer..." Afterwards, wrapped in warm towels we walked into the master bedroom. Harry led me to the bed and removed my towel and kissed my shoulder. There on my pillow was a round dimensional gold brooch in the form of a Chinese dragon, the eyes set with cabochon sapphires. "It's an 1890 Louis Wièse design from Paris," said Harry. I saw it at Delphi Antiques in the Powerscourt on Friday and it must have followed me home..."

August 1986
Nantucket

Nantucket, an island thirty miles south of Cape Cod, Massachusetts was settled by the English in 1659. Jonah Coffin's ancestors were one of the original families on the island. Nantucket's fortunes originally were tied to the whaling industry begun in 1712 and entered a golden age after the War of 1812 to the 1850s. At its height, Herman Melville wrote Moby Dick, the tale of Captain Ahab and the great white whale. Now a tourist destination, Nantucket had the finest collection of 18th century homes amid sophisticated restaurants, boutiques, hotels and bed and breakfast inns.

The first sight most people saw when approaching Nantucket by water or air was the golden dome of the Unitarian Church on Orange Street. Built in 1809, the church was going to be the site of Jonah and Phoebe's wedding ceremony. We were all in attendance; Jonah's family, Phoebe's parents, her brother Stephen Ingersoll, Sarah Townsend and Luke Gardiner, Carl and Pamela Eckhart, Andrew and Jessica Townsend and Harry and I. Andrew and Jessica, back from their honeymoon in France, were going to extend it a few extra days before they had to fly back to Virginia for the fall school term at the university. They were surprised and pleased to see Luke Gardiner, their good friend and Best Man from Dublin who was spending time with Sarah at her family's home on Martha's Vineyard.

Harry and I flew in from London on Friday. After arriving at the Jared Coffin House and a relaxing bath and nap, we were refreshed and ready for the rehearsal dinner at the Chanticleer Restaurant in Siasconset, a village at the eastern end of the island, known simply as "Sconset" to the locals. Chanticleer, where Jonah proposed to Phoebe was a romantic French restaurant with climbing pink roses on a traditional gray cedar covered building. At dinner, Jonah and Phoebe made a special toast to me thanking me for hiring Jonah at H.R. Grasso & Daughter in January thus setting the stage for their romance to bloom.

Jonah and Phoebe Coffin's Wedding Day
August 16, 1986
Nantucket

Phoebe, dressed in a strapless white lace fitted gown slightly flaring at the bottom, her pale blonde hair swept up in a soft chignon, walked up the aisle to a smiling Jonah dressed in a navy blue double breasted blazer with brass buttons, white trousers and a navy blue and white striped tie. She looked like a mermaid just risen from the sea and he, her dashing sea captain as the song *My Jolly Sailor Bold* was played on the piano and sung by Jonah's sister Mariah. After their vows Mariah played an early piece of music by Stephen Foster, *the Tioga Waltz* as they left the church to a waiting horse and carriage and then back to the reception at the Jared Coffin House.

At the reception I had the opportunity to speak privately to Sarah Townsend about her budding relationship with Andrew's friend Luke Gardiner. "So, how is Luke enjoying his stay with you on Martha's Vineyard?" "This is the first time he's been to America, he loves it! He's been invited to visit Andrew and Jessica in Virginia and wants to come to Delaware for Christmas to see Winterthur." "Does he have any *other* reason to come to Delaware?" I teased. "You *know* he does..." Should I start booking our plane tickets now?" "Oh don't worry, I'll keep you posted," she said as we hugged each other.

After the wedding, Jonah and Phoebe planned to stay on Nantucket until it was time to return to their fall classes at Penn. Harry and I were scheduled to leave on Monday morning so they had a day of activities planned for our small group on Sunday. First a walking tour of the historic district and then a sunset picnic on Madaket Beach, considered to be one of the prettiest beaches on the island. Jonah took us on a tour of the Three Bricks, the stately Greek Revival homes built in 1837-1840 by Christopher Capen for Joseph Starbuck's three sons and the Atheneum, the elegant white Greek temple designed by Frederick Brown Coleman in 1847 as the town's library. Andrew, Jessica and Luke, as preservation architects, were particularly impressed not only with the 19th century craftsmanship but the quality of preservation of these buildings on an island thirty miles out at sea.

Later in the afternoon we headed to Madaket Beach for our picnic. Jonah had ordered a special meal from the Jared Coffin House – jumbo shrimp cocktail, homemade fresh salsa with tortilla chips, chicken salad with avocado, tomato, bacon and blue cheese all to be washed down with ice cold Samuel Adams beer and white chocolate banana tarts for dessert.

It felt wonderful to be together; Harry and I, Jonah and Phoebe, Andrew and Jessica, Luke and Sarah, eating the delicious food, feeling the warm sand between our toes and laughing at each other's jokes - but bittersweet too. As the sun set in the Atlantic, we all knew it would be a long time before we were together again and I wondered what the future held in store for us.

The Ghost House

September 1986
Dublin

After a busy year watching our twins grow like dandelions in a summer field and attending our friends' weddings, Harry and I were ready to finalize the new plans for H.R. Grasso & Daughter, Dublin. Harry discovered the 1774 Georgian townhouse when we attended Andrew and Jessica Townsend's wedding in July. Located at No. 59 South William Street, the Powerscourt Centre was now a shopping venue and the perfect location for our antiques shop. We hoped to be open for business in time for Christmas. Through Luke Gardiner and the Irish Georgian Society we were able to make important contacts in the area and employ two graduates from Trinity College, Ian Byrne and Molly Ryan, to manage the shop. Jonah Coffin suggested a replacement for his position at H.R. Grasso & Daughter, Philadelphia, a former student of his, Colin Tyler who would start in January. We were looking forward to our annual visit to Philadelphia for the first week in October when I would see James and Melinda and meet Colin. Thanks to the hiring of Mrs. Avery, our housekeeper and Mrs. Thompson, the twins' nanny, we had the time to devote to our new business.

Harry and I flew into Dublin on Friday morning for the weekend to meet with Ian and Molly to discuss the design of the shop, review the calendar for local estate sales, set up delivery of inventory and plan the grand opening. We were also going to see Luke Gardiner for a tour of the Henrietta Street project and discuss my previous decorative arts work on the restoration of John Penn's house, The Solitude in Philadelphia. Upon arrival, we went to meet Ian and Molly in our new space at the Powerscourt Centre. They had set up a temporary table and chairs with fresh coffee, hot Irish scones and Kerrygold butter from the food court.

I liked them immediately! Young and enthusiastic, they both came from academic families – Ian was now studying furniture restoration, his father having written the definitive book on Irish Georgian furniture and Molly had extensive knowledge in Irish decorative silver and porcelain. Together they were the perfect team to manage our new shop in Dublin. I showed them the shop design and color scheme, business stationery design and photographs of the pieces we were shipping from both my mother's shop in Bath and the Philadelphia shop. The upcoming local estate sales were already booked on the calendar.

Ian and Molly were going to oversee the transformation of the empty space into a showroom; the walls painted in Farrow & Ball Drawing Room Blue, the same cobalt blue I chose for our sitting room in Bath, the better to showcase the gilt wood mirrors, sconces and picture frames and the blue & white Chinese export porcelains. A carpenter was to build one wall of bookcases, the reception desk and install dental molding around the ceiling to be painted a high gloss white to complement the Irish Georgian white marble mantel and the black and white marble checkerboard floor. An electrician was hired to install the trio of neoclassical bronze and crystal chandeliers. The design for the shop's business cards was a dark blue engraved Georgia typeface on white card stock with an embossed gold Chinese dragon copied from one in Harry's collection. We chose this particular dragon because it had a very celtic look.

After breakfast on Saturday, we took a tour of the Francis Street antiques shops known as the Art & Antiques Quarter. The street reminded me of Antique Row in Philadelphia. We planned to extend an invitation for a private preview to the local dealers to get to know them. In the afternoon we were to meet Luke for lunch at the Shelbourne Hotel and then head to Henrietta Street.

Henrietta Street was the earliest Georgian Street in Dublin, started in the mid-1720s, on land bought and developed by Luke Gardiner. There was a friendly dispute about for whom the street was named - Henrietta, the wife of Charles FitzRoy, 2nd Duke of Grafton or Henrietta, the wife of Charles Paulet, 2nd Duke of Bolton. Luke Gardiner, Trinity College graduate and present day preservation architect, ironically was no relation to the 18th century Luke Gardiner. The street fell into disrepair during the 19th and 20th centuries but had been the subject of restoration efforts in recent years being the single remaining intact example of an early 18th century street of houses.

Luke and his team from the Irish Georgian Society were restoring No. 12 Henrietta Street designed by Edward Lovett Pearce and built by Luke Gardiner along with No. 11 between 1730-1733. The house would become a museum and an educational resource center for anyone wanting to learn about the history of the street and proper restoration techniques. Luke was planning a Christmas event as a fund raiser the weekend of December 5th the same date as our opening. The Irish Baroque Orchestra was performing Handel's Messiah at Christ Church Cathedral that same weekend and Harry and I looked forward to attending the concert, our first during the Christmas season in Dublin.

Luke met us back at the hotel for lunch in the Lord Mayor's Lounge. "Lord and Lady Atherton, it's a pleasure to see you again," then hugged me and shook Harry's hand. We had been in close contact with Luke since we met him at Andrew's wedding in July and had spent time with him on Nantucket when Phoebe married Jonah in August. We already felt like old friends. It was because of him that everything was going smoothly in the setting up of our new business. "How did it go yesterday with Ian and Molly?" "Oh Luke, they're perfect! I'm looking forward to working with them. You could not have suggested a better pair." "Yeah, they're pretty special; I got to know them through their work with the IGS. Only the best for you, Henrietta, Andrew has often spoken so highly of you both." "Well, we think the same about him and you," replied Harry.

Over lunch, Luke outlined the progress at No. 12 Henrietta Street. "The two main rooms on the first floor will be completed for Christmas and we are asking the antiques dealers on Francis Street to decorate the rooms for the fund raiser the weekend of December 5th." "We would be happy to participate, Luke," I replied. "Great, thank you both for that. Henrietta, I would also like you to be our decorative arts consultant as you were with Andrew on The Solitude. I can't promise a salary, we are all volunteers, but we have a budget to purchase furniture and accessories and it would give your new business plenty of exposure and introduce you to the local community." "That's an excellent idea, Luke but Henrietta, sweetheart, do you think you will have the time to do this?" Harry asked. "I think I will now that I have Ian and Molly managing the shop. What's our time frame Luke?" "Our target completion date is the beginning of October next year so we can participate in Open House Dublin. Let's drive over to Henrietta Street and I'll show you No. 12."

Henrietta Street was less than two miles away from the Shelbourne Hotel and the Powerscourt Centre, my two bases of operation when in Dublin. I smiled to myself that yet another handsome man asked me to participate in a house museum restoration but this time under very different circumstances. Now that I was married, no other man would hold any allure for me, or so I thought.

Luke unlocked the door to No. 12 and said, "William Stewart, 3rd Viscount Mountjoy who later became 1st Earl of Blessington was the first resident of the house." I could see what a grand home it once was. The rooms were in various stages of restoration. The walls showed the discovery of multiple layers of paint in muted colors of mauve and ochre and brought to mind the painted walls of the ruins in the ancient city of Pompeii. This house, unlike The Solitude, was in decay and had spent its life in the nineteenth and twentieth centuries as tenement housing for multiple families. It was an archaeological dig, an excavation site. It was fascinating!

"We are going to have the main entrance and foyer, the drawing room and dining room decorated for the Christmas fund raiser with fresh seasonal greens, food and live music, all donated. The Royal Horticultural Society is providing the decorations, the Shelbourne Hotel is donating the food and students from Trinity College Music Department will perform over the weekend." "We have an Irish

George II mahogany console table and a gilt wood Rococo mirror that would look wonderful in the foyer. I can see it displayed with a fresh Christmas arrangement and bronze and gilt candlesticks." "…And don't forget; with H.R. Grasso & Daughter business cards prominently displayed," smiled Luke in response. "While you're here, let me get you a set of floor plans, a key and the budget guidelines for the furnishings. Sarah Townsend told me you were able to use Winterthur's resources when working on The Solitude. I've also included a list of similar resources I can introduce you to at Trinity and IGS." Harry saw the sparkle in my eyes and squeezed my hand and smiled. "Luke, you have made my wife very happy today, she loves doing this. It's going to be an intriguing project for her, especially coming on the heels of the opening of the new shop." Just how intriguing we were yet to discover…

November 1986
Dublin

When we returned from our week in Philadelphia, Harry and I reserved the remaining weekends in October and November for the grand opening of H.R. Grasso & Daughter, Dublin. Preparations in the shop were going well and every weekend we were able to see progress. The invitations were sent to the Francis Street antiques dealers for the preview party on November 29th and for the grand opening party on December 6th. Mother and Arthur and Harry's parents, William and Frances were coming for the opening, the twins to be in residence with Harry's brother and wife and Mrs. Thompson in Bath. It would give them a chance to spend time with their cousins.

Ian and Molly were very successful at the estate sales which added more Irish antiques to our inventory of English and American including antique prints of local scenes of Dublin and Ireland. By the end of November, everything was in position for our preview party and they had arranged for the delivery and installation of the Irish George II mahogany console table and gilt wood Rococo mirror at No. 12 Henrietta Street. I arrived from London on Friday morning the 28th. Harry was coming on Saturday afternoon as he had an important Asian Art auction at Sotheby's in London on Saturday morning. It was the first time we were spending the night apart since I moved to Bath. "I'll be there in plenty of time for the preview party on Saturday night, then we can have a very *private* reunion afterwards at the hotel," he said as he took me in his arms and gave me a lingering kiss at the airport.

I was excited and looking forward to the weekend and after checking in at the hotel went straight to the Powerscourt Center. The 18th century townhouse looked glorious decorated for Christmas and our shop was breathtaking. Ian and Molly had completed the Christmas decorations; fresh greens with cobalt blue velvet ribbons, a tree with tiny blue lights and brass ornaments in the shapes of dragons I found in a shop in Bath and a brass dragon lamp finial as a tree topper. A magnificent circular 1810 Regency mahogany library table with four ormolu mounted scroll legs stood in the center. The lights were dimmed and the gas fire lit so I could get the full effect. It was like seeing the stage set for the opening of a new play.

"The shop looks so beautiful, beyond my expectations," I said as I hugged Ian and Molly. "You both did a spectacular job. I can't wait for Harry and the other dealers to see it tomorrow night." "The only thing left to do is for the caterers to set up the food and drinks tomorrow in time for the preview party at 7PM," said Molly. "We received the response cards, all the dealers are coming as well as Luke Gardiner and our colleagues from IGS," added Ian.

"Speaking of Luke Gardiner, how do the console table and mirror look at No. 12 Henrietta Street?" I asked. "I oversaw the installation and its very dramatic, the first thing you see when you walk in, along with our business cards," smiled Ian. "I think I'll stop by later today and see how the other dealers are decorating the first floor rooms of the house. We might be able to purchase some pieces for the permanent collection. But now I'm going to treat you both to lunch at the hotel, you've earned it." And off we went to the Shelbourne Hotel to have a leisurely lunch in the Lord Mayor's Lounge.

The Ghost House

Printed on a white tented card with our signature blue ink and golden dragon logo, the description of the console table and mirror looked elegant next to the cast bronze dragon holding our business cards. Ian was right, they did look dramatic. At that moment, Luke came through the front door. "Henrietta, it's so good to see you," he said and gave me a hug, "Did you just arrive?" "I got into town this morning and stopped by the shop, then took Ian and Molly to lunch. Luke you should see what they have done, everything looks fantastic." "I'm sure it does, I'm looking forward to the party tomorrow night. Is Harry here with you?" "He's coming tomorrow afternoon; he has an Asian Art auction in London Saturday morning. I wanted to see our installation and look at the other rooms, perhaps there might be some pieces we could use for the permanent collection." "Well, I definitely think we should purchase the table and mirror; that is, if it's within our budget." "I seem to have connections with the dealer, I'll see what I can do for you," I teased. "Good, Let me introduce you to the other dealers." Afterwards, I made some notes and told Luke I wanted to look around on the upper floors and take some photographs before we lost the daylight. This time of year dusk came quickly. We bid goodbye and said we'd see each other tomorrow night.

I was up on the second floor taking photographs, the light coming from the front windows just starting to fade when I heard the sound of footsteps behind me. I turned to see Luke Gardiner standing there; I thought he had left the house. "Luke, you came back..." He was just staring at me and had changed his clothes – he was wearing a white shirt with full, billowing sleeves, black breeches and boots. I laughed and asked, "Are you on your way to a costume party"? "Madam, what are you doing here?" "Luke, I'm taking photographs, as I told you." "I'll ask you once again, Madam what are you doing in my private quarters?" I felt a sliver of fear run down my spine. This man looked and sounded like Luke Gardiner but was obviously not him. "My name is Henrietta Atherton and I'm working with Luke Gardiner and the Irish Georgian Society in the restoration of this house." "I'm afraid you are mistaken...I am Luke Gardiner, the builder of this house. And pray tell, what is the Irish Georgian Society?" My first instinct was to run but he held me in his penetrating gaze and I was frozen to the spot. "It is inappropriate for a lady to be in a gentleman's bedchamber unless she has a very good reason to be," he said as he came closer.

"Your attire is very odd; you are wearing men's trousers and your hair is shorn but upon closer examination you are quite beautiful. Are you a witch come to enchant me?" The empty room started to fade away and in its place appeared a bedroom with a large tester bed, a fireplace and a pair of wing chairs. There was a sterling candlestick on a stand which he proceeded to light, I could see his handsome face and feel the heat from the wood fire burning in the grate. "Come and have a glass of Madeira with me and tell me from where you have come." I could actually feel the glass in my hand and taste the wine. "I don't recognize your accent." "I live with my husband, Lord Henry Atherton in Bath but I am originally from America...Philadelphia." "Oh, you are from the colonies, I have yet to meet someone who was born there. Your family must have arrived with Mr. Penn. I would like to discuss this with you further but it's getting late and I'm sure your husband will be waiting for you." We rose from the wing chairs by the fire and he took my hand and kissed it. I could feel the kiss; this was no spirit but a flesh and blood man. "Until we meet again Lady Atherton..." I turned to leave and when I looked back the room was again in its original state and Luke Gardiner was gone.

I returned to the hotel where there was a phone message waiting for me from Luke. "Henrietta since you are on your own tonight, would you like to get a bite to eat at the Temple Bar Pub? The Guinness is cold and the Irish oysters are fresh from the sea." I wanted to tell Luke what had just happened at No 12 Henrietta Street and I didn't want to be alone tonight. A crowded pub was just what I needed at the moment. "Luke that sounds like a great idea, I'll be waiting for you downstairs in the lobby."

We were seated at a table in the Temple Bar Pub, the recorded fiddle music of Kevin Burke playing in the background while the band was taking a break. Luke was explaining the types of Irish oysters on the menu as we sipped our foamy draughts of Guinness. "Ostrea edulis is the oyster lovers favourite, the Kelly oyster is a Galway native oyster and then we have the Pacific oyster. Why don't we sample all three so you can see which one you like best?" After Luke placed the order he said, "I want to thank you again for working with us on the Henrietta Street restoration. After Andrew raved about your work, I really wanted you on our team."

"Luke, I have to tell you what happened this afternoon after you left. I think I disturbed one of the ghosts in the house." I told him about my encounter with Luke Gardiner, the 18th century developer of Henrietta Street. "I was on the second floor in the front room when I saw a man whom I thought was you except he was dressed in a white shirt and breeches. When he spoke, I heard your voice and the room was transformed to his bedchamber with a fire burning in the grate. He invited me to a glass of Madeira and asked me who I was."

Luke looked at me in wonderment. "You might think I'm mad but I have had similar visions before. Dr. Wendt in Philadelphia seems to think I'm what you would call a sensitive." "Henrietta, I don't think you're mad; remember you're in Ireland where seeing ghosts is a normal part of life here and not only after too many pints of Guinness. Perhaps your connection to the original Luke Gardiner can be helpful to our work. Imagine being able to ask him questions and publish your findings – *Conversations with Luke Gardiner on the development of Henrietta Street* by Lady Henrietta Atherton." Then we both laughed and the tension building in my stomach was released.

My telephone was ringing as I opened the door to my hotel room. It was Harry. "I'm in our bed at the moment which feels very cold and empty. I was tempted to borrow a teddy bear from the twins to keep me company." I laughed. "Harry, how are the twins?" "They are very well, my love and have thoroughly exhausted their father tonight. Sweetheart how was your day?" "Oh Harry, the shop looks beautiful, Ian and Molly did an exceptional job, wait until you see it!" "I'm looking forward to it; I should be there around 4PM tomorrow and am also looking forward to having my bride all to myself later in the evening. Best get plenty of rest because I'm planning to keep you very busy for most of the night..."

The preview party was a rousing success. The Francis Street antiques dealers and Luke Gardiner and his IGS colleagues all came to wish us well. Harry was beaming as he took me aside and said, "Henrietta, I am so proud of you. Wait until our parents see what you have done when they come for the grand opening next weekend." "Thank you my love, for all your help and for suggesting this idea in the first place."

Later that evening when we were in bed, relaxed after making love, I told Harry about my ghostly visitor at No 12 Henrietta Street. "I suppose I was the one who was the intruder as originally it was his house." "I knew I might have competition for your affections but I never imagined it would come from a ghost. Just don't enchant the present day Luke Gardiner or I might have to challenge him to a duel," he said, his blue eyes twinkling. "Although I think it's too late," he sighed, "He's already smitten. You do have a way about you, Lady Atherton and I think it's time to have *my way* with you again." "As you wish M'lord," I replied as I placed a lingering kiss on his chest directly on the dragon tattoo.

December 1986

Dublin

The following weekend found us back in Dublin for the grand opening of H.R. Grasso & Daughter and the fund raiser at No. 12 Henrietta Street. I treated both our mothers to an afternoon at the hotel spa and tea in the Lord Mayor's Lounge on Friday while Harry entertained his father and Arthur. I decided to wear the vintage Balmain dark teal velvet lace mini dress and the Tiffany green tourmaline and diamond earrings I had worn to the Powel House New Year's Eve party in Philadelphia a few years before. "You look beautiful, I've never seen you in that dress but somehow it looks vaguely familiar," said Harry. "You have seen it before…in 1982." Harry gave me a puzzled look as I smiled my Mona Liza smile, remembering the spirits of John Singleton Copley and Caroline Blackburn Stuart as they appeared to me that night at the Powel House.

No. 12 Henrietta Street was aglow in candlelight and filled with the smells of Christmas, good food and the sweet sounds of music as we entered the house. A harpist from Trinity College's Music Department was playing the music of Turlough O'Carolan in the drawing room and in the dining room the Georgian pedestal table and sideboard were groaning under the delectable food and drink from the Shelbourne Hotel. The Royal Horticultural Society outdid themselves with the fresh seasonal displays and the antiques from Francis Street tastefully decorated the rooms. It was a wonderful turnout, Luke must be very pleased. We found him in the back hall talking to the caterers and introduced him to our parents. "Luke, well done," said Harry "The house looks fantastic. I'd like you to meet our parents – Mother and Father, Charlotte and Arthur, this is Luke Gardiner, the architect behind the restoration of this house and instrumental in the saving of Henrietta Street." "It's my pleasure to meet you and when you return a year from now you will see a fully restored house museum due in no small part to the efforts of our decorative arts consultant, one Lady Henrietta Atherton." I blushed as all eyes turned to me. "Brilliant as well as beautiful," said Harry's father, William as he kissed my cheek. "We are all so proud of you, my dear."

Later in the evening I excused myself to use the powder room discreetly tucked away in the back of the first floor. The second floor was off limits to the guests but I could not resist, my curiosity getting the better of me as I surreptitiously crept up the stairs. As I walked toward the front room I could see a fire burning in the grate and Luke Gardiner sitting in the wing chair. He stood as I approached and bowed. He was wearing a dark red velvet fitted coat with wide cuffs, an embroidered waist coat shot with gold and matching breeches. No periwig, his dark hair was pulled back in a simple queue from his handsome face. Extending from his cuffs were lace sleeves as he reached to kiss my hand.

"Lady Atherton, you have returned. I have been waiting for you." "Mr. Gardiner, I see you are dressed for the party tonight..." "And you, Madam are underdressed; I have not seen a piece of women's clothing so minuscule as that which you are wearing but I must say I prefer it to your trousers." His gray blue eyes gazed at my mini dress barely covering my legs and I blushed a second time tonight. "Has your husband accompanied you this evening?" "Yes… he is downstairs." "Well then, I must not keep you from him." He picked up something from the table and held it over my head. "Mistletoe is believed to possess life-giving power. At Christmas time a young lady standing under a ball of mistletoe cannot refuse to be kissed. Such a kiss could mean deep romance or lasting friendship and goodwill. I hope that we will be good friends," he said as he leaned in and I could feel the warmth and pressure of those perfectly shaped lips on mine as he kissed me. As I walked away I knew I would not tell Harry or Luke about my latest encounter with the ghost of No. 12 Henrietta Street.

That night I had a vivid dream where I was lying in the tester bed with Luke Gardiner making love in the firelight on Henrietta Street. Harry gently touched my face as I awoke in a sweat. "Sweetheart, I heard you cry out, were you having a bad dream?" "I must have been." What I didn't say was that my cry was not from pain but *pleasure*.

I was cheating on my husband with a *ghost*. How did this happen? Dr. Wendt would have a field day with this latest news. Was I unconsciously transferring my attraction to the present day Luke Gardiner to this 18th century ghost? No, I liked Luke but I loved my husband. This was something else, but what, I had no idea. Maybe it was simply a vicarious thrill of being desired by another man… and innocent because he wasn't alive. But he felt alive…I might have to abandon the Henrietta Street project before I committed adultery.

The grand opening of H.R. Grasso & Daughter, Dublin commenced at 10AM on Saturday, December 6th. We had a great turnout and our parents were duly impressed. "Darling, I may have to hire you to redo the shop in Bath, this is spectacular!" "Thank you Mother, I'm sure we can come to an agreeable price, shall we say in trade for baby-sitting services?" At 5PM Harry and I, with our parents left the shop to freshen up and relax before dinner at the hotel. We had tickets for the 8PM performance of Handel's Messiah performed by the Irish Baroque Orchestra at Christ Church Cathedral and wanted to have plenty of time to enjoy a leisurely meal.

"So, darling how are you going to manage your time with the twins, the new shop and your Henrietta Street project?" asked Mother over dinner in the Saddle Room Restaurant. "We're lucky to have Ian and Molly who can easily manage the shop and we can bring in a third person if needed as we did in Philadelphia. Harry and I plan to spend one long weekend a month in Dublin for now. The good news is everything is close by, the hotel, the shop and Henrietta Street and the travel time from Bath to Dublin is only two hours." "You see Charlotte, my beautiful wife, your brilliant daughter, has everything in hand, not to worry," said Harry. *Except that I've fallen in lust with a ghost*, I thought.

We were planning to fly back to London Sunday afternoon. I had a few hours to spare and wanted to stop in the National Gallery of Ireland on Merrion Square while Harry and Luke were giving our parents a tour of Henrietta Street. I picked up a brochure at the entrance and asked one of the docents if they had any images and information on Luke Gardiner, 1690-1755, the developer of Henrietta Street. "Yes we do, in Prints and Drawings there is a mezzotint engraved by John Brooks after a work by Charles Jervas and I believe there may be a book in the gift shop about Henrietta Street." I made my way to the gallery and found the image. There he was; those same eyes and lips with the defined philtrum and now I had kissed those lips. I checked my brochure to see if there was anything else I wanted to see in the galleries before I headed to the gift shop. In the brochure was a photograph of an intriguing 1864 watercolor by Sir Frederic William Burton, in the style of the Pre-Raphaelites entitled *Hellelil and Hildebrand, the Meeting on the Turret Stairs.* I went to the location and there was a group of people studying the painting. It wasn't that large, approximately 38" x 24" but the image and the color were intense – the medieval lady wore a cornflower blue gown and was turning away from the knight who clasped her right arm in his and tenderly kissed it. The painting reminded me of Harry and our conversation in his parents' garden about courtly love in June 1984 when we first fell in love.

I went to the gift shop and purchased the Henrietta Street book along with a post-card of *Meeting on the Turret Stairs*. As I hurried back to the hotel, I felt this great urgency to see Harry, to touch him and hold him in my arms. At the museum I awoke, as if from a dream and knew whatever hold the ghost of Luke Gardiner had had on me, the spell was broken.

December, 1986
Bath

We were back home at No. 28 Royal Crescent Sunday night. Mrs. Thompson was bringing the twins from Harry's brother on Monday morning. Harry made a phone call to check in with one of his clients he was sponsoring. I took a shower and waited for him in the master bedroom. He came in a little later, his blonde hair damp, a towel around his waist. He stood by the bed and saw the postcard from the museum I had placed on his pillow. "What's this, love?" "I was thinking of you today while at the museum, I saw this painting and it reminded me of how much I love you." "My love, I'll never need reminding of how much I love you…you are my life." That night as we slept peacefully in each other's arms there were no more haunted dreams of ghosts on Henrietta Street.

Christmas 1986
Bath, Dublin, Nantucket, Heidelberg

In the third week in December Luke flew to Delaware to see Sarah at Winterthur and took her to Virginia to visit Andrew and Jessica. All four were to return to Dublin to spend the Christmas holidays on the Emerald Isle. Phoebe and Jonah were on Nantucket with his family and Pamela and Carl were in Heidelberg, Germany with his children and grandchildren. Harry and I were spending Christmas in Bath with the twins and our family but we were going to see all our friends in Dublin for New Year's Eve. I couldn't wait for them to see our new shop at the Powerscourt

Centre and the progress we had made on No. 12 Henrietta Street. What an international group of friends we had become, and to think, it all started in Philadelphia. My thoughts drifted back to the past and realized how enriched all our lives had become since we met one another.

Luke mentioned that Andrew and Jessica wanted to join forces with him and open a Dublin branch of Townsend, Moran & Gardiner. Sarah was reviewing an offer as Curator of Furniture at Thomas Jefferson's Monticello in Charlottesville. I think she missed her cousin and it would give her an opportunity to see him and also be in close contact with Luke. Perhaps in the future they would be living in Dublin not far from Harry and me. All three H.R. Grasso & Daughter shops in Philadelphia, Bath and Dublin did a brisk business for Christmas. Harry teased that I had become "quite the entrepreneur." Harry was now heading the Asian Arts Department at Sotheby's in London and his work with the addiction recovery program for returning vets gained national attention through the support of Princess Diana.

New Year's Eve 1986
Dublin

The Shelbourne Hotel was bustling with activity as the hotel guests assembled. The fireworks were scheduled for 8PM on St. Stephen's Green, then pre-dinner drinks in No. 27 Bar & Lounge, dinner in the Saddle Room and dancing to an orchestra in the Great Room as everyone rang in the new year at midnight. We all had arrived the day before. Harry and I gave everyone a tour of the Powerscourt Centre and our new shop and Luke took us on a tour of Henrietta Street and No. 12. We gathered in the lobby, the men looking handsome in formal white tie and the women beautiful in long black gowns. I wore a sleeveless deep vee neck fitted black taffeta gown with the gold Chinese dragon brooch with sapphire eyes on my left shoulder and the St. George and the Dragon gold sovereign bracelet on my wrist.

As I looked around the dinner table at the familiar faces, I was reminded of when and where I met each of these dear people and how they had changed my life. There was Phoebe and Sarah, my closest college friends, then dearest Pamela, Andrew, my first love and finally Harry, my loving husband.

I hadn't danced with my husband since Phoebe and Jonah's wedding in August. In the Great Room the orchestra played a slow Irish waltz and he took my hand and led me to the dance floor. "I can't think of anywhere I would rather be than here with you in my arms, I love you, Henrietta, always and forever."

At midnight the music changed and the first slow familiar chords of a piano were joined by the sweet strains of violins and finally the poignant sound of a lone flute:

Should *old* acquaintance be forgot,
and never brought to mind?
Should *old* acquaintance be forgot,
and *old* lang syne?
For auld lang syne, my *dear*,
for auld lang syne,
we'll take a cup of kindness yet,
for auld lang syne.

John and Caroline's 2nd Birthday
March 27, 1987
Bath

It was John and Caroline's second birthday and we celebrated in the yellow dining room at No. 28 Royal Crescent. Our parents and Harry's brother William and family were happily in attendance and I was glad we had the foresight, when Harry was still a bachelor, to purchase a dining room table that expanded to fit twelve. Mrs. Avery prepared a birthday luncheon complete with yellow sponge cake with layers of thick Devonshire cream after which she and Mrs. Thompson retreated to the cozy kitchen to enjoy their meal in relative peace and quiet. Among the twins' birthday presents were more dragon toys thanks to their doting father who couldn't help himself. I wore my favorite necklace; the thin platinum chain with the two round diamonds Harry had given me on our wedding night to represent the future arrival of our twins. We had been married just over two years and my prior life in Philadelphia seemed like a distant dream.

Long after kissing the twins goodnight we cuddled in our bed, a fire in the grate. It was still chilly outside even though spring had arrived a week earlier. Harry's mother had given me a bouquet of daffodils now sitting in the Chinese blue & white vase on the night stand. "I have a present for you I think you are going to like very much," said Harry. "You've already given me a present tonight, M'lord but I'd be happy to receive it again," I teased. "I was speaking to our neighbors upstairs and they are going to relocate to the states for his job in a year's time and they want to sell their two story flat. The twins will need their own bedrooms, we'll have plenty of room for guests to stay and I thought we could reserve the top floor for our private suite, offices and library." "Oh Harry, that's a wonderful idea. I knew we would outgrow the flat soon but I love it here…this is where we began." "I know, I feel the same way. So, if you agree, I think we should buy it. Remember how much fun we had decorating this flat," he whispered as he rolled on top of me. "Besides, we're running out of room for my dragon collection. And speaking of dragons, you know how dangerous it is to awaken a sleeping dragon…"

October 1, 1987

Dublin

We delayed our annual trip to Philadelphia to be in Dublin for the first week-end in October for Open House Dublin and the grand opening of the Henrietta Street Museum. Luke and I with Ian and Molly and the rest of the IGS team had been working on the project over the last year. Harry and I flew into Dublin from

London on Thursday morning the day before. After unpacking in our hotel room we set out for No. 12 Henrietta Street for one last walk through. In all the months leading up to this day I had not seen the ghost of Luke Gardiner again, not since the Christmas fund raiser and was both relieved and strangely disappointed that he did not appear. Perhaps all the activity in the house kept him away.

As we entered No. 12, there on the console table were the new color brochures Luke and I co-wrote and designed. On the cover was a photograph of the fully restored exterior while inside was written a history of the house and street, a biography of Luke Gardiner as the visionary developer of Henrietta Street and a photograph of the mezzotint of him I had seen at the National Gallery. Then a series of before and after photographs of the interior were pictured with the story of the restoration and finally information about the museum and its programs and services.

I wondered, as we walked around his house, what the ghost of Luke Gardiner thought of our work. I was particularly sensitive to what might be his reaction if he ever appeared to me again. Chances were slim now that the building was open to the public. I had tried to reconstruct his bedchamber as I had first seen it, hoping this would please him. As crazy as that sounded, it was important to me that I had his approval.

I decided to take one last look at the front room on the second floor. Harry was downstairs talking to Luke who had just arrived. The room looked beautiful. I had found a Georgian tester bed and covered it with floral crewel embroidered bed hangings in tones of blue and green on ivory linen. The velvet Chippendale wing chairs flanking the fireplace were the same pale aqua green of the walls. The carved mahogany tea table by the wing chairs held a pair of sterling candlesticks but there was an addition to the table I had not placed there.

On the tea table was a three piece Irish Georgian silver tea service highly embossed with scrolling floral designs, the handles depicting classical figure heads and an eagle's head for a tea spout. There was a letter on the table sealed with wax addressed to me —

The Ghost House

Lady Henrietta Atherton

Dublin, October 1, 1733

My Dear Lady Atherton,

Please accept my gift of this tea service designed by William Nowlan for you. You have enchanted me since the first moment my eyes gazed upon your fair countenance. I have chosen to name this street Henrietta Street in your honour. I look forward to the day we meet again.

Your Humble Servant,

Luke Gardiner

Discovering the gift of the exquisite Irish Georgian tea service and letter from our 18th century resident ghost profoundly moved me and I knew I must tell Harry and Luke. They were still downstairs; I called to them to come to the second floor and said I had something to show them. When they arrived I handed Harry the letter and then he gave it to Luke. Harry was very quiet. Luke spoke first. "This is amazing, Henrietta. The handwriting looks authentic based on the letters we have seen in the National's Gardiner archives and the William Nowlan tea service is of the period; the pieces are beautifully rendered. And now we have solved the mystery of the naming of the street; he named it after *you* although no one would believe it if we told them."

"I don't think we should ever tell them," I replied. "There's more…" I said reluctantly. "The night of the Christmas fund raiser last year I came upstairs and he was here. The room was as I described it the first time I saw him and he was dressed in a dark red velvet jacket and breeches. We had a conversation about the party and he commented on my dress, asked if my husband was downstairs then held up a sprig of mistletoe and…kissed me. I haven't seen him since that night." "So, our ghost

143

got into the Christmas spirit, no pun intended," joked Luke. Harry just stared at me, his eyes questioning mine.

"I would like to donate the tea service to the museum, I think it belongs here." "Thank you, Henrietta, that's very generous of you," replied Luke. "The museum looks amazing, thanks in no small part to you. I'm sure Mr. Gardiner must be very pleased with your efforts and I'm looking forward to the public's response during the open house this weekend." Harry finally spoke. "…Luke we have to go but we'll see you tomorrow."

We walked out and went back toward the hotel. Harry said, "Let's take a walk in St. Stephen's Green." We walked in silence past a lone violinist playing Vivaldi's *Autumn*, approached a bench and sat down. The trees in the park were dressed in lush colors of reds and golds reminding me of Washington Square.

Harry looked at me intently and said, "Henrietta, what just happened, what in *God's* name is going on?" "I was afraid to tell you, afraid I would have to abandon the project. Harry, I was awe-struck, I felt as though I was under some kind of spell. I don't know why these things keep happening to me." "I remember you were very emotional that weekend but I assumed it was because you were opening the new shop, our families were here and there was a lot going on."

He hesitated, and then said, "Does this have anything to do with Luke? Please tell me the truth." Luke was the spitting image of the 18th century Luke Gardiner, they even sounded alike. "No, in fact Luke is quite taken with Sarah Townsend. My interest in Luke is as a friend and colleague, nothing more…please believe me Harry." "I do, my love, perhaps it was the stress of getting married and having the twins almost immediately. We never really had a chance to have a honeymoon. Now we have responsibilities…" "And I've loved all of it, I really have," I said. "So have I," he said quietly, trying to control his emotions. "Can you ever forgive me?" "I already have," he replied as he pulled me into his arms and held me.

Open House Dublin
October 1987
Dublin

Open House Dublin with over one hundred private buildings open to the public was a success. The city was teeming with tourists on this fall weekend and as a result both the Henrietta Street Museum and our shop received extra attention. Harry and I divided our time between the shop, the museum and taking selected tours. Ian's father, Dr. Michael Byrne held court in the shop signing copies of his book on Irish Georgian furniture. At the museum, I acted as docent and responded to visitors' questions about the interior furnishings; some of which were highlighted in the brochures. Everyone admired the William Nowlan sterling tea service in the second floor bedroom. I made sure I did not linger in the room alone not wanting to rouse or *arouse* a ghost.

By Sunday afternoon we were all exhausted. When the last visitor left the museum Luke locked the front door and the IGS team gathered in the drawing room for a cold glass of champagne. "You all did an amazing job – thank you - here's to your dedication over the last year – the Henrietta Street Museum is now officially open." As we were all leaving I remembered I needed to re-plenish the console table in the foyer with H.R. Grasso & Daughter business cards and take additional brochures for our shops in Bath and Philadelphia. The foyer was deserted when I returned but as I looked up and gazed into the gilt wood mirror, there in its reflection was the ghost of Luke Gardiner dressed in a black velvet jacket with gold embroidery and ivory waistcoat, smiling.

The Journal of Henrietta Grasso

October 1987

Bath

Harry and I flew back to Bath arriving home just after 9PM. The twins were asleep; as we closed the door to their room we could hear the faint sounds of Mrs. Thompson's television coming from her bedroom. We decided to take a soothing bath together. Once in the tub, the steamy air infused with lavender, Harry gently rubbed my back as I leaned against him. "Harry, I saw him again..." I didn't need to explain who *he* was. "When I went back into the foyer I saw his reflection in the mirror." "Well, my love, I can't compete with a ghost nor do I ever want to. I'm just very glad that the Henrietta Street project is now successfully completed and...I'm never going to let you out of my sight while in that house again."

The Quiet Street

October 1987
Philadelphia

Harry and I had a very memorable visit to Philadelphia after Open House Dublin. I met Colin Tyler, the newest addition to our staff at H.R. Grasso & Daughter, Philadelphia. James and Melinda, impressed with the Henrietta Street Museum brochure and the photographs of our new shop in Dublin, were eager to start working with Ian and Molly on an advertising campaign for both shops. We had a candlelit dinner at Pamela and Carl's apartment on Washington Square with Phoebe and Jonah. Carl was now a guest lecturer in Jonah's history classes at Penn and they were talking about taking future trips to Heidelberg and Nantucket together. Pamela and Phoebe were glowing; married life agreed with them, they had chosen their husbands well. Harry and I shared recent photographs of the twins and the brochures from the Henrietta Street Museum.

Andrew and his cousin Sarah called from Virginia to congratulate me on the Henrietta Street project. Sarah was enjoying her new position as Curator of Furniture at Monticello and living near her cousin and his wife Jessica in Charlottesville. Andrew asked if I would present a paper to the Irish Georgian Society at their next annual meeting in Dublin in March. He and Jessica were going to make a special trip to attend. The topic of the ghost of Luke Gardiner did not come up. In deference to Harry, I had sworn the present day Luke to absolute secrecy. I smiled to myself; regardless of its questionable academic merit, the story of the ghost of No. 12 Henrietta Street would surely have spiced up the annual meeting.

Harry surprised me with tickets to hear the Philadelphia Orchestra at the Academy of Music where Riccardo Muti vigorously conducted an all Verdi program. Listening to the Overture from *La Forza del Destino*, it felt comforting sitting in those plush crimson velvet seats under the dramatic crystal chandelier in the 1857 opera house, the oldest in the country. We had dinner at Ralph's restaurant at the Italian Market and met Sam Jacobson at the Saloon for lunch. Hand in hand, we took meandering walks around Society Hill and afterwards the George III tester bed provided a familiar welcome in the blue bedroom over the shop on Antique Row. Harry was wooing me all over again; he didn't want to take any chances that the ghost of Luke Gardiner in Dublin or the present day Luke might steal me away.

October 1987
Bath

Back in Bath, a new project was under way - the updating of my mother's shop. She wanted a fresh look after she saw what we had accomplished in Dublin. I had a few months to work on it before we would begin renovations at No. 28 Royal Crescent. The twins needed to have their own bedrooms and Harry and I were looking forward to setting up our private suite on the third floor. As much as we loved listening to our two active toddlers chattering away, he and I were working at home more and needed a separate place to work.

The four storied building at No. 3 Quiet Street was the home of H.R. Grasso & Daughter, Bath. Located in the historic district of the Georgian city, Quiet Street was bustling and home to jewelers, women's clothing boutiques, antiques shops, banks and real estate agents. The street, its name now a misnomer, originally was made up of wooden cobbles instead of stone, making it one of the *quietest* streets in Bath. The building's limestone façade had two display windows on the first floor, a circa 1900 replacement shopfront with a deep set door, three windows across on the upper floors and decorative cast iron balconettes on the third level. Described as commercial Victorian architecture "at its most confident", it was designed in 1871 by local architect Charles Edward Davis. Mother, always the astute business woman, purchased the building a hundred years later in 1972, used the first two floors for her antiques business and rented out the upper floors as flats.

I proposed a layout similar to the Philadelphia shop where we would create rooms as they might appear in a home. The first floor would have a drawing room, dining room and library and the second floor - bedrooms and sitting rooms. We would create a design center with paint and fabric samples, update the lighting with crystal chandeliers and install a sound system for classical music. The original wooden floors would be restored and the oriental carpets cleaned.

Since the building was in the middle of the block with minimal natural light, I chose a bold wall color for the first floor – Farrow & Ball's Charlotte's Locks No. 268, the color of persimmons, a rich, vibrant orange and high gloss white for the crown molding and trim. We already had an antique Heriz oriental carpet in colors of peach with a light and dark blue floral pattern for the library. Upstairs, the softer color of F & B's Hound Lemon No. 2 would complement the bedrooms and sitting rooms. For the business cards I chose the same persimmon color in an engraved Georgia typeface on a beige card stock. The symbol was an embossed St. George & the Dragon gold sovereign, a sentimental image keeping with the dragon theme for good luck.

December 1987

Bath

Everything was in readiness. The party for the newly refurbished H.R. Grasso & Daughter, Bath was about to begin. Decorated for Christmas with garland adorned with fresh oranges, lemons and deep orange velvet bows, the balsam tree twinkled with tiny white lights reflected in the crystal chandeliers overhead. Clove studded oranges and fresh greens filled sterling bowls, their heavily spiced scent lingering in the air. The dining room pedestal table and side board held seasonal food offerings and the catering staff raised chilled champagne on silver trays, the crystal flutes catching the candlelight. The gas fires in the library and drawing room created shadows on the warm persimmon walls and the oriental carpets glowed jewel-like on the restored wooden floors. Handel's Messiah played softly through the new sound system and another stage was set for the play to begin.

Before the guests arrived, Harry hugged and kissed me and said, "Another fantastic job, well done, my love." Harry's parents came over and Frances said, "Your mother must be so pleased and proud of you, my dear, we certainly are." "Thank you Frances, it was fun doing this for Mother and she was a most accommodating client. Now I'm looking forward to the work ahead at No. 28 Royal Crescent." "No more than I, we adore our children but it's getting to be close quarters," Harry chuckled. "We're going to need a room just for the toys Harry keeps bringing home…" Mother interrupted our conversation and said, "Harry, Frances and William, would you mind if I borrowed my daughter for a moment? Henrietta, there is someone I would like you to meet." Mother took me by the elbow and led me to a man standing alone, watching intently as we approached.

"Henrietta, this is Dr. Thomas Cameron, the new Headmaster of King Edward's School. Dr. Cameron, this is my daughter, Lady Atherton." "Lady Atherton, it is a pleasure to meet you," he said taking my hand. Tall and fine featured with a high forehead and auburn hair, his intelligent blue eyes met mine from behind tortoise shell eyeglasses. I detected a slight Scottish burr in his voice. "Dr. Cameron, I've heard wonderful things about the school." "I'm looking forward to the challenge." "Henrietta, Dr. Cameron just purchased The Oaks in Norton St. Philip and wanted to talk with you about it." "I just moved from London where my former wife lives with our two children and I was hoping to make it a comfortable home for when they are visiting on weekends and holidays." "When would you like to get started?" "I'd like to settle in at the school first and was hoping to start at the end of spring term in April." "That should work with my schedule," I smiled in reply. "Lady Atherton, would you have time to have lunch next week and see the house before we begin?" "Yes, Dr. Cameron, I would." "In that case, please…call me Thomas."

December 1987

Norton St. Philip

I met Thomas Cameron for lunch the following week on an overcast day at the George Inn, a 700 year old establishment in Norton St. Philip. It looked as if it was going to snow. We sat down at a table by the fire; his handsome face was ruddy from the cold as he removed his eyeglasses and Burberry scarf. "Lady Atherton, thank you for coming." "Thomas, since we'll be working together, please call me Henrietta." The specials of the day were written on a chalkboard over the large hearth. We ordered a hearty beef stew with rustic bread for our lunch and two glasses of the local ale. Once we were settled Thomas said, "Henrietta, let me tell you about The Oaks…" *His words brought to mind the lunch Andrew and I had over four years ago at the Water Works Café in Philadelphia when he first told me about The Solitude. I felt a shudder run through me.* "The Oaks is a late 18th century Regency house made of Bath stone with a tile hipped roof and end chimney stacks. It really looks like a house you would find in a child's picture book." *I remembered thinking the same thing when I first saw The Solitude.* His voice continued, "I think that's why it appealed to me, working with children as I do…"

He paused and was silent for a moment, his pleasant expression changed to one of sadness. "I want to make a home for my two children; my son Alistair is 8 and my daughter Blair, 6. They have had a hard time since the divorce without family around." "Where is your family?" "Their grandparents are in Scotland…in Aberdeen. Unfortunately, they don't get to see them as much as they would like. The children will be with them during Christmas and the spring and summer school recesses and I would like to have the house ready for them when they return to school in September." "I think we can do that," I replied.

After lunch we drove to see The Oaks. The village of Norton St. Philip was less than six miles from Bath, a short fifteen minute drive, convenient for the new Headmaster of King Edward's School and close to my home at No. 28 Royal Crescent.

The house was exactly as Thomas described it. The first floor had a kitchen, powder room, dining room, living room and study. On the second floor were three bedrooms and a full bath. The top floor under the hipped roof housed the fourth bedroom, an open loft-like space. "I was thinking of putting in a bathroom on the top floor and reserving the second floor for the children, making the third bedroom a TV/playroom." "Good idea, we are going to do the same thing in our home" I replied. The house just needed some updating and freshening up – new carpets, fabrics and paint, perhaps a few pieces of furniture. We would also select fixtures and tiles for the master bath. Thomas said he had family antique pieces he would have shipped from Scotland. As we left the house he showed me around the winter garden which, with proper landscaping would be lovely come summer. Then he thanked me and wished me a Happy Christmas as I got into the Range Rover. On the drive home I prayed that Thomas Cameron and his children would also have a happy Christmas and suddenly felt a strong desire to be home with Harry and our twins as the first snowflakes started to fall.

January 1988
Bath

No. 28 Royal Crescent was finally ours – *at last*! After living on the ground floor for the past three years, we were going to occupy the upper floors, over 5000 square feet in total. The first project was updating the bedrooms and baths on the second floor for the twins and Mrs. Thompson, adding a TV/playroom for them and a sitting room for our beloved nanny. We also had our plans for the third floor; it was going to be our private retreat with master bedroom and bath, library/sitting room and our offices. To keep the decorating plan simple, we chose Farrow & Ball Archive No. 227, a warm neutral taupe for the walls with all woodwork done in a white satin finish. We would add color and texture with framed prints, oriental carpets and upholstered sofas and chairs in the living areas and patterned comforters and pillows in the bedrooms.

The renovation proceeded according to plan and as the workers came and went we were able to live very comfortably on the ground floor as we always had. I instructed Mrs. Avery to hire a weekly cleaning service to help with the construction clean up. The ground floor bedrooms would become guestrooms for our overseas friends and Harry teased that we should rename it *The Hotel Atherton*.

March 1988
Dublin

The annual meeting of the Irish Georgian Society was on March 16th. I promised Andrew I would present a paper on the restoration of No. 12 Henrietta Street. Harry and I arrived in Dublin on Tuesday night at the Shelbourne Hotel just in time to have dinner with Luke, Andrew and Jessica. Luke and I were co-present-ing the paper at the Society's headquarters at the City Assembly House on South William Street and the Townsends flew in from Virginia just for this event. I was so glad to see Andrew and Jessica, we had only seen them briefly at Christmas when they were in Dublin visiting their family. The good news was that, in January, Luke opened the Dublin branch of Townsend, Moran and Gardiner, Preservation Architects.

"We have another piece of good news to share with you," said Andrew, smil-ing. "Jessica and I are going to have a baby, a boy in August." "Oh Andrew that's wonderful," I said as I hugged Jessica and Andrew. Harry and Luke kissed Jessica and gave Andrew bear hugs. "We'll be here in Dublin for the baby's birth," said Jessica "which will make my mother happy." "And Sarah can't wait to be an aunt," said Andrew. "Congratulations to both of you, this calls for a celebration; champagne and sparkling cider all around," said Harry as he sig-naled to our waiter.

March 1988
Bath

At the end of March, just in time for the twins' third birthday, the No. 28 Royal Crescent renovation was complete. When they arrived for the birthday luncheon, we gave our family the grand tour. That night, after the twins and Mrs. Thompson were settled in their new bedrooms, Harry took my hand and we ascended the stairs to the third floor. He had turned on the gas fire in the bedroom; Bach's *Air on the G String* was playing softly, our wedding night music. He led me into the master bath where a bottle of Perrier Jouet champagne was chilling in an ice bucket with two Waterford crystal flutes. There was the large tub, perfect for two, ringed with tea lights, the scent of lavender filling the air. He removed my clothes first and then his own until the only thing remaining was the dragon tattoo on his chest. The tattoo glowed in the candlelight as it had the first time I saw it almost four years ago. He seemed to read my mind and said, "Who would have thought when you arrived on my doorstep that fateful day in June, we would be standing here like this tonight?" "And to think I didn't want to come to Bath at all," I replied. "But you did and for that I shall be forever grateful, my love." He lifted me up in his arms and placed me in the warm water, got into the tub and poured two glasses of champagne and said, "To my dearest love Henrietta, without whom this life would not be possible, I love you." "And I love you Harry… always and forever."

April 1988
Norton St. Philip

At the beginning of April, the spring term at King Edward's School ended, the summer term not to begin until the end of the month. Dr. Thomas Cameron and I were ready to concentrate on a new project - his home, The Oaks. We met again for lunch at the George Inn, this time on a warm spring day. He was in a jovial mood as he stood and kissed my hand. "Lady Atherton…Henrietta it's a pleasure to see you again. "And mine as well, Thomas, how was your first term at King Edward's?" "It went better than I expected. I must admit I was a bit nervous going in, the former head master had been at the school for thirty years and was much loved by the students – a hard act to follow."

We sat comfortably together and he asked me about my background. I told him about my schooling at the University of Penn and Winterthur, my antiques shops in Philadelphia and Dublin, the discovery of the John Singleton Copley painting and my projects with The Solitude and the Henrietta Street Museum. "My life is not as exciting as yours, I'm afraid," Thomas replied. "I grew up in Aberdeen and attended Aberdeen University where I received my doctorate in early childhood education. Before I came to St. Edward's I was the assistant rector of Aberdeen Grammar School founded in 1257. The school's claim to fame is that it is one of the oldest schools in the United Kingdom and its infamous claim is that Lord Byron was one of its students," he said with a chuckle. "Back in the 1870's my ancestor Robert Cameron was Headmaster at King Edward's so I suppose that's what drew me to the school."

"And how are your children?" I asked. "They are very well; in fact I'm to see them on Friday for the weekend before they travel to Aberdeen to be with their grand-parents. Your mother told me you have a boy and a girl, twins…" "Yes, John and Caroline just turned three. We would like to enroll them in the school's nursery program in September." "Well, I seem to have an *in* with the Headmaster so that shouldn't present a problem," he said teasingly.

King Edward VI School, founded in 1552, was a private school for students aged three to eighteen in Bath. Harry and I had discussed the pros and cons of sending the twins to boarding school and decided with such an excellent school right here in Bath, it made perfect sense for them to live at home. "They'll be on their own soon enough when they go to college," said Harry, "Why not have them at home with us until then…besides we'd miss them terribly." "M'lord are you breaking with tradition? I think that's a wonderful idea." "I'm full of wonderful ideas; the first one was when I met you."

After lunch Thomas and I drove to the Oaks and sat in the kitchen looking at the floor plans the former owner had given him. "The creation of the master suite should begin first," I commented, "We can install the new master bath and you'll still have use of the second floor bath and bedrooms. I'll prepare suggestions for tiles and bath fixtures and paint samples for the whole house along with fabric swatches for window treatments and upholstery. The floors should be done last. I suggest new carpeting in the bedrooms and having the wooden floors refinished in the first floor rooms. This kitchen was recently remodeled. I like the gray and white tile floor and the yellow Aga stove and gray window pane cabinets. The terrace and gardens should be landscaped with perennial flower beds but we should wait until early summer to see what flowers come up on their own."

"Now that you mention it, come out to the terrace and see for yourself," said Thomas with a smile. We walked through the French doors leading to the terrace and the garden beyond. I laughed with delight. There before our eyes were hundreds of daffodils. "Behold the majestic King Alfred daffodil, Latin name: Narcissus, with its giant ruffled trumpet head," said Thomas. "Named after one of the greatest medieval kings, Alfred the Great and cultivated by John Kendall in the late 1800's, the King Alfred daffodil is considered to be the greatest of all the species." "How do you know all this?" I laughed. "I was an only child and spent a lot of time alone. When I was in school, I fell in love with William Wordsworth's poem. It gives me comfort when I think of these flowers. When I bought this house last fall I didn't know they were here lying dormant under the earth waiting to surprise me in the spring." "I think this house was waiting for you to find it," I said. "I think you may be right," he replied.

August 1988
Norton St Philip

The renovations were finally coming to completion at the Cameron residence, The Oaks. The house was not large so I suggested using a light palette throughout in whites, grays and gray greens to continue the gray color used in the kitchen. The master suite on the third floor now had a new master bath. All the bedrooms had new comforters, bed linens and accent pillows. For Alistair's room I found six vintage colored prints of Scottish military uniforms and for Blair, whimsical Scottish terrier prints, the 1940's work of Lucy Dawson. The dining room received a Brunschwig and Fils wallpaper in the Bird & Thistle pattern, a green floral on a white ground, the thistle, a nod to the Cameron family's Scottish roots and a complement to their antique barley twist round oak table, matching chairs and side board. In the entrance hall, the walls were lined with colored Highland sporting prints in gilt frames, a Robert Bryson mahogany drumhead Longcase clock, another Cameron family heirloom and an Axminster carpet runner in Green Palmette, a floral pattern on the restored wooden floors.

The living room was painted in Farrow & Ball Breakfast Room Green, a gray green with white high gloss trim matching the original wood and gesso Regency mantel. A soft green velvet highback chesterfield sofa with matching club chair and ottoman and the Axminster Green Palmette area carpet completed the room.

The iron verdigris dining table and chairs on the gray flagstone terrace looked out onto a newly landscaped garden flanked by stone planters overflowing with variegated vinca vine and white geraniums with the promise of King Alfred daffodils in the spring.

August 1988
Bath & London

One of the final items on my check list for The Oaks was the purchase of a painting I had seen in a London gallery catalog — it was a 19th century landscape by Arthur Perigal (1816-1884) titled *On the Moors Inverness Shire* and perfect for over the mantel in the living room. I called to make an appointment to view the painting. Harry was working at home that day so he drove me to the Bath train station. "I should be home in time for tea." "Don't worry, my love, we're fine here, enjoy yourself, do a little shopping, just stay away from the John Singleton Copley paintings at the

National…" "Why, M'lord don't you trust me?" "Oh I trust you, it's the male popu-
lation I don't trust," he said as we both remembered where we first met.

London is not the most comfortable place to be on a summer's day in August and
the humidity made it feel like 100 degrees. After I purchased the Perigal painting,
I asked them to ship it to No. 28 Royal Crescent and abandoned my plans for shopping and headed back to Paddington Station, deciding to take the twins for a dip in
the pool at the Old Rectory. It must have been the heat, for once on the train; I fell
instantly into a deep sleep.

I awoke just in time to hear the conductor say "…*next stop, Bath Station*" and felt a
rush of humid air as he opened the door to the compartment. "Your stop is next,
Miss." I was sweating and my clothing felt restrictive, particularly around my ribs.
I looked up and saw men and women dressed in hats and coats sitting on tufted
red velvet banquets, too much clothing to wear on a day in August. My own clothing had *changed* – I was no longer wearing my white blouse, khaki slacks, navy
espadrilles and straw boater, the clothes I wore when I left Bath this morning,
but a fitted sapphire blue jacket and long skirt. On my head was a straw hat with a
matching blue ribbon tied under my chin. My long curling hair felt hot on my neck.
At my feet was a tapestry bag. The train slowed as it pulled into Bath station and I
rose from my seat, picked up my bag and descended the steps of the train.

"Miss Harrington…Charlotte Harrington?" Calling my name was Thomas Cameron.
"Thomas, what's going on?" "I beg your pardon, Miss but my name is Robert Cameron,
Headmaster of King Edward's School. The agency in London said they were sending a
Miss Charlotte Harrington for the governess's position." I thought *Charlotte Harrington
is my mother's maiden name. What in God's name is happening?* "I have my carriage waiting
to take you to my home, The Oaks in Norton St. Philip." I felt like I was going to faint,
the corset I was wearing made it hard to breathe and the heat was almost unbearable.
He grabbed me by the arm as I started to fall. "Let's get you inside the station out of
the sun and perhaps something cool to drink." He found a bench, sat me down and
then quickly returned with a glass of water. "Are you feeling better now?" "Yes, thank
you…Dr. Cameron." "Allow me to get your trunk and bring it to the carriage."

August 1870
Bath

He helped me into his carriage, loaded my trunk and handed me my bag. Then he got in beside me and gave the horse's reins a shake. I was beginning to feel better as the country air filled my lungs. Who was this man? As I looked at his profile, he was the spitting image of Thomas Cameron. Then a memory of a conversation came to me "...*Back in the 1870's my ancestor Robert Cameron was Headmaster at King Edward's so I suppose that's what drew me to the school...*"

"You come highly recommended, Miss Harrington. I and my children, Archie and Julia are looking forward to having you with us. You see, they lost their mother a year ago." "How old are your children, Dr. Cameron?" "Archie is eight and Julia is six. My responsibilities at school keep me busy and I don't get to spend as much time with them as I would wish. Our housekeeper, Mrs. Aubrey and her assistant, Mary have been filling in until I found someone suitable. The autumn term starts in a few weeks and I would like to get them settled before I have to go back to school. Julia will need full instruction whereas Archie is enrolled in King Edward's and I will supervise his studies."

August 1870
Norton St Philip

We finally arrived at The Oaks. I didn't know what else to do but go along with this experience as it was unfolding. I had somehow traveled back in time to the very place I last had been in 1988. Dr. Wendt would have yet another chapter for his book. I just hoped I would be home in time for tea with Harry and the twins.

It was exciting to see the house as it was in 1870. As the carriage wheels came to a stop the front door swung open and two copper haired children came running out to greet us. "Father, is she our new governess?" they both asked. "Yes, please say *how do you do* to Miss Harrington, children." Archie bowed and Julia curtseyed. I think I fell in love with them at that moment. "May we show her to her room?" "Let's help her get inside first," their father said as he looked at me and smiled.

My bedroom was on the second floor near the children's room. It had a tester bed with green and white floral bed hangings and a white counterpane. A wood burning fireplace and a green velvet wing chair were opposite the bed. There was a desk and chair in front of a window overlooking the garden. Dr. Cameron followed us up the stairs with my trunk as the children hurried into my room. "Do you like it?" they both asked. "I like it very much." "Children, we should let Miss Harrington refresh herself after her journey and then she can come and have tea with us."

Mrs. Aubrey had prepared a lovely tea especially for my arrival. I came downstairs and was introduced to her and Mary. We were now sitting at the table in the dining room listening to the children chatter away; they reminded me of what John and Caroline would be like in a few years. After supper, Dr. Cameron offered to read a story before the children went to sleep. They chose Lewis Carroll's *Alice's Adventures in Wonderland*. As I listened, I felt like *I was the girl who had fallen down the rabbit hole*. How was I going to get back to my home in 1988? I didn't want to worry Harry and the children but I had no way of communicating with them.

A month went by and I settled into a routine of tutoring Julia during the day and reading to Archie and Julia each night after I helped them prepare for bed. On weekends, their father took us on picnics and sometimes to London to go to the museums. I was getting attached to them and knew when I left it would be difficult for all of us.

Finally at the end of the month after the children were asleep, Dr. Cameron asked to speak to me in the parlor. The fire was burning in the grate as I entered the room. "Please have a seat, Miss Harrington...may I call you Charlotte?" "Yes, you may." "Please, call me Robert. I must tell you how happy you have made the children…and me," he said as the firelight played on his handsome face, so similar to the future Dr. Cameron. "They have become attached to you and so have I in the short time you have been with us. When their mother died I didn't think I would ever know happiness again and then you came along. What I'm trying to say, what I mean to ask you is would you consider becoming their mother and my wife?" He rose from his chair and walked over to me and took my hand and kissed it. "You don't have to give me an answer now, all I ask is that you think about it. Dear Charlotte, I bid you good night," he said as he slowly released my hand.

That night in bed I couldn't sleep. What was I to do? What if I could never return to Harry and the twins and had to remain here in 1870? I know I could grow to love Robert Cameron and his children but never to return to the life I already had was heartbreaking. Finally, right before dawn, I fell into a troubled sleep.

"*…next stop, Bath Station.*" I woke up to find myself on the train. I was wearing my white blouse and khaki slacks, the laces of my espadrilles securely tied around my ankles. It was all a dream, an amazing, wonderful yet frightening dream. As I descended the train, there was Harry leaning against the Range Rover. "May I give you a lift Ms. Grasso?" "Yes, Lord Atherton, you may," as I ran to him. He picked me up and I covered him with kisses. "My, my Ms. Grasso, such public displays of affection…" "You don't know the half of it, M'lord."

August 1988
Norton St Philip

The Arthur Perigal landscape painting finally arrived from London. I drove over to The Oaks in the Range Rover to install it, the last piece of the puzzle. It looked wonderful in its gilt frame over the mantel in the living room, the room where Robert Cameron asked me to marry him. It felt strange to be back in this house where I had lived. I hadn't seen Thomas Cameron since I returned from my visit to 1870. He was due back with the children from Aberdeen today. I was getting ready to leave when I heard the front door open. "Close your eyes…okay now you can open them." Alistair and Blair screamed with delight as they ran from room to room and then up the stairs to see their new rooms. "Welcome home, Thomas," I said as I kissed his cheek. "You did a fantastic job, Henrietta. You can tell by the reaction you just got from my children." The children came running back down the stairs. "Thank you, Henrietta, we love our rooms," said Alistair. "I love the pictures of the dogs in my room," said Blair. "Daddy, can we get a dog?" We both laughed as Thomas looked at me and said, "We'll see…" The children ran off again, delighted with their new home.

"Oh, I almost forgot, I have something very intriguing to show you," Thomas said. "You'll have to tell me where you think I should hang them." He came back with two large packages wrapped in cardboard and brown paper. "They arrived right before I left for Aberdeen." He carefully unwrapped the packages and leaned them on the floor against the mantel. "They are two oil portraits of my ancestors. One is of Robert Cameron, Headmaster of King Edward's in the 1870's, I think I mentioned him to you, and the other is of his second wife, Charlotte and their two children Archie and Julia. I realize now that I do bear more than a passing resemblance to him but you, my dear Henrietta, are the spitting image of Charlotte."

September 1988
Bath

Saturday, found Harry and me at the entrance to King Edward's School on Weston Lane for the Open Morning tour of the nursery school. Dr. Cameron asked us to stop by his office afterwards to say hello. "Welcome Harry and Henrietta, it's good to see you both. Did you enjoy the tour?" "You have a wonderful facility here, Thomas, we're impressed," replied Harry. "I think John and Caroline will love it here," I said enthusiastically. "I'm so glad you like the school, I wish I could persuade Helen to allow Alistair and Blair to attend. By the way, the children and I love The Oaks; it feels like a real home now, thanks to you, Henrietta. They can't wait to arrive on the weekends. You'll have to come by with the twins and visit when my children are here. I'm sure Harry would like to see the finished product after I've monopolized his wife's schedule these last months." *In more ways than one* I thought, thinking about the time I spent with his ancestor Robert Cameron. "We'll have to show Harry the portraits and your uncanny resemblance to Charlotte Cameron. I'll give you a call when the children are down from London." Thomas and Harry shook hands and he kissed me on the cheek.

"What was that all about?" asked Harry, on the drive home. "It's a long story...preferably told in the bath with a large glass of champagne," I said reluctantly. "And when were you going to tell me?" "Well, definitely not when you were sober." "Did you, by any chance, have another one of your adventures, my love?" "You could say that..." "Then we'll need to pick up a magnum of champagne on the way, I have a feeling it's going to be a long night." I would then also have to tell him about the book I found in my leather satchel upon my return from London that day in August – the 1865 first edition of Lewis Carroll's *Alice's Adventures in Wonderland* with the bookplate - Ex Libris *Dr. Robert Cameron.*

Americans Abroad

September 1988
Norton St. Philip

On this late summer afternoon we were sitting around the wrought iron table on the terrace after lunch watching the twins play in the garden with Thomas Cameron's children, Alistair and Blair. John and Caroline had started nursery school at King Edward's this past week and already were enjoying their independence from their parents. Harry and I were teary-eyed that first day as they headed into the school in their uniforms with the maroon Tudor Rose emblem embroidered on their crisp white polo shirts and navy blue sweaters. "How did John and Caroline enjoy their first week of school?" asked Thomas. Dr. Thomas Cameron was the school's Headmaster and my client. I had helped him renovate and re-decorate his Regency home, The Oaks. "They enjoyed it immensely but we were *emotional wrecks*," replied Harry with a chuckle. "I know that feeling very well," sighed Thomas, having been divorced the previous year. "I still feel it at the end of every weekend when I have to return my two to London to their mother."

"I think I have something that will perk you up," I said and removed the red cloth volume from my leather satchel and handed it to Thomas. It was the 1865 first edition of Lewis Carroll's *Alice's Adventures in Wonderland*. "Look inside the cover." He opened the book and discovered the book plate - Ex Libris *Dr. Robert Cameron*. "Where did you get this?" I couldn't tell him the truth - that I had traveled back in time to 1870 and married his ancestor - so Harry and I came up with a small falsehood. "When I was setting up your library, it was among the books you had shipped from Aberdeen. I took it to have it appraised at George Bayntun's on Manvers Street in Bath. They gave me an appraised value of 15,235 pounds, $25,000 dollars but it could go for far more in the appropriate auction. You should probably have them clean and restore it and create an archival slipcase for it." "Henrietta, I don't know what to say. You have been a blessing to me and my children since we met."

Earlier in the day, Thomas showed Harry the 1870 portraits of Robert Cameron and his second wife Charlotte with their children Archie and Julia. Harry tried to look surprised as he gazed upon the face of Charlotte Cameron and saw my face staring back at him. I had confessed all to him a month ago when we were drinking champagne in the bath. "It was as though I walked into Mr. Cavendish's jewellery shop in London. One minute the shop was there and then it wasn't," I told him. "But this time you traveled back and Robert Cameron, Thomas' ancestor asked you to marry him," Harry replied painfully. "I know, Harry; I was so worried I wouldn't be able to return to you and the twins. I had to make the best of unimaginable circumstances. I thought it was just a dream I had on the train coming back from London but then I found the book in my satchel and I knew I had been there." "It seems during that ninety minute train ride you lived another life time – no wonder you were so glad to see me at the train station. I do like Dr. Cameron but let me say I am *very glad* your work with him is completed. Please Henrietta, no more time travel or ghosts – I don't think I can take it."

October 1988
Bath

We postponed our October trip to Philadelphia since the twins were starting school. Andrew Townsend and his wife Jessica now had a son, Andrew Jr. We would get to meet him at Christmas in Dublin. For the first time in our married life, things seemed to be settling into place or so I thought until I received an amazing phone call.

Peter Blakeley, a curator at the National Portrait Gallery in London was on the other end of the line. Established in 1856, the National Portrait Gallery located at St. Martin's Place off Trafalgar Square, housed the most extensive collection of portraits in the world. We had corresponded and spoken on the phone back in 1983 when I was curating the John Singleton Copley exhibit at the Historical Society of Pennsylvania. He was responsible for the loan of the Copley portrait by Gilbert Stuart. "Henrietta, I called the Historical Society of Pennsylvania and then your business in Philadelphia and was told you moved to Bath and married Lord Atherton. Our spring/ summer exhibition fell through and I am looking for a replacement show from the end of April through August. I was thinking about the newly discovered Copley portrait of Caroline Blackburn Stuart and thought it could be a centerpiece for a new show - an exhibition of portraits by American artists who lived in England during the 18th and 19th centuries. I would like to know if you would be interested in being the guest curator." I thought, *an opportunity like this came along only once in a lifetime.* "Peter, I'm honoured that you thought of me and I am very interested." "Good news, can you come to London one day this week so we can go over everything?" "Yes, I can."

October 1988

London

Two days later I was on the train to London with Harry; he to his job at Sotheby's and I to my appointment with Peter Blakeley at the National Portrait Gallery. We planned to meet at the end of the day and return home to Bath together. He was as excited as I was. "Please, darling, no more time travel until after the exhibit opens, we shall need you to stay in the present," he said with a smile. "I think we may be able to get Princess Diana to attend and the American ambassador as well."

I met with Peter and his staff at the National. After several hours, we toured the gallery which would be used for the exhibit, ordered lunch in and continued to work into the afternoon. By tea time we had hammered out the overall plan. The title of the exhibit would be *Americans Abroad: 1700-1900 American Artists Living in*

England and include the works of John Singleton Copley, Benjamin West, Gilbert Stuart, James McNeill Whistler, Edwin Austin Abbey and John Singer Sargent. I was standing in Room 14 admiring Copley's painting *the Death of the Earl of Chatham* when I heard a familiar voice behind me. "You are an admirer of Copley too, I see." "Yes, I am." "Could I interest you in a cup of tea, Ms. Grasso?" Harry came up behind me and hugged me reminding us both of the moment we met and the first words we ever spoke to each other. I had declined his invitation back then but now I said, "I would be delighted M'lord," as I turned to kiss him and off we went to have the long awaited tea before our train was to leave for Bath.

Working with Peter Blakeley and his staff on the *Americans Abroad* exhibit was pure joy. Once we selected the paintings, twenty four in all including the artists' self-portraits, we contacted the museums in America and Europe for permission to have the paintings on loan. The paintings were coming from the most prestigious museums in America - the Metropolitan Museum of Art, New York, the National Gallery, Washington DC, the Philadelphia Museum of Art, the Pennsylvania Academy of Fine Arts and the Isabella Stewart Gardner Museum, Boston. The Uffizi Gallery in Florence, Italy and the Musee d'Orsay in Paris were sending paintings as well as the Tate Gallery in London. This was going to be an exciting event sure to garner extensive international press coverage.

A very special painting was coming from the Metropolitan Museum of Art in New York. It was John Singer Sargent's notorious portrait of Virginie Amelie Avegno Gautreau, referred to as *Madame X*. Virginie was an American expatriate who married a French banker, Pierre Gautreau. We were working with Guy Pierce, the curator of 19th century American Paintings at the Met and had just received permission to use the image of Madame X on one of a pair of banners announcing the exhibit at the entrance to the National Portrait Gallery. Guy Pierce, a native of Durham, North Carolina was a graduate of Duke University and was well known in the art world as a brilliant curator and a specialist on John Singer Sargent. I was looking forward to meeting him. He was going to escort the painting to London and oversee the installation.

With the twins now in school, I was able to spend more time with Harry in London taking the train with him in the mornings and returning to Bath together in the evenings while I was working on the upcoming exhibition. Some of our best conversations were on that train and sometimes we would nap on each other's shoulders. Harry would gently kiss me when we arrived at Bath Spa Station and whisper playfully in my ear, "We've arrived, my love, what century are you in?" Sometimes we would attend events at Sotheby's or have a romantic dinner and take in a concert. But the best part of our day was when Mrs. Avery would prepare supper for the children and leave two plates warming in the oven for when we arrived home. Then, after the children were asleep, we would sit in the kitchen around the French farmhouse table, near the still warm Aga and eat our supper with a glass of Cabernet in candlelight, Debussy's music playing softly in the background.

November 1988

London

On this particular Monday morning in early November, the London air was too cold and crisp to linger outside. I hurriedly kissed Harry through the open window of the taxi and turned to rush inside to the warmth of the museum. "I'll pick you up at 5PM." "I'll be waiting."

Room 14 at the National Portrait Gallery was the location of John Singleton Copley's painting *The Death of the Earl of Chatham* and the exact spot where Harry and I first met in the summer of 1984. We were going to use the painting in the *Americans Abroad* exhibit and feeling sentimental, I made it a habit to visit the room at some point during the day when I was working at the museum.

At lunch time I wandered down to Room 14 for my daily visit. There, standing in front of Copley's painting with his back to me, was Harry. I thought, *how sweet, he's just in time to take me to lunch.* I walked up behind him and started to kiss his cheek when he turned and the kiss landed full on his lips. I smiled and looked up into a pair of eyes, the deepest brown, so dark that the pupil and iris melted into one. Embarrassed, I said, "I'm so sorry; I thought you were my husband." "*I'm* not...," he replied as he looked at me appraisingly and smiled. His face and build were very similar to Harry's; tall, blonde hair and an easy smile but his eyes were brown, not Harry's bright blue and he had a soft southern accent, an American. "Now that we've shared a kiss, I suppose we should introduce ourselves," he said flirtatiously. "I'm Guy Pierce from Durham, North Carolina." *This was Guy Pierce, the curator from the Metropolitan Museum.* "I'm Henrietta Atherton from Philadelphia, Pennsylvania." "So, you're a Philly girl, how long have you lived across the pond?" "Almost four years. Mr. Pierce - I'm the guest curator for the *Americans Abroad* exhibit and want you to know how thrilled we are that the Metropolitan Museum has agreed to lend Sargent's Madame X to us." "So, you're Henrietta Atherton, Lord Atherton's wife; I've heard wonderful things about you from Jamie Cadwalader at Sotheby's. I'm here to bid on paintings at the American Art auction this week that Jamie has organized." "Yes, my husband is head of the Asian Arts Department at Sotheby's and I know Jamie from Philadelphia." "Well, Lady Henrietta Atherton, now that you and I are intimate friends, you'll have to call me by my first name and tell me all about it over lunch." Then he touched my elbow and led me out of Room 14 to the third floor of the museum.

The windows of the museum's rooftop dining room, the Portrait Restaurant, looked out on one of the best vistas in London; an unparalleled view of the statue of Lord Horatio Nelson in Trafalgar Square and across Whitehall to the Houses of Parliament and Big Ben. We sat at a table by the window and ordered the spiced butternut squash soup with crème fraiche, homemade chips and a salad. Also on the menu was the Portrait Bellini – lychee liqueur, pomegranate juice and prosecco, a variation on the famous drink from Harry's American Bar in Venice. "I think our first collaboration deserves a toast," said Guy. Dashingly handsome, oozing southern charm from every pore, he was a bit of a rogue and I would have to keep my wits about me if we were to successfully work together. "Here's to the success of *Americans Abroad* and our beautiful guest curator," he smiled as we sipped our Bellinis. "By the way, has anyone ever told you that you look like Audrey Hepburn? But you're taller and your eyes are green." If I could handle the ghost of Luke

Gardiner in Dublin, Ireland, I could certainly handle Guy Pierce from Durham, North Carolina. I later realized what a foolish thought that was.

After lunch, mellowed by the Bellinis, we sipped our coffee with plates of rum raisin ice cream. "I see you have a sweet tooth too," Guy said. "You would love my mama's sweet potato pie - have you ever been to the Carolinas?" "I used to do the Charleston antiques show in March every year until I moved to England. Now, my staff in Philadelphia does the show." "Ah, Charleston, the Holy City, one of the most beautiful places on earth..."

> "...But when the dusk is deep upon the harbor,
> She finds me where her rivers meet and speak,
> And while the constellations ride the silence
> High overhead, her cheek is on my cheek.
> I know her in the thrill behind the dark
> When sleep brims all her silent thoroughfares..."

"That's lovely, what's the quote from?" "It's a poem by DuBose Heyward called *Dusk*. I'll have to send you a book of his poems." Dubose Heyward was a writer born in Charleston best known for his novel *Porgy* from which George Gershwin wrote his seminal opera *Porgy and Bess*.

I thanked Guy for lunch as we said goodbye at the museum's entrance. He said he would see me in London again in the spring for the installation of the Sargent painting, if not sooner.

That night, on the train going back to Bath, I told Harry about my awkward first meeting with Guy Pierce and having lunch with him. "From behind, I thought he was you coming to take me to lunch and when I kissed him on the cheek, he turned and I realized my mistake." I started to blush all over again thinking about the kiss. "I'm sure you made his day but please be careful darling, Jamie knows him and said he is quite the playboy leaving a trail of broken hearts. The art world is really a small place." "I guess it takes one to know one," I replied and we both laughed. Thanks to Harry's sponsorship, Jamie Cadwalader, a former boyfriend and an abusive man due to his cocaine addiction had turned his life around and was now in a serious relationship with another Sotheby's employee, Cynthia Chapman.

The next day, when I arrived at the museum, waiting for me was a florist's box from Paul Thomas Flowers Ltd. in Mayfair. Inside was a single white gardenia, its heady, hot house fragrance reminding me of a tropical summer day on this cold November one. The card read:

Madam Curator,

The scent of Charleston to brighten your day,

as yesterday you brightened mine.

Warm Regards,

Guy Pierce

The second package arrived a week later and contained *Carolina Chansons: Legends of the Low Country*, a book of poetry by DuBose Heyward and Hervey Allen. It was a 1922 first edition autographed by DuBose Heyward with Guy's business card marking the page for the poem, *Dusk*. On the back of the card he had written:

To Lady A,

"...But when the dusk is deep upon the harbor...

...her cheek is on my cheek..."

It reminded me of our accidental kiss that day in Room 14 in front of the Copley painting. This was neither a ghost nor a man I had traveled back in time to meet but a present day, red blooded American who bore an uncanny resemblance to Harry. Thank goodness there would be an ocean between us...

November 1988
Philadelphia

The annual trip to Philadelphia was long overdue with the children starting nursery school and the planning of the exhibit at the National Portrait Gallery. We decided I should go for a shorter stay and take care of business at H.R. Grasso & Daughter and Harry would stay behind with the twins. He was planning a trip to Sotheby's in Hong Kong in the new year and until they were older, we would have to take short solo business trips.

As the yellow cab traveled east on Pine Street through Antique Row I felt a strong pull of nostalgia. I rolled down the window and breathed in the crisp autumn air. I couldn't wait to see the shop, James, Melinda and Colin and my old apartment on the top floor with the George III tester bed. I whispered quietly, *"Dad, I'm home."*

It was like old times as we sat around the round George IV mahogany table in the library, the gas fire lit, drinking Darjeeling tea from the Coalport Indian Tree Coral tea cups and discussed our current news. I gave them an update on the shop in Dublin where Ian and Molly were doing a thriving business. The Philadelphia shop was busy as well. James told me he received a phone call from *Antiques* magazine and they wanted to do a cover story for their fall 1989 issue on H.R. Grasso & Daughter; its history, a profile on me and the three shops in Philadelphia, Dublin and Bath. I told them about my guest curatorship of the *Americans Abroad* exhibit at the National Portrait Gallery opening at the end of April. "I'm sure they will want to include the exhibit information in the article as well," added Melinda. Colin reported that the antiques shows in Charleston, Philadelphia and Nantucket had done well. My good friend Sarah Townsend, curator of furniture at Monticello in Charlottesville, Virginia, was still doing the Charleston show with Colin and my best friend Phoebe and her husband, Jonah Coffin were helping him at the Nantucket show while they visited their family on the island every summer. I had a wonderful group of friends and colleagues who had stayed with me over the years.

After the meeting I called Pamela and Phoebe to tell them I had arrived in town and we arranged to meet at Pamela's apartment on Washington Square on Friday afternoon for tea to catch up with all the news. Then I made a quick call to Sam Jacobson on Jewelers' Row to set up our lunch date at the Saloon. The Historical Society of Pennsylvania, the PA Academy of Fine Arts and The Philadelphia Museum were next on my list to make courtesy calls to view the paintings to be given on loan for the exhibition. Later in the afternoon, finally feeling the effects of jet lag, I nestled in the George III tester bed and called Harry and the twins. "Hello, darling, I allowed them to stay up past their bedtime to wait for your call," said Harry. "Mummy, when are you coming home?" they asked together. "Hello my sweet ones, I'll be home on Sunday to kiss you goodnight." "Will you bring us a present?" asked Caroline. "Yes, I shall bring you a present. Now be good and listen to Mrs. Thompson and take good care of Daddy until I return." "Okay, Mummy, we love you." "I love you both very much," I replied. "You sound tired," said Harry when he returned to the phone. "I'll be fine; I'm in our favorite bed at the moment and looking forward to a good night's sleep." "I hope you dream of me," he whispered, his voice growing husky. "Always, my love."

The next morning, feeling refreshed, I rose early and brewed a cup of French Roast. After a quick shower, I dressed and went downstairs just as Melinda was opening the shop for business. James and Colin were off to the estate sales and would be back in the early afternoon. The bell over the door jingled and we both looked up to see Guy Pierce standing in the entrance. "I called the museum in London and they told me that you were in Philadelphia," he said, his deep brown eyes staring at me intently. "So, I decided to come down on the train and surprise you." I introduced Melinda to Guy and then she excused herself to work in the library. "Did you get the gardenia and the book I sent you?" he asked. "Yes, I did… thank you." There was an awkward moment of silence and then he said, "How's the exhibit shaping up?" "Very well, in fact I have appointments today to visit four of the paintings we will be using." "May I accompany you? I came to invite you to lunch but we can do that around your appointments. I'm very interested in viewing your selections." I hesitated for a moment and then decided it couldn't hurt my credibility as guest curator to be seen with Guy Pierce, the acclaimed curator from the Metropolitan Museum.

I called for a yellow cab and soon we were traveling along the Benjamin Franklin Parkway toward the Philadelphia Museum of Art. The first painting we viewed was James McNeill Whistler's *Arrangement in Black; the Lady in the Yellow Buskin - Portrait of Lady Archibald Campbell*. Whistler's painting was going to be reproduced on a banner outside the National Portrait Gallery facing Sargent's *Madame X*. Both paintings featured a full length portrait of a woman. The actual paintings were quite large, over seven feet tall. The women were both dressed in black and very provocative. Madame X wore a figure hugging gown exposing her bare arms and low décolleté, her head glancing to the right. Lady Archibald Campbell's figure was completely covered in furs and a hat; only her face was exposed as she glanced over her left shoulder.

Guy commented, *sotto voce,* "Lady Campbell's family rejected the painting, claiming it 'represented a street walker encouraging a shy follower with a backward glance.' One woman has the look of a courtesan and the other of a street walker. Perfect for attracting the public – we should have a large turnout - good choice, Madame Curator," teased Guy. The next painting was Benjamin West's *Benjamin Franklin Drawing Electricity from the Sky*. "Mr. Franklin always enjoyed the company of beautiful women, something he and I have in common. Make sure you hang him next to those ladies." "Mr. Pierce, behave yourself or I will have to send you home," I whispered, trying to hold in my laughter as we left the gallery and headed to the museum store. There, I purchased two snow globes featuring Rodin's *The Thinker* in front of a miniature Rodin Museum for the twins.

Our next stop was the Pennsylvania Academy of Fine Arts on North Broad Street where we found another Benjamin West painting, the famous *Treaty of Penn with the*

Indians. I tried to give Guy my sternest look, as if to say *don't say another word.* He looked at me like a little boy and placed his hand over his mouth and crossed his eyes. I started laughing all over again. Afterwards, in the museum store I found Charlie, the Artist Bear, a teddy bear dressed in an artist's smock holding a palette with a miniature easel and purchased three bears; two for the twins and one for Guy for good behavior.

Our appointment at the Historical Society of Pennsylvania wasn't until 3PM so we took a cab to the Garden Restaurant; the perfect place on a cold winter's day. The waitress recommended the fettuccine with wild mushrooms with the Garden salad and we ordered glasses of pino grigio and tiramisu for dessert. "Thank you for the teddy bear, Miz Henrietta. He reminds me of a bear I had back in Durham. I used to sleep with him every night," he said wiggling his eyebrows. "You are incorrigible, Mr. Pierce, how do you get away with it?" "It must be my southern charm. Southern boys are raised to please their women folk, at least that's what my mama used to say."

We were enjoying our dessert and coffee when Guy said, "Henrietta, I hope I didn't offend you by sending the gardenia and the book of poetry. I enjoy your company and they were gifts to show my appreciation. I hope we have the chance to work together on other projects in the future. I have a feeling you're going to be in much demand after *Americans Abroad* opens in London." "Guy, I also hope we work together again and I enjoyed your gifts but you know I'm married and I love Harry and our children very much. They mean the world to me and I would never do anything to jeopardize my family." "Then please forgive this ole southern man for his schoolboy crush and consider him your friend." "I will," I replied and secretly hoped it would be enough, for both of us.

"So this is the famous beauty who broke the heart of John Singleton Copley," said Guy as he gazed upon the portrait of Caroline Blackburn Stuart. We were standing in the gallery at the Historical Society of Pennsylvania as I related the story of the painting's discovery. John Bentley, the curator, also brought out the star ruby ring and the love letter dated 1768 from Copley to Caroline. "And they never saw each other again after that one time at the Powel House?" "No, but I have the feeling they are together again in another lifetime." "You are one mysterious, amazing woman, Miz Henrietta." "Thank you, kind sir, I'll take that as a compliment."

As the late afternoon sun set over Philadelphia turning the clouds the color of rubies, we shared a cab to take me back to Antique Row and Guy to 30th Street Station to board his train for New York City. "Henrietta, thank you for allowing me to spend the day with you, it was very special and meant a lot to me. On the train ride back to New York, Charlie the Bear and I are going to have a long conversation about you." "Goodbye, Guy, thanks for lunch today and your company. I'll see you in London." He hesitated and then briefly kissed my cheek. I got out of the cab, waved goodbye and he was gone. It was funny, but I missed him already.

Sam Jacobson and I had our annual lunch at the Saloon on Friday. "Sam, please promise me you'll come to Bath this summer when you take your vacation. We have one of the guest rooms all ready for you and you know I, Harry and the twins would love to see you. We may even get lucky and see Mr. Cavendish's estate jewellery shop in London, although the shop is like Brigadoon, appearing out of the mist and then disappearing again." We laughed and I gave him a picture of the twins in their school uniforms. "Caroline is looking more and more like you, Henrietta and John is the spitting image of Harry. They are beautiful children and growing up so quickly." I could see his blue eyes tear up behind his John Lennon glasses. I secretly decided I was just going to mail him an open ended ticket to London and send it to him every year for Christmas.

After walking back with Sam to his shop, I stopped at Old City Flowers and picked up a bouquet of russet and gold chrysanthemums for Pamela and two red roses and wandered around Society Hill finding myself at the Powel House. I made my way up to the second floor and walked into the back parlor where I had witnessed the spirits of John Singleton Copley and Caroline Blackburn Stuart on New Year's Eve 1982. I knew I would not find them there now. Harry and I had been John and Caroline in 1768 and had found each other again in this life. This is what I could never tell Guy. So where did Guy Pierce fit into this picture, if at all and why had he come into my life at this time?

I left the Powel House and walked over to St. Peter's churchyard nearby to visit my father's and the Stuart family graves before it was time for tea with Pamela and Phoebe. There they were as I had left them a year ago, still firmly planted in the earth.

Henry Richard Grasso 1918-1981
Dearly Beloved Father Who So Loved This City

Charles Peter Stuart 1740-1793
Caroline Blackburn Stuart 1750-1727

"Dad, I'm home for just a short while and stopped by to say hello," I said as I placed one of the red roses on his grave. "Harry sends his love, the twins started nursery school." I could feel the warm breeze kiss my cheek and I knew he was there. "I'm the guest curator of a new exhibition at the National Portrait Gallery. I met this man, Guy Pierce whom I am working with. He's a curator at the Metropolitan Museum in New York." I could hear the faint words, *Be Careful* as they carried on the breeze. "I will, I love you, Dad." *Love you* his words came back to me.

I came to the Stuart family grave where I placed the second red rose and sent a heartfelt prayer for all of us, the living and the dead that we would be happy and at peace and slowly turned and walked out of the churchyard into the autumn afternoon.

Pamela Stuart Eckhart, tall and elegant with her bobbed silver hair and trademark gray South Sea pearls, was waiting for me at the entrance to her apartment on Washington Square. "My darling girl, it's been too long since we've seen you," she said as she hugged and kissed me. "Phoebe is already here; Carl and Jonah are at the university but will be home soon." I handed Pamela the bouquet of chrysanthemums. "Thank you, my dear, you always remember how much I love flowers.

Come into the sitting room, Phoebe is anxious to see you." Phoebe jumped up and ran to hug me. "Henrietta, we didn't think you were coming to Philadelphia. How are Harry and the twins?" "They're all doing very well. I have a lot to tell you but first let me hear what you both have been up to."

Over tea, Phoebe revealed her plans to publish her first book the following October, titled *The Removal of Clothes and Halos: Humanism in Italian Renaissance Art.* "That's a very provocative title." "That's the idea; sex sells," replied Phoebe, smiling sweetly. Phoebe herself still looked like a Botticelli angel with her curly pale blonde hair and sparkling blue eyes. "Carl and Jonah are also collaborating on a book of Carl's memoirs," said Phoebe. Carl was now a guest lecturer in Jonah's classes and Pamela was lecturing at the Historical Society of Pennsylvania telling the amazing story of John Singleton Copley and Caroline Blackburn Stuart. They traveled to Germany to see Carl's children and grandchildren and entertained them when they came to visit Philadelphia. Carl's youngest grandson, Charles was applying to Penn for the fall term next year.

"I have some news of my own...," I replied. "I've been asked to curate an upcoming exhibition at the National Portrait Gallery in London in the spring and you are all invited to the preview reception and dinner on April 28th. It's called *Americans Abroad: 1700-1900 American Artists Living in England.* They requested Copley's portrait of Caroline to be part of the exhibition. I'm inviting Dr. Spiller and his wife Dorothy as well. You and your dear husbands are invited to stay in Bath with us. Phoebe, I would like you and Dr. Spiller to collaborate on a statement about the portrait for the catalogue. And I've saved the best part for last; *Princess Diana will be attending the preview with the American ambassador and his wife."*

At that moment, Carl and Jonah walked through the door amid the excitement. "What's happening? Did we miss anything?" asked Carl. Carl, tall and silver haired and Jonah, with a close cropped auburn beard, looking like one of his Nantucket ancestors walked into the sitting room. Phoebe jumped up to kiss Jonah and said, "We're all going to London to meet Princess Diana!" Once I hugged Carl and Jonah and everyone settled down, I repeated the story about the exhibition. Carl said,

"Well done, Henrietta, we have much to celebrate; I'm treating everyone to dinner tonight. Ladies, where would you like to go?" We decided on Head House Tavern at 2nd and Walnut. It was going to be a memorable night for all.

November 1988

Bath

Back in Bath on Sunday, the twins were happy to finally have their mother home, laden with presents. They loved the snow globes and teddy bears. I fleetingly wondered if Guy was also enjoying his teddy bear; a token from our day at the museums. It was a memorable trip to Philadelphia. After Harry and I kissed them goodnight, we walked up to our bedroom on the third floor. Harry drew a bath and had a bottle of merlot with a plate of brie and crackers waiting.

In the bath, each sipping a glass of merlot, my head resting against Harry's chest, he said, "I really missed you sweetheart; I wish I could have come with you. I've gotten very attached to Philadelphia and our friends there." "I missed you too; the George III tester bed didn't feel the same without you. Everyone asked for you. Sam and I had lunch at The Saloon and Carl treated us to dinner at Head House Tavern. I extended the invitation to have the Eckharts and the Coffins stay with us for the preview party of the exhibit. Phoebe is having her first book published next October and *Antiques* magazine wants to do a cover story on H.R. Grasso & Daughter for the fall 1989 issue."

"Sounds like a very good trip, I'm glad you went. Did you get to the museums to see the selections for the exhibit?" "Yes" I hesitated, "That's what I wanted to talk to you about...Guy Pierce came down from New York on Thursday morning and came by the shop to invite me to lunch." "How did he know you were in Philadelphia?" "He called the museum in London and they told him. Harry, I didn't know what else to do so I invited him to the museums and we had lunch. He said I would be in much demand after the exhibit opened and hoped we would work together again." "Did he behave himself?" "Yes, he was the perfect gentleman."

"Good, but you *will* let me know if he steps out of line, won't you?" "I can handle Guy Pierce, Harry, please don't worry about it." And just to confirm it, I turned around and placed a deep kiss on his lips and we spoke no more for the rest of the evening.

March 1989
London

Spring had finally come to England. I was working at the museum and had completed the editing of the galley proofs for the *Americans Abroad* catalogue. John Singer Sargent's portrait of Madame X graced the cover. Peter Blakely had written the Forward and I, the Introduction. We received the curators' statements to accompany each of the twenty four paintings including Guy Pierce's regarding Madame X and Dr. Spiller and Phoebe Coffin's regarding the discovery and authentication of John Singleton Copley's portrait of Caroline Blackburn Stuart.

The beautiful Georgian Church of St. Martin-in-the-Fields, designed by James Gibbs in 1722 located across the street from the museum was having a lunch time concert. The Academy of St. Martin-in-the-Fields was founded in 1959 by Sir Neville Marriner. Today they were performing Antonin Dvorak's *Serenade for Strings in E Major*, one of my favorites. I invited Harry but he had a business meeting he could not re-schedule so I decided to take myself to the Café in the Crypt, a cafeteria style restaurant located in the basement of the church with dramatic whitewashed brick arches, for a quick lunch and then to the concert. Just as I had settled my tray down on the table, I heard a male voice with a soft southern accent say, "May I join you?"

"Guy, I didn't know you were in London, I'm just having a quick bite and then going to the lunch time concert." "I know, they're playing Dvorak's *Serenade for Strings*. That's why I'm here too; it's one of my favorites of his works," he said as he sat down beside me. "I just came from Sotheby's and Harry told me you were attending the concert when I asked if you were at the museum today." "I was editing the galley proofs for the *Americans Abroad* catalogue. It looks spectacular. All the curatorial statements are thoughtfully presented and the color registrations of the paintings are a perfect match. Your statement regarding Madame X is exceptional." "Let's just say I was inspired," he said with a wink. "Actually, Charlie the Bear helped me write it – he says hello, by the way."

After lunch we made our way upstairs to the church for the concert. It was crowded and we finally found two seats in one of the back pews. The acoustics in the church were superb; Dvorak's *Serenade* soaring majestically all around us. The 4th movement, the Larghetto began, enchantingly building to a culmination, bringing to mind Wagner's Liebestod from Tristan and Isolde, but sweeter and filled with a happy longing. Guy turned and looked at me, his dark eyes glistening.

After the concert, we sat in the pew as everyone got up to leave and the musicians packed up their instruments. The church was almost empty as we quietly walked through the nave. At the end of the aisle, Guy gently took my hand and led me to a quiet corner. He looked at me and said, "I am only going to do this once because I will never get another moment like this." And then he took me in his arms and kissed me. I could feel his longing as we broke apart. "I promise I won't kiss you again unless you ask me to," he said, his voice deep, his southern accent stronger. We then left the violet dimness of the church and went out into the too bright spring afternoon.

It was the middle of the night, I suddenly awoke realizing Harry was not in bed. Wearing only the thin platinum and diamond necklace Harry gave me on our wedding night; I slipped on the short silvery satin nightgown and went downstairs. As I walked pass the bedroom on the first floor, I saw Harry standing by the open French doors. The light from the full moon outlined his profile, his chest was bare; he was wearing only khaki pants with a brown leather belt and shoes. "Harry, is everything alright?" I asked as I approached him. He turned to look at me and as I looked at his chest, I realized his dragon tattoo was missing. I looked up at his face but it was shrouded in darkness as he turned away from the moonlight. "Harry. . .," I repeated softly. I walked over to him and heard him say, "Did you come to ask me, Henrietta?" In his voice was the sultry rhythm of the Carolina low country. It was Guy. He slowly walked over to me and gently put his hand under my chin and repeated, "Did you come to ask me?" "Yes," I answered. He placed his lips on mine and after a long moment, kissed the hollow of my throat where the diamond necklace was nestled and

*then lowered his mouth to my breasts. "Do you want me to. . .?" "Yes." His fingers gently lifted the
hem of my nightgown and, finding the place between my thighs, found entry.*

I cried out and woke up in a sweat. Harry came awake and felt my forehead. "You're
burning up, sweetheart." He came back with two aspirins and a glass of water
which I gratefully accepted and took my temperature with a thermometer. "I'm
afraid no work for you today, my love. I'll call the museum and tell them you're
staying home and will ask Mrs. Avery to make you a bowl of chicken broth. Mrs.
Thompson will get the children ready for school and I'll check in with you later
to see how you're feeling. Feel better, my love." He gave me a gentle kiss on the
forehead and left to get ready for work.

I drifted in and out of sleep the rest of the morning. Mrs. Avery came into my
room at noon carrying a blue & white porcelain vase filled with brightly colored
long stemmed French tulips. "These just came for you, Lady Atherton," she said
as she placed them on the bureau opposite the bed and handed me the card. "Lord
Atherton called but didn't want me to disturb you. Now that you're awake, perhaps you can take a little chicken broth. Oh, before I forget, I found your diamond
necklace on the floor in the first floor guestroom when I was cleaning the room,"
she said as she handed it to me. *I was wearing the necklace when I went to bed last night.*
The card was from Guy Pierce and read:

> *Henrietta,*
>
> *Thinking of you*
>
> *and*
>
> *Hoping you'll be feeling better soon*
>
> *Warm regards,*
>
> *Guy*

The card reminded me of the vivid dream I had the night before. *Thank goodness it was only a dream*, I thought as I drifted back to sleep.

That night Harry came home from London and came upstairs to check on me. "How are you feeling my love?" he asked as he kissed my forehead. "Everyone from the museum was asking about you and I ran into Guy Pierce at Sotheby's and told him you were home and not feeling well." "He sent me tulips," I said as I gestured toward the vase on the bureau. "I figured as much when he asked for our home address." "When you're feeling better, we should have him come to Bath for dinner one night while he's in London. I'm sure he would enjoy one of Mrs. Avery's home cooked meals. "You want him to come here?" "Well, you'll probably be working together in the future; besides, I would like to get to know him better." Harry paused and then looked at me and said gently, "I know what's been going on. He's in love with you and I can't fault him for that. I guess I should be flattered. He does bear a passing resemblance to me and I must admit he has excellent taste but as Sun-Tzu, the great Chinese military general and strategist said, *"Keep your friends close and your enemies closer."* It was impressive and humbling to see my golden dragon prepare to do battle to protect what he valued so highly.

April 1989
Bath

True to his word, Harry invited Guy to dinner when he returned to London the beginning of the last week in April. It was going to be busy these last few days before the preview party and the Philadelphia contingency's arrival on Thursday night. Harry suggested the three of us travel by train to Bath at the end of the day and that Guy should plan to stay over and return with us to London in the morning.

Guy and I walked through the gallery as the *Americans Abroad* installation was in progress. "It's going to be a spectacular show, Henrietta." "Your help and suggestions were invaluable… thanks Guy." "My pleasure, Madame Curator, by the way, the catalogue looks very impressive. The Met and I are very pleased you chose to place Madame X on the cover."

At the end of the day, Harry was waiting outside the museum in a taxi to take Guy and me to Paddington Station for the train trip to Bath. Ninety minutes later we arrived at Bath Spa Station and hopped in the Range Rover to drive the short distance to our home. The twins came running downstairs when they heard our voices in the foyer. "Guy, we'd like you to meet John and Caroline," said Harry. "Children, this is Mr. Pierce, our friend from America." Caroline stared at Guy and said, "You look just like Daddy." "Yes I have heard that," laughed Guy. "Just make sure you don't get us mixed up," said Harry with mock sternness. "Do you have a dragon tattoo on your chest too?" asked John. "No, I'm afraid I don't." "Then we won't get you mixed up." We all laughed at the innocence and logic of children.

After a tour of the townhouse and dinner, the children said goodnight and Mrs. Thompson took them upstairs to prepare them for bed. We sat in the blue sitting room where Guy admired Harry's blue and white porcelain collection and dragon artifacts as we sipped snifters of cognac. "You have a very lovely home and the children are delightful," said Guy as he sat on the dark blue velvet chesterfield sofa. "All credit goes to Henrietta," said Harry. "Both for the creation of the home *and* the children." We all laughed. After awhile Harry excused himself saying he wanted to finish up some work in his office. "Don't keep Guy up too late sweetheart; we all have a busy day tomorrow." Then he shook Guy's hand and wished him goodnight.

"So, tell me about this dragon tattoo of Harry's," said Guy when Harry left the room, "I'm intrigued." "Well, as you know Harry is the head of the Asian Arts Department at Sotheby's. He explained that more than any other image, the dragon is associated with the Orient. A symbol of the emperor himself, it can take many forms and can be victorious in any circumstance. He got the two inch dragon tattoo above his right breast when the vets came home from the war in the Falklands. He said it reminds him of their determination to protect and defend against all odds." Guy gave me a long look and then said, "Duly noted; I shall be very mindful of that In the future."

"I should go upstairs too in a few minutes; let me show you to your room." At the entrance to the guest room, I stopped, remembering the vivid dream I had about making love with Guy in this room. "There are fresh towels and soap in the bathroom; we'll need to catch the 8AM train tomorrow so I'll knock on your door at 7 for breakfast…" I was nervous and rambling when Guy placed his hand on mine. "I know this is awkward for you but I want you to know I appreciate your effort, and Harry's. He is very protective of you and the children and if you were mine I would feel the same way. I don't want to cause a problem for you but I think you know how I feel," he said his eyes searching mine. Then he looked around the room and said, "This bedroom looks very familiar; I think I had a dream about it. It was a full moon and the light was streaming in through the French doors over there and you were here with me. I remember you wore a necklace with two diamonds around your neck and a silver night gown. The rest of the dream I won't repeat but let's just say I woke the next morning with a smile on my face and hugging Charlie the bear." We both laughed. *I didn't dare tell him I had the same dream.* "Sweet dreams, Henrietta, thank you for a lovely evening," he said as he kissed my hand and I went upstairs to my bedroom and Harry.

April 28, 1989
London

The preview party for *Americans Abroad: 1700-1900 American Artists living in England* was about to begin. The National Portrait Gallery was lit up like a Christmas tree; the long royal blue banners hung on either side of the entrance; John Singer Sargent's portrait of Madame X and James McNeill Whistler's portrait of Lady Archibald Campbell facing each other. Harry, handsome in black tie whispered, "You look beautiful, my love" as he admired my royal blue satin fitted strapless gown with my grandmother's pearl necklace and ruby and pearl earrings. We waited nervously in the reception line next to John Hayes, the director, Peter Blakeley and Harry's parents, the Earl and Countess of Bath, William and Frances Atherton. Finally, a black limousine slowly eased to the curb, the door opened and as the cameras flashed out stepped Princess Diana looking radiant in a navy blue sequined form fitting gown. Behind her was the new American ambassador, Henry Catto, Jr. and his wife Jessica. They approached the reception line and when they came to us, I curtseyed and Harry bowed saying, "Your Royal Highness I'd like you to meet my wife, Henrietta." Princess Diana extended her hand and said, "Good evening Harry, nice to see you, I've heard so much about you, Lady Atherton, please call me Diana. We'll have time to talk later."

The twenty four portraits in their gilded frames glowed on the gallery walls, painted a rich royal blue. Among them were Gilbert Stuart's 1796 regal *Portrait of George Washington*, Edwin Austin Abbey's 1896 *Richard Duke of Gloucester and the Lady Anne from Shakespeare's Richard III*, Benjamin West's 1806 *Death of Nelson* and John Singleton Copley's 1768 *Portrait of Caroline Blackburn Stuart* in her claret red satin gown. The one hundred specially invited guests walked around the gallery, catalogues in hand, enthusiastically commenting on the portraits. The curators were stationed by their paintings answering questions - Dr. Spiller and Phoebe standing by the Copley *Portrait of Caroline Blackburn Stuart* and Guy Pierce next to Whistler's *Portrait of Madame X*.

Director Hayes asked Peter Blakeley and me to accompany Princess Diana and Ambassador Catto and his wife through the exhibit. We stopped at Copley's *Portrait of Caroline Blackburn Stuart* and I introduced the Princess to Dr. Spiller and Phoebe. "I've heard about this portrait and the fascinating love story...a case of star crossed lovers," remarked Princess Diana. We finally came to Sargent's dramatic *Portrait of Madame X* and I introduced the Princess to Guy Pierce. "Mr. Pierce, when next I'm in New York, I would love a tour of the Metropolitan Museum. "It would be my pleasure, Your Royal Highness," replied Guy with a bow.

The dinner was in the Portrait Restaurant - the view of nighttime London dramatically lit through the windows. It was magical. The round tables for ten encircled by gilt chairs were covered in royal blue linen, white china plates with gold star borders sat atop gold chargers and the crystal sparkled in the candlelight amid floral bouquets of red roses with miniature flags of the Union Jack and Ole Glory. Harry and I were seated at the table with the Princess. During dinner she leaned in and asked me about my children. "I hear you have twins, a boy and a girl." "Yes, they started King Edward's last year and just celebrated their fourth birthday in March." "William and Harry are six and four now and I would love to have a little girl." "She would be beautiful," I replied. "...Unless she looks like Charles," she said with a giggle and we both laughed.

Afterwards there was dancing to a small orchestra playing old standards from the Great American Songbook. Harry asked the Princess to dance and Guy came to our table and extended his hand to me. The music was Irving Berlin's 1923 song *What'll I Do* and as Guy took me in his arms, he sang the words softly in my ear:

> *What'll I do*
> *When you are far away*
> *And I am blue*
> *What'll I do?*
> *What'll I do?*
> *When I am wond'ring who*
> *Is kissing you*
> *What'll I do?*

All too soon the evening came to an end and I felt like Cinderella after the ball. It had been a heady experience working with the museum these last six months, meeting Guy Pierce and finally, Princess Diana. As we prepared to take the limousine with our guests back to Bath I replayed the evening over again in my mind and wondered what the future held, what new adventure would beckon. And in my thoughts, came unbidden, the image of a diamond necklace lying on the floor in the moonlight, in a bedroom in Bath.

Where or When

April 1989
Bath

After the opening night of *Americans Abroad* at the National Portrait Gallery, British, European and American newspapers rushed to cover the event with the photograph of Princess Diana, Henry Catto Jr., the American ambassador to England, Guy Pierce and me standing next to John Singer Sargent's portrait of Madame X – all Americans abroad. At brunch surrounded by the Sunday newspapers, the Athertons, Tuttenhams, Eckharts and Coffins sat at the dining table at Bathampton Hall conducting a post mortem.

"Henrietta, you looked lovely standing next to Princess Diana," said my mother, Charlotte. "Yes she did, they made a beautiful portrait, two princesses, one fair and one dark," replied William, Harry's father. I was glad I wore my three inch heels standing next to the willowy princess, topping six feet in height as we stood shoulder to shoulder smiling for the camera. "And Harry, you looked so handsome dancing with Princess Diana," His mother Frances said. "...But the bloody bastard was holding my wife a bit too close," groused Harry referring to Guy. "...It was almost indecent." My usually patient husband was also not amused when a large bouquet of showy pink peonies arrived from Guy first thing Saturday morning upstaging Harry's tasteful bouquet of blue hydrangeas and red and white roses. Our mothers were still swooning over Guy, having danced with him at the party while my stepfather Arthur and Harry's father looked on in amusement. "Harry, you have to step up your game when competition threatens," teased his father. Frances leaned over and whispered in my ear, "It's good for him to see other men desire you, it fuels the passions." His parents knew their son well, for that night, after our houseguests flew back to Philadelphia, my husband declared an early bedtime and made good on his efforts to remove all lingering thoughts of the charming Mr. Pierce.

May 1989
Dublin, Ireland

After the purchase and yearlong renovation of No. 7 Henrietta Street, the Dublin branch of Townsend, Moran and Gardiner, Preservation Architects was finally open for business. The double wide four story brick townhouse with the elegant tracery fanlight over the aqua blue painted door was built in 1730 by Nathaniel Clements and across the street from the Henrietta Street Museum at No. 12. The first two floors housed the architectural offices and the top two floors were Luke Gardiner's apartment. He was now teaching at his alma mater, Trinity College, had established an internship program for the architectural students and was still very involved with the Irish Georgian Society restoration projects. Andrew Townsend, Luke's business partner, still taught at the University of Virginia in Charlottesville. Sarah Townsend, Andrew's cousin was having a long distance romance with Luke but neither wanted to move. Sarah loved her job as curator of furniture at Monticello and Luke loved Dublin where he was born and raised.

I tried to visit our Dublin antiques shop at the Powerscourt Centre at least once a month and Harry often came with me. When not at the shop, we enjoyed our stay at the Shelbourne Hotel, visiting the other antiques dealers on Francis Street, going with Luke to the Temple Bar Pub to hear live Irish music and just strolling around St. Stephen's Green. Harry, always on the lookout for antiques to add to his dragon collection, and Ireland being such a magical place, we were sure a few dragons could be found here.

I was in Dublin to meet with the people from *Antiques* magazine and Ian and Molly for the fall cover story on H. R. Grasso & Daughter. Earlier in the week, we met in Bath at Mother's shop and they already had interviewed James, Melinda and Colin in Philadelphia. We sat around the Regency mahogany library table with Deidre Lloyd and Tom Bailey, the writer and photographer from the magazine.

"We're going to stop by the Henrietta Street Museum, take some photographs and pick up the brochure after we're finished here," said Tom. "We have everything we need from the Philadelphia and Bath locations. The photograph of you and your mother looks great as does the vintage black and white one of you and your father standing in front of the Philadelphia shop. We met with John Bentley at the Historical Society about the Copley exhibit and photographed the star ruby ring and the love letter. He gave us a photograph of Caroline Blackburn Stuart's portrait. We also have interior and exterior shots of The Solitude, the house museum in Fairmount Park and received a written release from them and a quote from Andrew Townsend about the project."

"Which reminds me, Tom, Luke Gardiner will meet you both at the Henrietta Street Museum and give you a release and quote as well," I said. "We also obtained permission to use the photo of Princess Diana, the American ambassador, Guy Pierce and you from the *Americans Abroad* opening," declared Tom. "We have an appointment with Peter Blakeley at the National Portrait Gallery in London on Monday to see the exhibit, take a few photographs and pick up a copy of the catalogue before we fly back to New York," said Deidre. "And speaking of New York, I received a call from Mr. Pierce wanting to give a quote about working with you on the exhibit. It seems you left *quite* an impression on him." *I was thankful Harry was back in Bath and could not hear Deidre's innocent comment.*

July 1989
The Palladian Bridge, Prior Park
Bath

The summer term at King Edward's was finally at an end and the twins were looking forward to swimming in their grandparents' pool and picnics with Harry and me at our special place, the Palladian Bridge in Prior Park. Harry was happy to have his little family all to himself again as he showed John and Caroline where he carved our initials on the bridge on our wedding night on Christmas in 1984. "Did Santa give you presents?" they asked. "Oh yes, lots of presents," Harry responded as he looked intently at me. "Why didn't *we* get presents?" asked Caroline. "You hadn't arrived yet but we were waiting for you," I replied remembering how we felt the twins move for the first time that night. That seemed to satisfy them for the time being. Harry leaned over and whispered to me, "I'm glad they didn't ask us where babies came from, I don't think I'm ready for that question yet," and we both laughed.

Fortunately changing the subject, John asked, "Can we go and play with Alistair and Blair?" "They're going to Scotland for the summer to visit their grandparents," I replied. "Can't we visit them too?" asked John. "Where's Scotland?" questioned Caroline. Thomas Cameron and his children were on their way to Aberdeen and we wouldn't see them again until the start of the autumn term in September. "Maybe next summer we'll take the train to see them," said Harry. "Scotland is many miles away." "…And your granddad Henry's best friend, Sam and baby Andrew are coming from America in a few weeks," I replied. Sam Jacobson was finally coming for a visit and Andrew and Jessica Townsend were bringing little Andrew to meet John and Caroline. We had shown them a photograph of my late father with Sam and one of Andrew and Jessica's new baby, soon to be a year old and they were excited to finally meet them.

I continued to receive congratulatory phone calls and letters about *Americans Abroad* with requests for interviews and Peter Blakeley called to say the exhibit was breaking all attendance records, thanks in part to Princess Diana's endorsement. Harry and I were taking some time off for the summer and looked forward to spending quiet evenings on the terrace overlooking the small garden at No. 28 Royal Crescent. This garden reminded us of another one; my pocket garden behind the antiques shop on Pine Street in Philadelphia and those very first summer nights that July of 1984.

September 1989
Bath

After the summer the children were happy to see their friends again when they returned to King Edward's at the start of the new school term. Harry was back to work at Sotheby's - I missed riding with him on the train when we were both working in London. That afternoon, feeling at loose ends, I went through the mail. There were two letters; one from Guy Pierce and the other from Dr. Wendt. I put Guy's letter aside and opened the one from Dr. Wendt. He and his wife Martha were going to be at a psychiatry conference in London at the end of the month and wanted to meet us for dinner. I picked up the phone and called his Philadelphia office.

"Henrietta, how are you and your family?" asked Dr. Wendt upon hearing my voice. "We are all very well, how are you and Martha?" "She exhausts me; I should have considered this before I decided to marry a much younger woman." I could hear the humor in his voice. Martha Wendt had been his most brilliant student and now they were co-writing books and giving seminars together. "I'll confirm with Harry but I know he would want to have dinner with you and Martha." "Good, good, we'll be flying in on the 22nd and are staying at the Dorchester. "How about dinner at The Grill on Saturday the 23rd, say 8PM?" That sounds delightful, Dr. Wendt."

Then touching Guy's letter I said, "By the way…would you have time for a session with me while you're in London?" "For you, my dear, always; your experiences have fascinated my readers and I'm always looking for fresh material." We said goodbye and I immediately made another call to the Dorchester to reserve a hotel room for the night of the 23rd as a surprise for Harry.

I looked at Guy's letter, his handwriting a bold cursive; black ink on heavy white stock. Inside was a beautiful little watercolor portrait of Charlie the Bear he had painted. The words on the back of his enclosed business card simply said:

Missing You.

The Journal of Henrietta Grasso

September 23, 1989

London

Harry and I took the train to London early Saturday afternoon, the twins now ensconced at the Old Rectory for the weekend. We arrived at the Dorchester, overlooking Hyde Park in Mayfair, in time for tea in the Promenader Room followed by a nap and a long soak in the tub before our dinner with the Wendts. Relaxed and looking very handsome, Harry escorted me downstairs to The Grill restaurant. "Thank you sweetheart for arranging the sleepover at the Dorchester, we should do this more often." It was the least I could do for my husband who had been so supportive during my work on the *Americans Abroad* exhibit.

On the golden walls of The Grill were painted large heroic figures of Scotsmen in traditional dress kilts. The chairs were upholstered in jewel toned clan tartans and the Moorish style banquets were covered in tufted cerise red velvet matching the silk lampshades on the tables and chandeliers. We were warmly greeted by Dr. Wendt and Martha and were shown to a quiet corner table where once seated, Dr. Wendt ordered a bottle of champagne. "I'd like to make a toast to Henrietta for her recent success with the *Americans Abroad* exhibit. We're very proud of our hometown girl. Harry you're very fortunate to have found this precious gem." Harry smiled as he looked at me and said, "No one knows this better than I."

At the end of the dinner as we lingered over coffee, Dr. Wendt asked me when I was available for a session with him. "At your convenience," I responded. "Well, how about tomorrow after brunch?" "I have some shopping to do," said Martha, "You could come to our suite." "Harry would that be okay with you?" "Yes, sweetheart, I could stop at the office for a few hours and get a head start on the work week before we return home."

The next day after brunch found me sitting in Dr. Wendt's suite. The cozy sitting room was paneled in a honey colored wood with a carved mantel over the fireplace.

The room faced the park allowing the early afternoon light to filter through the tall windows. All was quiet as I leaned my head against the high back wing chair, Dr. Wendt sitting comfortably on the loveseat next to me.

"So, tell me what's been going on," he said. I started with the story of meeting the ghost of Luke Gardiner in Dublin then moved on to the time travel event on the train where I returned to 1870 and married Robert Cameron and up to the meeting with Guy Pierce and the vivid dream I had.

"It seems that all these events occurred while you were working intensely on a project. It's interesting that in each instance, the project triggered a connection to a past life. It started with your discovery of the star ruby ring. What's more interesting this time is that the men in the past physically resemble those in the present. Now you have met Mr. Pierce whom you say looks like Harry and that you and he both had a dream of a sexual encounter at the same time." "Yes, that's true." "... And now both men exist in the present. I remember you and Harry had a similar sexual dream when you met." "Yes and I broke off my engagement to Andrew Townsend to marry him. There is a lot more at stake now, Dr. Wendt. I love Harry and we have the children..." "But you are drawn to Guy Pierce and want to know why..." "Yes, that's it. Harry knows about all the events except for the dream I had last March about Guy. He's been very patient, if unsettled, about the ghosts and time travel and would prefer they don't happen, as I would."

"Well then, let's begin. Let's start by getting comfortable in your chair and closing your eyes. Next take a series of deep breaths..." With these words Dr. Wendt started the familiar process.

My legs and feet were bare; I could feel wet sand between my toes and smell the strong briny scent of the sea. "Jules, please don't!" I protested as he chased me along the water's edge then grabbed me around the waist pulling me into an oncoming wave. A moment later I came up choking and gasping for air. "A little salt water is good for you, Audra, it stimulates the blood." His brown eyes were laughing as he eyed my wet bathing costume clinging to my body. "Well, you certainly have grown up since last summer." It was the summer of 1912 and I had just turned sixteen. *"I promise I won't pull you into the ocean again if you let me escort you to the dance at the Pavilion tonight." "You know your brother Jonathan already asked me." "Well, Miss Layton, my brother and I can share you but I want to take you for a ride on the Ferris wheel, tonight…alone. There's going to be a full moon and they say you can see Charleston and the houses on the Battery from the top." I had come from Richmond, Virginia and was staying with my Grandmother Layton at the Hotel Seashore on the Isle of Palms for the summer where I had met the Allerton brothers the previous season.*

The scene changed and I was wearing a pale pink silk gown with a matching satin sash. "That color looks so pretty with your dark hair, my dear," said my grandmother. "You are growing up so quickly, soon it will be time to choose a suitable husband for you." We were sitting in the hotel lobby when in walked Jonathan and Jules Allerton, identical twins. Both tall with blonde hair, the only way to tell them apart was their eye color; Jonathan's eyes were bright sky blue while Jules were the deepest shade of brown. At eighteen years old, they already looked like the handsome men they would become and were entering the Citadel, the Military College of South Carolina in the fall. Jonathan said, "Good evening, Mrs. Layton, we've come to escort you and your granddaughter to the dance tonight." They were each holding a small box which when opened contained a single white gardenia. "Here my dear, let me pin it on your waist," said Grandmother. "Thank you boys, that was very thoughtful," she said as I helped her attach her gardenia to her lavender silk gown.

The Pavilion, newly opened this summer, had a four hundred foot long dance hall with high ceilings and windows open to the sea breezes on three sides. When we arrived the orchestra was playing Scott Joplin's "New Rag". Jules quickly took my hand and led me to the crowded dance floor and into a fox trot. Jonathan, always the gentleman, asked Grandmother to dance and soon we were lost in the crush of dancers.

The rest of the evening, in between icy glasses of lemonade, was spent dancing with Jonathan and Jules to more Joplin tunes; the Bethana Waltz, Solace and the popular Maple Leaf Rag. The last dance was Claude Debussy's Clair de Lune in honor of the full moon tonight. Jules took me in his arms for the final waltz. "You look beautiful tonight, Audra." The sweet exotic scent of the gardenia, warm against my body, rose up between us. Holding me closer, Jules took the opportunity to kiss me on the cheek, barely missing my mouth. "This is what I want to do with you on the top of the Ferris wheel tonight," he whispered, his breath against my ear, causing an unfamiliar sensation through my body.

When the dance was over, the brothers walked us back to the hotel and said goodnight. Jules whispered in my ear, "I'll be back to take you for that ride on the Ferris wheel. I'll wait outside the hotel. Can you make some excuse to your grandmother and get away for an hour?" "I'll try."

The full moon, a pale opal in the night sky, hung low as we reached the top of the Ferris wheel, the cages swaying slowly before coming to a complete stop. "I paid the operator a little extra to stop the ride when we reached the top so I could do this..." He pulled out a silver flask which caught the reflection of the moonlight. Opening it, he moistened his finger and rubbed the amber liquid on my lips. "Do you like the taste?" "...Yes." "Here, take a deep sip, you'll enjoy the ride much better." Then he took me in his arms and kissed me. I felt the earlier sensation, now stronger, deep inside. He parted my lips and placed his tongue, inside my mouth, slowly moving it in and out. "This is what they call a French kiss, do you like it?" His tongue tasted of mint and lemons and something else, something rich and sweet. After he took a sip from the flask, his lips, now moist with the liquid, kissed my throat and wandered down to my breast. At that moment, the cage started to move again. He swore softly under his breath as we made the slow descent.

That fall I moved into my grandmother's house at 20 South Battery Street in Charleston. Since my grandfather died, she was lonely in that big house on the Battery and had expressed interest to have me come live with her. Now cadets at the Citadel, the Allerton brothers often came to visit; Jules sneaking out against orders; his silver flask filled with bourbon. He would climb up to the second floor veranda and lightly tap on my window. Then he would kiss me as he had on the Ferris wheel and I was finding it harder to resist his advances. "What's the harm?" he would say. "We'll be getting married in a few years and I can't wait that long..."

But the summer of 1914 changed everything. War broke out in Europe and Jonathan and Jules were anxious to go. Citadel graduates volunteered with Allied forces prior to America's entry into the war. Upon graduation in 1916, the Allerton brothers became officers in the Marine Corps and left for Europe. I wrote to them often and prayed for their safe return. The United States entered the war in April 1917 and by November 1918 it was all over. Except that only *one brother came home. During the battle of Belleau Wood, outside Paris, in June 1918, Jules was killed. Jonathan and I deeply mourned his loss and over the course of the following year slowly fell in love and married in a quiet ceremony at St. Michael's Church. But I would never forget Jules; wild and impetuous and so full of life...*

"...Take a deep breath and exhale," said Dr. Wendt and I was back in his suite at the Dorchester. The afternoon sun coming in through the windows was now lower in the sky. "How do you feel?" "Like I lived another lifetime, again." I told him the story of my life in Charleston, South Carolina in 1912 as Audra Layton with the twin brothers, Jonathan and Jules Allerton.

"Well, Jonathan is definitely your husband Harry and Jules sounds a lot like Guy, from what you've told me about him. Perhaps it's a case of unfinished business between you and Guy. Henrietta, everything happens for a reason. Through your discovery of the star ruby ring you met Pamela Stuart and Andrew Townsend and their lives have been changed because of you, for the better I might add. Through Jamie Cadwalader, you met Harry and he helped Jamie recover from his addiction and make amends with you. You now have a wonderful life with Harry and your children. You helped restore Luke Gardiner's home in Dublin to its original beauty and so his spirit is now at rest. And you became a much needed mother to Dr. Cameron's children in 1870 and created a delightful home for the present day Dr. Cameron. Perhaps, it is now time to make peace with Jules Allerton. I'm sure you'll know what to do."

September 24, 1989
Bath

On Sunday evening on the train back to Bath, Harry asked me how I was feeling and how did things go with Dr. Wendt. I told him it was amazing and would tell him everything once we were home in the privacy of our bedroom. We picked up the twins from my mother's home outside Bath and went home to No. 28 Royal

Crescent. After they were asleep, we went upstairs to our bedroom with a bottle of merlot. The night had turned chilly so Harry turned on the gas fire and poured the wine. Now thoroughly relaxed and happy to be back in our own bed, I told him the story of Audra Layton, the Allerton brothers and Dr. Wendt's interpretation of all my experiences leading up to the present.

"When you present it like that, it all makes complete sense," he said. "I know, I feel more at peace with it now." "Forgive me, my love for not always understanding what you have been going through. Dr. Wendt was able to show us the bigger picture and as you say, it is quite amazing." "He's also thrilled that he can write about it in his next book; he said I'm the perfect case study for his on-going research."

"May I make a suggestion about Guy and your unfinished business? "Yes, you know you can." "We have to be in Philadelphia in two weeks for Phoebe's book signing and your reception in New York for the *Antiques* magazine issue. I think you should call Guy and ask him to meet you in Charleston afterwards. Take a few days to revisit the scenes of your lives back in 1912 and finally put the ghosts to rest. "You would trust us?" "Yes, because I know more than ever that you love me and that will never change but I think you have to do this so you both can move on and hopefully remain friends. And I'll be waiting for you back in Philadelphia."

October 1989
Philadelphia and New York

We flew into Philadelphia to attend Phoebe's reception and dinner for her book *The Removal of Clothes and Halos: Humanism in Italian Renaissance Art*. The reception was held at the Fisher Fine Arts Library on the University of Penn campus with a dinner afterwards at La Terrasse. The library, a Venetian Gothic building designed by Frank Furness in 1890 was a spectacular setting for the event and the place where Phoebe and I studied during our student days at Penn.

Etched into the large leaded glass fanlight over the entrance was a quote from Elizabethan poet Samuel Daniel:

"O Blessed Letters That Combine In One All Ages Past and Make One Live with All
By You We do Confer With Who Are Gone and The Dead Living Unto Counsel Call"

That quote which I had seen daily for four years as I entered this building took on a new meaning as I considered the past lives I had lived.

We gathered in the seminar room off the two-story Rotunda Reading Room. The red sandstone, brick and terra cotta building - part fortress, part cathedral was called by architect, Frank Lloyd Wright, "the work of an artist." Phoebe's family, the Ingersolls were there as were Jonah's parents, the Coffins. Dr. Spiller and Dorothy, Dr. Wendt and Martha, Carl and Pamela Eckhart, Sam Jacobson, Phoebe and Jonah's colleagues and students were all in attendance.

"Phoebe you did it! I'm so proud of you," I said as I hugged and kissed her. "What a turnout and you couldn't ask for a more perfect setting for the launch of your book." "Henrietta, I've waited a long time for this moment, thank you both for coming." "You know Harry and I would not miss this special night of yours." "It's like winning the Academy Award. I know I felt this way too at the opening of your exhibit in London. Imagine meeting Princess Diana and now this! In fact, a journalist from the Philadelphia Inquirer is here to interview me."

After a wonderful evening reveling in Phoebe's success, the very next afternoon, Harry and I along with my staff in the Philadelphia shop, James, Melinda and Colin took the Metroliner to the New York office of *Antiques* magazine for the reception for the new issue featuring H.R. Grasso & Daughter. Deirdre Lloyd had sent me advance copies of the magazine. Mother was thrilled as were Ian and Molly in our Dublin shop. "This should increase traffic in all three shops," said Melinda, "And improve sales in the Charleston, Philadelphia and Nantucket antiques shows this year." Her mention of Charleston touched a nerve and I started thinking about my trip to meet Guy Pierce. I had called Guy and he was intrigued about my invitation to meet me in Charleston for a few days. I made up an excuse about meeting with the curator of exhibitions at the Gibbes Museum regarding a future show.

Late that night, after arriving back in Philadelphia, Harry and I were in the George III tester bed in the apartment above the shop on Pine Street. I was flying to Charleston the next morning and Harry planned to meet me at the Philadelphia airport on Saturday for our trip back to England. "I have to admit I'm feeling nervous about this, Harry, I hope I haven't given Guy the wrong idea." "If he cares about you and I believe he does, these next few days will be as much of a breakthrough for him as when you and Jamie met at Bath Abbey." "But you were there to facilitate the meeting and to make sure nothing went wrong," I reminded him. Harry had been Jamie Cadwalader's sponsor through his addiction recovery and arranged a meeting for Jamie to apologize to me for his past abusive behavior. It was a courageous thing for both men to do and I had forgiven Jamie. "I'll be as close as the phone and can fly down to Charleston if you need me. You can do this, my love and now…come over here so I can give you something to remember me by." I have to say that was one of the most passionate nights we encountered in the George III tester bed.

October 1989
Charleston

Even in October, the air was warm and humid as I walked up the steps of 20 South Battery Street, formerly the home of Audra's Grandmother Layton in 1912, now a bed and breakfast inn. I had reserved two rooms on the second floor off the veranda and Guy was going to meet me here. As I checked in at the reception desk I asked if Mr. Pierce had arrived. "Not yet, Ms. Atherton but a delivery came for you, we placed it in your room." I was given the key and my luggage was carried upstairs. Upon entering the room, I was greeted by the intoxicating aroma of gardenias. There on the night table by my bed was a miniature gardenia plant in a footed white porcelain pot overflowing with white flowers. The attached card said:

Henrietta,

A flower a day

To wear in your hair

Guy

I inhaled the sweet fragrance and was reminded of the day when a single gardenia arrived at the National Portrait Gallery; a gift from Guy sent the day after we met, almost a year ago.

I unpacked my clothes and freshened up in the bathroom and soon I heard a light tap on my door. Charlie the Bear poked his head in as I opened it. "He just couldn't stay away, he missed you too," said Guy with a smile as he enfolded me in his arms and gave me a hug. He smelled of citrus and bergamot. "Did you receive the gardenias?" he asked as he reluctantly released me. "Yes, they're lovely, thank you." "I asked the innkeeper to send up a pitcher of lemonade to the veranda. Let's have a seat and you can tell me about the meeting at the Gibbes Museum."

We sat on the dark green wicker chairs on the second floor veranda, sipping ice cold glasses of lemonade laced with fresh mint leaves, the afternoon sun reflecting on the harbor across the street. The taste of the lemonade reminded me of the first kiss Jules gave Audra on the Ferris wheel. "There is no meeting at the Gibbes Museum," I said quietly. "I know, I called the curator to say hello and that we would see her soon. She sounded puzzled and said she had not contacted you."

"Something happened in London..." "Are you alright; did something happen with Harry, the children?" "No, everyone is fine. Guy, remember the vivid dream you had about us last spring? It was the night after we went to the concert at St Martin-in the-Fields." "Yes, how could I forget? I remember mentioning it to you when I came to your home in Bath." "Well, I had the same dream that night and Mrs. Avery found my diamond necklace on the floor in the guestroom the next morning." Guy looked at me, his brown eyes intense. "I've been having these experiences for the last seven years, since after my father died. Have you heard of past life regression? Dr. Wendt, a psychiatrist and a friend from Philadelphia has treated me twice before and most recently when he was in London. It involves a hypnosis technique where the person is taken back to visit past lives which have an impact in their present life. I wanted to understand our strong attraction to each other. I'm very much in love with my husband and yet..." my speech trailed off. "You have feelings for me," he said softly. "It's not as simple as that." And as the sun lowered over Charleston Harbor, I told Guy the story of Audra Layton and Jonathan and Jules Allerton.

That night we had dinner at the elegant Charleston Grill in the Charleston Place Hotel on Meeting Street. I wore one of the gardenias in my hair. After dinner, we went into the lounge to listen to a jazz ensemble. They started playing the Rogers and Hart song *Where or When* and Guy said, "They're playing our song – let's dance."

When you're awake, the things you think
Come from the dreams you dream
Thought has wings, and lots of things
Are seldom what they seem
Sometimes you think you've lived before
All that you live today
Things you do come back to you
As though they knew the way
Oh the tricks your mind can play

We finally arrived back at 20 South Battery Street and Guy walked me to my room. "Guy, thank you for a lovely evening." "It was my pleasure, Miz Henrietta. What would you like to do tomorrow?" "I think I would like to visit the Isle of Palms and then the Citadel Archives and Museum to see if we can get information on Jonathan and Jules." He took me in his arms for a warm hug and removed the gardenia from my hair. "A keepsake to remind me of you – sleep well, I'll see you in the morning."

The next morning after breakfast we drove to the Isle of Palms, about twenty minutes away. In 1912 there was a ferry that left Charleston to go to Mount Pleasant and from there a horse drawn trolley took you the rest of the way to the island. We walked along the beach and looked back at the sites where the Hotel Seashore, the Pavilion dance hall and the Ferris wheel once stood, now long gone. It was a warm day; the temperature in the seventies with a breeze coming off the ocean. Guy took my hand as we strolled along. "So this is where I pulled you into the ocean. You must have looked adorable at sixteen in your bathing suit. What young man could resist," he said as he teasingly tug on my hand. "You were incorrigible even then," I said and our laughter melted away any lingering ghosts of 1912 in the fresh salt air.

By lunchtime we were hungry from our walk on the beach and made our way to the Long Island Café on Palm Blvd. Known for its seafood, we ordered cups of she crab soup and shrimp and grits and glasses of cold lemonade. Guy smiled and said, "My, my, you sure can eat Miz Henrietta; I like my women with an appetite." Satisfied and with a promise of ice cream back in Charleston for dessert, we left the Isle of Palms.

The Citadel Archives and Museum was located at the Daniel Library on 171 Moultrie Street in Charleston. I turned to Guy and said, "I called ahead and made an appointment to access the archives." As we approached the reception desk, I gave my name and after a few minutes, a tall dark haired woman about my age came out to greet us. "You must be Henrietta Atherton, I'm Audra Jones." I introduced Guy to Audra and saw a look of recognition on her face. "As I requested on the phone, we would like any information on Jonathan and Jules Allerton who were cadets here from 1912 to 1916." "Well, you are in luck. I am the granddaughter of Jonathan and Jules was my grand uncle. If I may ask, what is your interest in them?" I had to think quickly for a reply. "…My grandfather served with them at the Battle of Belleau Wood in France. He was with the British Armed Forces and always spoke highly of them." Guy looked at me and smiled as if to say *"right answer."*

"Well, come this way, I have a lot to show you. After my grandfather died, my father gave all of his and Uncle Jules' military artifacts to the Museum." Over the next few hours we reviewed school records, letters, held the cadet rings and saw the uniforms belonging to the Allerton brothers. Finally we saw their pictures in the Sphinx, the Citadel yearbook. Side by side, they smiled for the camera, identical twins, so young and handsome. The black and white images could not reveal their eye color but I knew Jonathan's eyes were bright blue and Jules were the deepest brown.

At the end of the afternoon, we thanked Audra whose full name was Audra Layton Allerton-Jones after her grandmother who died in 1950 the year before she was born. Little did she know I had been her grandmother. As we were leaving, she hesitated and said, "Would you like to come by and meet my father?" He lives with us since my mother died last year. I know he would love to meet you. We live nearby." I looked to Guy and he nodded. "We would like that," I replied. *I was finally going to meet the son I had had with Jonathan Allerton!*

His eyes were the deepest brown, like his Uncle Jules. At sixty-nine, Jules Allerton was still handsome, his once blond hair now silver. When he saw Guy, his eyes lit up. "You remind me of my father and his brother. And you, young lady bear a striking resemblance to my mother."

With that said, he went to get the family photo album and there they were – Audra, Jonathan and Jules together again. The photograph of the three of them was taken at the Homecoming Dance at the Citadel in 1915. Audra wore the same gown she wore at the Pavilion dance with a white gardenia pinned at her waist. I felt tears come to my eyes as I looked at the photograph and Guy squeezed my hand. "Would it be possible to get a copy of this photograph?" he asked. "In exchange, I would like to take one of the four of us and I will send you a copy." At that moment, Audra's husband Charles walked in the door and happily obliged us.

As we took our leave, we hugged everyone goodbye as though we were long lost friends. I suppose in a way we were. This trip to Charleston had been a very memorable one and I had Harry and Guy to thank for it.

That night, our last in Charleston, Guy took me to a cozy Italian restaurant on Church Street called Bocci's. I wore another gardenia in my hair. We ordered Chicken Piccata with glasses of Pino Grigio and fig gelato with ricotta cannoli for dessert. These last two days I felt as though I had been far away from my normal life. After dinner Guy suggested a walk on the Battery. The night air had turned cool and he placed his jacket around my shoulders. I could feel the heat from his body in the jacket's fabric. There was a quarter moon in the sky and a million stars were out.

"This has been quite a trip, one I'll never forget," Guy said. "And I didn't even have my way with you," he smiled. "Well, Jules did and I'll never forget our first ride on the Ferris wheel," I replied. "There is that and our dream of an unforgettable night in your guestroom in Bath last spring and the kiss in St. Martin -in –the-Fields. I turned to him and said, "Thank you Guy for coming to Charleston and being the wonderful friend that you are – I hope we will always be friends." "Don't ever doubt it, Henrietta; I will always be here for you if you need me." And because the words had to be said, I asked him to kiss me. "I thought you'd never ask," he smiled and then he did.

The next morning as I was packing I heard a light tap on my door. "I had the most vivid dream last night," Guy said. It involved you, me, Charlie the Bear and a jar of honey…" "Guy, stop…" I laughed. "Are you ready to have breakfast? We have to be at the airport in an hour."

At the airport we hugged, said goodbye and went our separate ways – he back to New York, I to Philadelphia to meet Harry; the ghosts of Charleston finally laid to rest.

October 1989
Bath

A few weeks later, two packages arrived in the mail. I opened the first to find two photographs in a double sterling silver frame; the one of Audra, Jules and Jonathan at the Citadel Homecoming Dance in 1915 and the more recent one of Guy and me with Audra's son and granddaughter. There was a card from Guy:

Henrietta,

I made copies of the Allerton Family photographs for you and myself

and will remember our time in Charleston always.

Love,

Guy

The second package contained a beautiful burled walnut box. Inside was a dried gardenia wrapped in an embroidered handkerchief with the initials *AL*. It was a music box and when I turned the key it played Claude Debussy's *Clair de Lune*. There was also a note from Audra's son Jules:

Dear Henrietta,

Please accept this music box which belonged to my mother and was a gift to her from my Uncle Jules. It was a pleasure meeting you and Guy and we look forward to meeting your husband, Harry someday soon.

With sincere regards,

Jules Allerton

The Nightingale

November 1989

Bath

Life is full of surprises and my husband, Harry would wholeheartedly agree. His life has been turned upside-down since we met but he said he has enjoyed it all immensely. As we flew home to England I told him of my adventures in Charleston with Guy Pierce and how we parted as good friends. Harry's plan worked and the ghosts from our past life in 1912 were at peace. A few weeks later when the packages arrived, he looked at the photograph of Audra Layton and the Allerton Brothers and the music box with the dried gardenia and smiled.

"I wish I could have been at Jules Allerton's home just to see the look on his face when he saw Guy and me together," Harry said. "I had enough trouble making up an excuse to view the Allerton archives at the museum; I never expected to meet Audra, their granddaughter." "I'm sure Guy appreciated having you all to himself for a few days and I'm glad he behaved like a gentleman." "Harry, Guy's an honourable man and I know he will continue to be a good friend to us." "Well, I know if I wasn't in the picture he would leap at the opportunity to be with you." "…But you are in the picture and will always be along with those two little ones upstairs."

The two little ones were excited. They were going to be in the Christmas play at King Edward's school. John was going to be a shepherd and Caroline, an angel. Harry and I were busy making preparations for the coming holidays. As usual we were having supper on Christmas Eve at Harry's parents' home, Bathampton Hall after services at St. Nicholas's Church and brunch on Christmas Day at the Old Rectory, home to my mother and Arthur. We were hosting New Year's Eve at our home at No. 28 Royal Crescent. The twins were anxious to see Father Christmas and give him their wish lists. We planned a day in London to take the twins to Harrods Department Store to meet him for the first time and for tea afterwards at Fortnum and Mason. I wanted to show them the mechanical clock outside the store.

After the visit, Harry and the twins said they had some very special shopping to do and would meet me back at the entrance to the store in an hour. Caroline whispered in my ear, "Mummy, we're going to buy you a Christmas present but don't tell anyone." I nodded and smiled as they skipped away each holding on to Harry's hands. I hadn't been on the Old Brompton Road in a while and curiosity getting the better of me, I walked down the block to see if Mr. Cavendish might be in residence. The estate jewellery shop, perpetually stuck back in the year 1910, had a habit of appearing and disappearing at whim, my own personal Brigadoon.

As I approached 159 Old Brompton Road I saw the lights were on in the shop! The bell over the door jingled as I entered and instantly I was back in time, everything in the store looking exactly the same as when I was last here. "Good Afternoon, Lady Atherton, it's been a long time since your last visit." There he was, the perfect Victorian gentleman with his mutton chop whiskers. Even for 1910 he and the store were hopelessly out of date. "And how are your husband and children?" "They are very well, I left them at Harrods to do some shopping and thought I might stop by and say hello." "I knew you would come today. So…you have settled everything in

America with Mr. Pierce?" "...Yes." *How did he know about Guy Pierce?* "Good, I knew you would, so now, let's move on. "I have something very special that may interest you. From the display case he removed a miniature gilded bird cage. Inside was a painted metal bird which when he turned a key lifted up its wings and opened its mouth to sing the most beautiful song. "It's a nightingale," he said. Engraved around the base of the cage were the words *Je ne chante que pour toi.* I translated the French words - *I only sing for you.* "It was made in Paris by Bontems in 1880. Mr. Ravel has a similar one; he has an interest in automatons. I was at the Proms at the Queen's Hall in 1907, wonderful acoustics there, for the premiere of his *Introduction and Allegro.* Do you know it?" "Yes, I enjoy his music." He would never know that the Queen's Hall was bombed during World War II and that the annual concerts known as the Proms were now performed at Royal Albert Hall. "This would make a perfect present for your husband for Christmas." "Yes, I think you may be right." "Good, shall I wrap it for you?"

Christmas 1989
Bath

The Christmas play was a great success; Caroline looked adorable as a Christmas angel and John in a black beard played his part as a shepherd very well. On Christmas Eve after church services we were at Bathampton Hall. After a festive meal, we exchanged the first of our presents. From the children I received a 1913 edition of Hans Christian Andersen's *Fairy Tales* with the beautiful illustrations by W. Heath Robinson and a silver necklace with an antique silver wax seal depicting a nightingale dated 1820, France. Around the seal were the words *Je ne chante que pour toi – I only sing for you.* "Our teacher, Miss Frobisher read the story of The Nightingale to us in school," said Caroline. "Now you can read it to us at home," said John, "And wear the necklace." From Harry I received a vintage Butler and Wilson blue enamel and rhinestone Chinese dragon brooch from Nightingale Antiques. Finally Harry unwrapped the Bontems miniature bird cage with the automaton nightingale inside and the inscription around the base *Je ne chante que pour toi.* The children were delighted as I wound the key and the bird came to life and sang its song. "Daddy, now we have our very own nightingale," said Caroline. Harry and I looked at each other and knew all the nightingale references were not a coincidence. "We have to talk," he said softly.

Late Christmas night, the children were sound asleep and we were snug in our bed at No. 28 Royal Crescent. Harry lit two candles and turned on the gas fireplace, our goblets of Merlot glowing like rubies in the firelight. The stage finally set, he said, "I am going to tell you the real story of The Nightingale, not to be found in any of Mr. Andersen's books." And so he did.

The Year Before
Hong Kong, China
January 1989

Harry's trip to Sotheby's office in Hong Kong was long overdue. As the new head of the Asian Arts Department, he was supposed to travel there at least twice a year for the major auction events in April and October. The Christmas holidays were over and I was knee deep in the *Americans Abroad* exhibit planning. This would be his first trip to meet the staff, some of whom he knew from the London office before they transferred to Hong Kong. The 6,000 mile trip would take 13-15 hours and we had never been this far away from each other since our marriage and the birth of the twins.

The phone rang the following evening at No. 28 Royal Crescent. I had just returned home from London. "Hello, darling, I've arrived at the Peninsula Hotel." "How was the flight, Harry?" "In a word...*long*. I wanted to say goodnight to you and the children before I go to bed." "What time is it there?" "It's 1:30 in the morning, about seven hours ahead of London time." "Children, your father is on the phone from Hong Kong. Hurry, he wants to say goodnight to you." "Daddy, we looked up Hong Kong on the map at school, it's very far away from here," said John. "You won't get lost coming back, will you?" asked Caroline. "No, sweetheart, I won't get lost, not to worry, I'll be home at the end of the week." "Will you bring us presents?" asked Caroline, always the little *mercenary*. "Yes…and now children take care of your mother, sweet dreams, I love you both every much." "We love you too, Daddy." I quickly got back on the phone, "Harry, I miss you so, the train ride to London and back was lonely – I turned and started a conversation and you weren't there. People must have thought I was talking to myself." We both chuckled. "Well, we'll be back together on the train next week, I'm going to try and wrap this trip up quickly so I can be home by the weekend." "At least try to enjoy your first visit to Hong Kong" I replied. "Perhaps you'll find some dragons while you're there, that would be nice." Harry was an avid collector of antique dragon imagery and our home was beginning to look like a museum. "I'll do my best and now I must say good night darling, I'm exhausted, I love you," he said as he yawned deeply. "Goodnight, sweetheart, I love you too."

As I hung up the phone, I suddenly felt a shiver run down my spine and had a dis-quieting image of an antique map with the Latin inscription *hic sunt dracones* – there be dragons. Ancient mapmakers would draw dragons and sea monsters around the outer edges of maps to show dangerous or unexplored territory. *Beyond this point there be dragons.* Little did Harry know that instead of a dragon he would find some-thing even more threatening - *a nightingale.*

As he slowly removed his shirt and tie, Harry thoughtfully gazed out the win-dow of his suite onto a picture perfect view of Victoria Harbour and across to the iridescent lights of Hong Kong Island dramatically reflected in the water. The Peninsula Hotel in Kowloon was opened in 1928, the Grande Dame of British colonialism. With its gilded Rococo lobby and fleet of Rolls Royces, the hotel epitomized British rule. Kowloon on the Chinese mainland was named for the mountains that surrounded it in the north: gaulung "nine dragons" - there were actually eight mountains - the ninth representing the emperor who named them. It was still the Year of The Dragon until February and a most auspicious time to be in Hong Kong. His main objective on this first trip was to simply meet the staff of Sotheby's tomorrow, review operations, check sales figures for the preceding year and view their projections for the new year but his mind kept wandering back to the ancient city of Bath and Henrietta and their children…

Had it been less than five years since his life changed completely? It felt like she had always been a part of his life and according to Dr. Wendt, she had been... for many lives. There had been a time when he first started working at Sotheby's that he only dreamed of coming to Hong Kong. But now his thoughts traveled back again - to his clients in the addiction program. The program also meant a lot to him. Jamie Cadwalader, one of his early success stories, was now a sponsor and still working at Sotheby's. Jamie married Cynthia Chapman, another Sotheby's employee at Christmas and he and Henrietta attended their wedding at the Connaught. Jamie was taking care of his clients while he was away this week and they had become good friends. It was through Jamie that he had met Henrietta and for that he would always be thankful to him. He thought he might bring back a token of his appreciation for Jamie and he wanted to pick up presents for the children and Henrietta – perhaps a dragon boat for John, a tea set for Caroline and an antique piece of jewelry for Henrietta. He yawned again, now it really was time for bed.

He was watching Henrietta and the children; they were standing on the promenade overlooking Victoria Harbour, calling to him as he drifted out toward the South China Sea in a dragon boat, without oars. As the figures of his family grew smaller and smaller he heard a sudden knocking sound and the boat began to sink. It was too far to swim back - he was going to drown. He started to panic as his head went under the waves – he couldn't breathe!

He awoke with a start, his head and heart pounding. He was back in his suite at the Peninsula Hotel and there was someone knocking at the door. After a busy day at Sotheby's Hong Kong office, he had returned to the hotel and too tired to dine out, had ordered room service and promptly fell into a deep sleep. He opened the door expecting to find his supper and instead standing there before him was a mirage. *I must still be dreaming,* he thought. "Hello Harry ...may I come in?" asked Susanna Nightingale. Eye level to Harry, she was tall with a sensuous figure, shiny black hair cascading around her shoulders, full lips, porcelain complexion and those piercing blue eyes; her jasmine perfume an all too familiar scent.

His thoughts flew back to Oxford where he first met Susanna Nightingale. He was starting his second year at Christ Church planning to major in International Studies. His father wanted him to go into diplomatic service. She was the daughter of Sir Edward Nightingale, a career diplomat and his wife Lily, a beautiful Asian art dealer who Sir Edward had met at the British Embassy in Hong Kong. Raised in Hong Kong, Susanna was fluent in Mandarin and English and had come to Oxford to study art history. Word traveled quickly about this exotic creature known simply as *The Nightingale*. Legend had it she would come into your room in the middle of the night and slowly wake you by making love to you and then disappear before the dawn. She was said to have a small tattoo of a nightingale on her inner right thigh with the words Je ne chante que pour toi - *I only sing for you.* Harry knew it was no legend. It had happened to him and it was one of the most thrilling experiences in his young life. Before he knew it, she was gone but his love of all things Asian began with her and changed the course of his life. Upon graduation from Oxford he was accepted into the Internship program at Sotheby's, making Asian Arts his area of expertise. He tried to find her but his friends said she had returned to Hong Kong. And now she was standing in front of him as he had once hoped and dreamed those many years ago.

"It's been a long time, Harry." *Just fifteen years,* he thought. "Susanna what are you doing here?" "I heard about your appointment as head of Asian Arts at Sotheby's and of your visit this week. It's a small arts community here in Hong Kong and word gets around quickly." At that moment there was another knock on the door – this time it was room service. "Don't let me keep you – I wanted to know if we could have tea tomorrow at the hotel – to catch up and …I have something to ask you. Say 4PM?" Curious about her request, he agreed. "Good, I'll see you tomorrow." And then she was gone – only the scent of her perfume lingering in the air.

That night, still suffering from jet lag, he tossed and turned in bed; his mind restless. He thought of Henrietta and the children and the strange dream he had earlier that evening. He also wondered what Susanna wanted from him after all these years. *She was still beautiful… and seductive*, he thought as he fell into a troubled sleep.

He was asleep in his room at Christ Church when he was awakened by a hand stroking him, a voice whispering in his ear, sweet breath on his cheek, a warm body pressed against him, the scent of jasmine. "Je ne chante que pour toi," the voice said. He could feel her breasts touching his shoulder blades, her hips moving against him. As if in a dream, he turned and caressed her and she guided him down to the place where the nightingale tattoo awaited his kiss and then into her, going deeper until she cried out. When he awoke again she was gone, only the scent of jasmine lingering in his bed told him she had been there.

He awoke in a cold sweat, it was morning and he was in his bed at the Peninsula Hotel in Hong Kong, not Oxford. But his lovemaking with the Nightingale seemed so real. Had she cast another spell on him all these years later? He took a cold shower and prepared for his day. He would need to keep his wits about him when he met her later that afternoon.

He went about his business like an automaton, his mind preoccupied with the dream from the night before but no one seemed to notice at the office. At 4PM he was seated at a table in the lobby of the hotel waiting for Susanna Nightingale. In the background a string quartet was playing the second movement of Bach's *Double Concerto in D Minor for Two Violins*, the sensual Largo ma non tanto. Suddenly she was before him in an indigo blue cashmere sweater dress that hugged every curve and high-heeled black suede boots. "Thank you for meeting me," she said as she tossed her long dark hair over her shoulder, those laser blue eyes focusing on his as he stood and pulled out her chair. The tension broke when a waiter came over to their table and they placed their order for afternoon tea.

Her long fingers curled around a steaming cup of Lapsang Souchong, she finally spoke. "I hear you're married to an American and have two children, a boy and a girl." "Yes, they're twins." "I have a daughter, Lily. My husband, Mark Chang is American. He works for Merrill Lynch and I'm curator at the University Museum and Art Gallery. My mother passed away last year and my father has since retired. He's living in London now. I've tried to convince Mark to move to London so we can be near my father but so far he has refused. I've decided to leave him and take my daughter with me to London." "How can *I* help you?" "Well, you work at

Sotheby's and have contacts in London. I will need a job and a place to live near a good school for Lily. She's six. My father lives on Berkeley Square in an apartment and I would like to live near him if possible. He says that a Nightingale should always live on Berkeley Square – he and my mother always loved that song. Will you help us Harry? "Does your husband know you're leaving?" "Yes, we are currently living apart." "What about your daughter, won't she miss her father?" "It can't be helped; he'll have to make the effort to visit her in London. He travels there often for business so she will still see him." "How soon do you want to move?" "As soon as possible." "Let me think on it, Susanna." "That's all I can ask…thank you Harry.

She slipped a white envelope out of her purse and handed it to Harry. "Here is my contact information and my father's in London, my resume and letters of reference." "Susanna, I'll call you before I leave and let you know my decision." He signed the bill, then they both rose from the table and he walked her to the entrance of the hotel. "It's so good to see you again, Harry," she said as she caressed his cheek. "I'll wait to hear from you." He watched as she walked away. The Nightingale had cast her spell over him yet again.

The next morning, under a bright azure blue sky with white puffy clouds, the sun sparkled on the water as Harry took the ten minute ride on the green and white Star Ferry across Victoria Harbour to Sotheby's office on Hong Kong Island. At lunchtime he decided to visit the University Museum and Art Gallery nearby at 94 Bonham Road where Susanna worked. Established in 1953 it was the oldest museum in Hong Kong and known for its excellent collection of Chinese antiquities, some dating from 3,000 BC, including ceramics and bronzes, fine paintings, lacquer-ware and carvings in jade, stone and wood. As he entered the museum the soft plucking sound of a Chinese harp commingled with the faint odor of incense and floated on the air. He heard a child's laughter and as he turned he saw a young girl with dark hair and amazing blue eyes coming toward him.

"Lily, where are you?" It was Susanna's voice. The little girl was beautiful - the image of her mother. "Harry, what a pleasant surprise! I'd like you to meet my daughter, Lily. Lily, this is Lord Atherton, an old friend from England." "Do you live near Grandfather? He lives in England. Mother says we are going to visit him soon." "It's a pleasure to meet you, Lily; yes I work near where your grandfather lives, in London." "Do you have children?" "Yes, John and Caroline, they'll soon be four." "Can they come and play with me?" "Lily, they are back in England; would you like to show Lord Atherton around the museum?"

It was a delightful tour; Lily at age six, thanks to her mother and grandmother, was already knowledgeable about Chinese art and antiques. Afterwards they escorted him to the museum entrance. "Harry, why don't you stop by after work for supper? We live in my parents' old apartment near the British Embassy. I'm sure you could use a good home cooked meal and our housekeeper is a wonder in the kitchen. "Yes, please come Harry, please?" asked Lily. "Well, how can I refuse such an enthusiastic invitation?"

After a delicious Cantonese meal of steamed chicken, shrimp dumplings, lotus leaf rice and sponge cake with molasses, it was Lily's bedtime. Susanna returned with a bottle of cognac and two glasses to find Harry gazing at a photograph of Mark Chang and Susanna on their wedding day. "I met Mark here in Hong Kong when he first came to work for Merrill Lynch. He had just graduated from the Wharton School with his MBA. He's been a good father to Lily but we've drifted apart and after my mother died he started traveling all the time." Susanna sat on the sofa and poured their drinks as Harry took the chair next to her. They sat for a time in silence savoring the cognac when she spoke. "Harry…have you had a chance to think about my request?" "Susanna, are you sure you want to do this?" "Yes, I'm sure." "Then I will help you and Lily return to England." "Thank you Harry; I'll never forget your kindness to Lily and me." At the door of her apartment, she paused and said, "Your wife must be a remarkable woman." "Yes, she is." "…And a very lucky one to have you. Goodnight, Harry, thanks again and have a safe trip home."

That night, on the ferry ride back to Kowloon and the Peninsula Hotel, the moon was full; its pale round orb reflected in the still waters of Victoria Harbour. Harry thought about what he was about to do, the ghostly images of Susanna and Lily imprinted in his mind.

The next day he tried to find the presents for the children but was unsuccessful. Back at the hotel after returning from the office, he wandered into one of the jewelry stores and found a beautiful antique bracelet of carved green jade medallions with a gold embossed dragon medallion in the center for Henrietta. He was leaving early the next day and decided to settle his bill. As he approached the reception desk, the concierge said, "Ah, Lord Atherton, two packages arrived for you this afternoon." Up in his suite he opened the packages and to his surprise and delight he found a miniature dragon boat carved in ivory and a tea set with a dragon motif. Harry read the enclosed note:

Harry,

Lily chose these presents for John and Caroline

and looks forward to meeting them someday soon.

Our love and thanks,

Susanna and Lily

January 1989
Bath

Harry was now back home in Bath; the children had really missed their father and loved their presents. I thought the bracelet exceptionally beautiful and wore it to bed that night. After a week away, Harry and I had much catching up to do. He was especially ardent in his lovemaking. "Hmmm…perhaps you should go away more often." "Oh no, *next time* you are coming with me – *no arguments.* Now…come here and let me show you how much I've missed you." After a restful weekend, I wore the bracelet on the Monday morning train to London.

April 1989
London

The opening of the *Americans Abroad* exhibit at the National Portrait Gallery was a month away and Susanna and Lily Nightingale had finally arrived in London. They were staying at Sir Edward Nightingale's apartment on Berkeley Square in Mayfair temporarily and had interviews with several schools in the area recommended by Dr. Cameron, Headmaster of King Edward's School in Bath. The summer term was due to start the last week in April. Harry had also arranged interviews for Susanna for positions at several museums. The last item on the list was to find a suitable apartment for them. Harry worked with the same estate agent who found him his own apartment when he first moved to London. The agent and Harry had narrowed it down to three good choices – one of which was in the apartment building where Susanna's father lived.

Harry left Sotheby's at lunchtime and met Susanna with the estate agent to tour the three apartments. The last one was a light filled, airy two bedroom apartment with fireplaces, a spacious kitchen, two baths and a small library which looked directly out on to Berkeley Square. The estate agent told them to take their time, look around and call him when they decided and left the apartment. Susanna giggled, "He thinks we're a couple. It's perfect Harry, I think Lily will love living here, her grandfather lives in the building and the Nightingales are back in Berkeley Square." "Good, I'm glad you like it, Susanna, I'll tell the estate agent. I have to get back to the office soon. Let's get a takeaway lunch and eat it on a bench in the square."

They soon found a bench under one of the 200-year-old plane trees said to be the oldest in London near the statue of the Woman of Samaria by the Pre-Raphaelite artist Alexander Munro. "Thank you, Harry, for everything – you have been a savior to Lily and me and we'll never forget it." "I almost forgot, Susanna, the children loved your gifts from Hong Kong – they were exactly what I was looking for."

"Well, they were chosen by a six year old with a *very* discerning eye," she replied and they both laughed.

They sat quietly for a moment and then Susanna said, "I wonder what would have happened if we had gotten together all those years ago." "Susanna, I've wanted to ask you for a long time, not that it matters now…but was it true?" "Was what true, Harry?" "…The legend of the Nightingale at Oxford." "No, Harry, it wasn't true, just a story one of my friends made up when I returned to Oxford with my nightingale tattoo. I had gotten it in Hong Kong over the summer and showed it to her." "But it was true for us, wasn't it?" "Yes, I had a crush on you from the first time I saw you and my friend dared me to do it." "But why did you leave? I was in love with you; I changed my course of study to art history, because of you and specialized in Asian Arts at Sotheby's." "We were so young, Harry, and I saw the prejudice my mother faced by marrying a British man. I didn't want us to have to go through that. Plus, you were the Earl of Bath's son; getting involved with a Eurasian girl was not for you. After two years at Oxford I returned home and received my degrees from the University of Hong Kong, took the position at the museum and eventually met Mark and married him. But if it means anything, I did love you and have never forgotten you."

Christmas 1989
Bath

The bottle of Merlot long empty, his story ended with the events of last April leading up to the opening of the *Americans Abroad* exhibit. "I didn't want to tell you while you were under pressure to open the exhibit and then we were dealing with Guy Pierce and his feelings toward you. There never seemed to be a good time…" "Harry, Mr. Cavendish knew. That's where I found the nightingale automaton. It was the day we took the children to see Father Christmas at Harrods. While you and the children were buying me the nightingale necklace and the book of fairy-tales I walked over to see if the shop might be there and it was! He asked me if I had settled things in America with Mr. Pierce and then showed me the nightingale and suggested it would be the perfect gift for you." "Mr. Cavendish is definitely the harbinger of future events," Harry said with a smile. "So, Susanna Nightingale was the reason you first became interested in Asian Arts and why you started your career at Sotheby's. "Yes, that's so." "Thank goodness or we might never have met…I should thank her." "Just like I thank Jamie Cadwalader every day for leading me to you, my love."

New Year's Eve 1989
Bath

It was New Year's Eve at No. 28 Royal Crescent. The townhouse was filled with music and children's laughter, good food and drink and dear family and friends from near and far. Harry's parents, his brother and wife and their children along with my mother and Arthur were there. Carl and Pamela Eckhart came from Germany after spending Christmas with Carl's family. Andrew and Jessica Townsend with their son Andy came from Dublin after visiting Jessica's family. Sarah Townsend came from Virginia to spend Christmas with Luke Gardiner in Dublin and they were here together. Jonah and Phoebe Coffin came after spending Christmas on Nantucket. Sam Jacobson, Dr Robert Spiller and his wife Dorothy and Dr. Frederick Wendt and his wife Martha came from Philadelphia. Jamie and Cynthia Cadwalader arrived from London, Dr. Thomas Cameron and his children Alistair and Blair were here and Guy Pierce was in from New York. Three new friends were on the guest list – Sir Edward Nightingale from London with his daughter Susanna and granddaughter Lily.

Everyone was finally together; all the people Harry and I loved with one exception. How I missed my father, Henry on this of all nights. I thought back to my parents' midnight suppers on Clinton Street in Philadelphia and to that fateful New Year's Eve at the Powel House when I saw the ghosts of John Singleton Copley and Caroline Blackburn Stuart. Just as we were approaching midnight there was a frantic knocking on our front door to rouse me from my reverie. Harry opened it to find a tall, handsome Asian man – Harry knew who it was immediately. "Is Susanna Nightingale here?" he asked. We invited him inside and Harry went to get Susanna. As she came into the foyer, she saw him and ran to him. "Mark, what are you doing here?" "I came to tell you I love you and never want to be apart from you and Lily again. Can you ever forgive me? I'm moving to London if you'll still have me." With smiles on our faces, Harry and I turned away to give them their privacy as the tall case clock struck the hour of midnight and everyone shouted "Happy New Year!" It was 1990 and we had our own celebrating to do.

After all our guests had gone, Harry went to the kitchen to get a special bottle of champagne, Perrier Jouet, the same champagne we drank the night of our engagement in Philadelphia, to mark our fifth wedding anniversary on Christmas Eve. "Are you coming to bed, darling?" asked Harry. "Yes, in a minute…" I was standing alone in the foyer in front of the dragon mirror when it started to glow softly and there appeared my father, Henry, smiling. I heard him say *Henrietta, I am so proud of you, I'll always love you.* Then his image faded and in his place was another Henry, Mr. Cavendish. *You have more stories to tell, my dear and you will.* And so I would.

To Be Continued…

Acknowledgements

Great love and thanks to my muse and first reader, John Christopher Seedorff, for being the inspiration for my story, cheering my efforts along the way and whose heart and soul are in each of the male characters. A most fond remembrance is sent to the late author, Guy Durham, my "partner-in-crime". My mother Mae loved historic houses, antiques and a good ghost story and my grandmother Henrietta, was a story teller in her own right. My dear father, Henry's heart was always filled with love for us. Thanks to my friend, Tara Dahl, who offered words of support and said, "Now you'll have time to write," when I reduced my work schedule. A special thank you to author, Cordelia Frances Biddle, who encouraged me to continue with Henrietta's story when it was just 8,000 words. Thanks to Missy Hart-Minemier, my guardian angel of years past and Judy Jarmer, former children's librarian, friend and colleague who retrieved the antique print of the Royal Crescent for me during her trip to Bath. Fond memories and thanks to Hollie Powers Holt and Denise DeLaurentis of FineAntiquePrints.com – *antique print dealers extraordinaire.* You made my visits to W. Graham Arader, III Gallery and Washington Square Gallery enjoyable and productive. Thank you Graham and Hollie for the wonderful trip to London and Paris – the Duke's Hotel and my memorable visit to Bath. Also thanks to antiques dealer, Amy Finkel of M. Finkel & Daughter who unknowingly inspired the name of Henrietta's antiques shop. You and your father, Morris were always kind and helpful. Many thanks to author Antonia Phillips Rabb and the members of the Writer's Café at the City of Parkland Library, Florida who listened to Henrietta's words every week and always offered invaluable thoughts and suggestions. A special thank you to Joe Green, Manager of the library and staff members:

Margaret, Diane, Shelly, Tim, Michele and Miles, for your support and listening to my singing. Thank you to Kyle Jeter and his son Kyle for providing a peaceful home in which to write. Finally, thank you to my beautiful home town of Philadelphia for its history, art and architecture which continues to be an inspiration.

Author's Note

This is a love letter to Philadelphia.

The locations throughout the story are real although the characters are a product of my imagination. The few exceptions include the most talented artist of 18th century America – John Singleton Copley and all other artists mentioned, the Right Hon. Luke Gardiner of Dublin, our beloved Princess Diana and the former United States Ambassador to Great Britain, Henry E. Catto, Jr. The venerable Cadwalader family does exist as does the time honored First City Troop, originally known as the Philadelphia Light Horse, noble protectors of George Washington during the American Revolution. Every story needs a charismatic antagonist and who better than a fictitious member of a historic Philadelphia family to add appropriate drama.

If you would like to take a tour around Philadelphia of Henrietta's story locations, visit her favorite restaurants and listen to the classical music she enjoyed, here is a list below. The Garden Restaurant at 16th and Spruce and Le Bec Fin at 15th and Walnut unfortunately are closed but were two of the finest and most romantic restaurants in the city. With the exception of the museums and restaurants, please be mindful these are private residences.

Henrietta's Story Locations in Philadelphia

- H. R. Grasso & Daughter and Henrietta's apartment (1800) 814 Pine St
- Clinton Street home of Henrietta's parents (1852) 922 Clinton St bwt Spruce & Pine
- Independence Park 3rd and Chestnut Sts

- The Powel House (1765) 244 S 3rd St
- Pamela Stuart's home (1830) 242 S 3rd St
- Main Library of Philadelphia (1927) 1900 Vine St
- Historical Society of Pennsylvania (1910) 1300 Locust St
- St. Peter's Church and Churchyard (1761) 313 Pine St
- Fairmount Water Works (1815) 650 Water Works Dr
- The Solitude at the Philadelphia Zoo (1784) 3400 Girard Ave (by appointment)
- The Union League of Philadelphia (1865) 140 South Broad St
- Andrew Townsend's home (1810) 126 Delancey St bwt Spruce & Pine
- Phoebe Ingersoll's apartment (1890) 2009 Pine St
- The Physick House (1786) 321 S 4th St
- Washington Square Walnut St bwt 6th & 7th
- Pamela Stuart's apartment on the square (1809) 228 Washington Square West
- The Italian Market, South 9th Street below Christian
- Swann Memorial Fountain (1924) 19th St and Logan Square
- The Philadelphia Museum of Art (1928) 2600 Benjamin Franklin Parkway
- Pennsylvania Academy of Fine Arts (1876) 118 N. Broad Street
- Rittenhouse Square Walnut St bwt 18th and 19th
- The Academy of Music (1857) Broad & Locust Sts
- The Fisher Fine Arts Library, (The Furness Library) University of Pennsylvania (1891) 220 S 34th St

Henrietta's Favorite Restaurants in Philadelphia

- The Water Works Restaurant & Lounge 640 Waterworks Drive *(where Andrew Townsend takes Henrietta for lunch before visiting The Solitude)*
- City Tavern 138 S. 2nd Street (2nd & Walnut)*(where Andrew Townsend takes Henrietta on their first date)*
- The Saloon 750 S. 7th Street (1/2 block below Fitzwater)*(where Samuel Jacobson and Henrietta have their monthly lunches)*
- Ralph's Italian Restaurant 760 S 9th St (9th & Christian) *(where Henrietta takes Harry Atherton when he first visits her)*

- Four Seasons Hotel, The Fountain Room One Logan Square *(where Harry Atherton takes Henrietta for dinner)*
- Valley Green Inn, Valley Green Road at Wissahickon *(where Harry and Henrietta make wedding plans over Sunday brunch)*
- Victor's Café 1303 Dickinson St *(where Henrietta takes Harry before they leave Philadelphia)*

Music from the Journal of Henrietta Grasso

- The Four Seasons – Vivaldi
- Messiah – Handel
- Requiem in D Minor – Mozart
- Violin Concerto in A Minor – Bach
- Brandenburg Concertos - Bach
- Moonlight Sonata - Beethoven
- Sussex Waltz - Michael Turner
- Orchestral Suite No. 3 in D major, BWV 1068 – 2nd Movement - Air on the G String - Bach
- Jesu Joy of Man's Desiring – violin solo - Bach
- Ave Maria – organ and voice – Schubert
- Harpsichord Prelude and Fugue in C Major - Bach
- Carolan's Dream – celtic harp solo – Turlough O'Carolan
- Carolan's Concerto – celtic harp solo – Turlough O'Carolan
- My Jolly Sailor Bold – piano and voice – Real Sailor Songs compiled by John Aston
- Tioga Waltz – piano solo - Stephen Foster
- Auld Lang Syne – piano and flute – Scots folk melody
- La Forza del Destino Overture - Verdi
- Serenade for Strings in E Major Opus 22 – 4th Movement – Larghetto – Dvorak
- What'll I Do? – Irving Berlin
- Clair de Lune - Debussy
- Where or When – jazz quartet - Babes in Arms - Rogers & Hart

- Introduction and Allegro for Harp, Flute, Clarinet and String Quartet - Ravel
- A Nightingale Sang in Berkeley Square - Maschwitz & Sherwin
- Double Concerto in D Minor for Two Violins and Orchestra BMV 1043 – 2nd Movement –Largo ma non tanto - Bach